Sing

SUITED FOR SIN: BOOK ONE

ANGEL PAYNE

Sing

SUITED FOR SIN: BOOK ONE

ANGEL PAYNE

WATERHOUSE PRESS

To my beautiful Mr. Payne, for the song that never ends.

CHAPTER ONE

So this was why they made up the term "conflicted emotions."

Dasha Moore punched the End Call button and winced at her phone's black screen.

It was the third night she'd sold out Madison Square Garden.

The third night Dad "just couldn't make it."

As she tried to breathe down the ache in her chest, the air in her dressing room shifted with the movement of its other occupant. A leg, long and commanding, invaded her view. A camel Kiton suit clung to it in all the right places. The other leg entered her view before the owner of those tense, braced thighs huffed, emphasizing a case of pissed-off that she'd recognize even if blindfolded.

"David," she pleaded. "Don't start, okay?"

"Don't start what?" came his rage-roughened voice. "Asking what lame excuse he came up with this time?"

"He's a senator. He has responsibilities." *So many, he has the perfect little aide leaving his voice mails for him.* Crystal had even done the deed in less than sixty seconds. Was there anything the woman wasn't good at?

"Right. Responsibilities greater than his own daughter. Responsibilities that come up *every* time you invite him to a show."

Dasha bit down her retort. What option did she have otherwise? David was right. There was no point arguing, because that was what they'd do. Same words, different setting. She'd protest about Dad's "duty" and "obligations" to his position. David would snarl about how the esteemed Senator Moore had an obligation to *her* first. Her frustration would mount with each word. His protective fury would climb in proportion.

Her adoration for him would grow because of it.

She grabbed a water bottle from the clutter on her dressing table and then downed a bunch, attempting to drown that thought, which had been attacking her more often lately. She kept telling herself it had nothing to do with David's recent breakup. What was this one's name again? Oh, right. Jasmine. Like the split changed anything between *her* and David. Like it ever would. Like Jasmine wouldn't be replaced in another month with another strawberry blonde who stood demurely at his side, quipping three-word sentences.

Dasha grimaced. Damn it, *she* was a strawberry blonde, give or take a shade or two. As for the vocabulary handicap... well, that was where she fell short. David didn't call her his "walking thesaurus" for nothing. She'd started wishing, with more frequency than she wanted, for just a few less IQ points, as well as a good dip in the sarcasm that earned her David's chuckles but not his heart.

Brooding was a completely unproductive pastime.

She put the bottle back down with a decisive *thud*, making the sequins of her stage outfit throw little prisms all over the room. Next to the bottle, she found an elastic band and used it to whip her long, thick curls into a high ponytail. In the mirror, she caught David's eyes on her. The dark-gray depths glittered like a wildcat watching from a forest.

She stopped, arms frozen in midair. "What?" she challenged.

His gaze narrowed, making him look even more predatory, tightening the knot in her stomach. "You're not going to say anything else?" he asked.

Dasha huffed. "Why? Because you *want* a fight? Because you don't have—"

She stopped herself from blurting something she'd regret later. Or even right now.

"Because I don't have what?"

"Forget it."

"No." His voice lowered. "I can't and won't read your mind, sweetheart. Spit it the hell out."

She was glad they now stared at each other via the mirror. She wasn't sure she could directly handle the do-it-or-else intensity underlining his words. Or the dark energy that saturated his gaze again. She watched a cord in his neck go hard, pulsing against the collar of his white dress shirt. Their sparring matches had always been part of their friendship, but the edge he'd carved to his end tonight was new. And strange. And turning her pulse into five kinds of *awake.*

"Fine. I was going to comment on how testy you get when there's no bimbette on hand for you to order around."

To her shock, he snickered. On the heels of the shock came the embarrassment, making her flush deeper—which, of course, made David laugh harder.

"'Bimbette,' huh?"

She flashed a tighter-than-Spanx smile. "If the shoe fits, Mr. Pennington."

"Hey, no hating. Unless you're auditioning for the job?"

"And if I am?"

"Ha-ha."

He kept grinning. Dasha didn't. She spun back toward him

but barely moved otherwise. She just waited, wordless, for...

What?

Idiot. Like after five years, he's ever going to see you as something, someone, *more than his employer. His paycheck. Maybe, just maybe, you qualify as a "friend"—but not a lover. No, you're not enough of a woman to be his lover.*

Not. Enough.

The words stabbed, sharp and accusing. Plunged into the heart that tonight, of all nights, felt exposed and trampled. Dasha bowed her head, but tears still speared to the front of her eyes.

"D?" David only made the torment worse with his concerned rumble. She felt him move closer, his steps strong and fast. "Hey. What—"

She cut him off by acting, for once, on pure instinct. She lunged into him with every ounce of her strength. Before he could turn his stunned grunt into words, she captured his lips beneath hers and tasted him greedily, desperately. Joy rained through her when she felt the answering pressure from his own mouth, the seeking tilt of his head, the eager response of his tongue, the hard grip of his hands at her lower back.

All too fast, he broke the kiss short.

"Dasha." The sound vibrated through his body, dark as his unblinking stare. "Wait. Whoa."

"No." It came out a sob, and she didn't care. "No *wait.* No *whoa,* damn it. Please, David, not tonight!" She slid a hand from his neck to his face, threaded her fingers through his hair. "Please, just for tonight...I need to know..."

"What?" he uttered into her hesitation.

"That I'm good enough." She squeezed her eyes shut against the humiliation of the words. "Damn it, that *someone* wants me." She shook her head. "No, that's not it. That *you* want me. I need *you* to want me, David. You have to know, just a little, how I feel. How I want it...from you."

Silence stretched. David released a heavy breath, though he didn't pull away. That had to be good, right?

But then he spoke again.

"Ohhhh boy," he muttered. "Dasha. Listen. *Listen.*" He captured both her wrists as she tried to yank away. "It's not that I don't want you too, okay? Christ, there's a reason your fans adore you. You're incredible and talented, vital and gorgeous—*beyond* gorgeous. But, you and I, as lovers..." He exhaled hard. "I can't take care of your heart the way it deserves to be taken care of. And sweetheart, you *do* des—"

"I'm not your sweetheart." She dipped her head again. "Got your message, mister. Loud and clear. Now let me go."

His grip tightened. "That's exactly my point." He tightened it again. The move, so deliberate, brought her stare back up in time to watch him slide an assessing stare all the way down her body. "If we were...together, you wouldn't be firing orders at me like that. Well, not without some punishment to follow. And I certainly wouldn't be letting you go. Not by a long shot. Not for a long time." One side of his mouth quirked. "As a matter of fact, I'd be thinking of which way to best hold down your pretty little ankles too."

Dasha got a shallow gulp in. "My—my ankles? And what do you mean, *punishment*?"

He locked his stare back to hers. A trace of dark marine blue danced in the gray depths now, giving her the smile his mouth only teased at. "I'm a Dominant, Dasha. I enjoy a lot of control in my personal relationships. Granted, it's freely relinquished, but I push those limits. *A lot.* Do you understand now?"

"No." She couldn't get out much else. The way his tone had gone lower...and harder...

Wow.

Things started happening to her body. Things normally requiring physical touches from other men. Her thighs began to ache. The intimate flesh between them... *Dear God.* Were her folds *pulsing*?

"Let me put it this way. I don't waste my time with women who can't think. All my 'bimbettes' have a master's degree or higher, some more than one. The reason they all took my orders is because they chose to, as my submissives."

"As your *what*?"

He chuckled again. "Surrender can be fun, you know. And a lot more."

At that, he changed his grip on her, making it possible to rub the pads of his thumbs into her palms. Her breath caught. The caresses were better than his foot rubs. Dasha dragged her eyes up. Forced herself to focus beyond the pleasure and accuse, "Fun for who?"

"Fair question." Though his gaze remained steady, a discernible tension began curling from him. No. Not tension. Something closer to...anticipation. A sensual Tesla coil, radiating deep into her, as well. "And I'll be honest with my answer." He pressed an inch closer. "You know you can expect no less."

Her lips twitched upward. "I guess I do."

David didn't return the smile. Instead, the Tesla coil cycled higher.

He squared his stance and nearly pressed their bodies together. "The full term for the dynamic is BDSM," he stated. "The letters stand for Bondage, Domination, Sadism, and

Masochism. The *S* is also sometimes for Submission." His gaze raked her face, which was surely stamped with every sizzling spark of her shock. "I know they're not words found on your usual Valentine's Day card—"

"You think?" she retorted.

"But to those of us who got created with the mental chip for it, those words are better than a Shakespeare sonnet." The angles of his face changed, riveting her with their deep conviction. "In D/s, it's not just an act of your body. We sometimes call them scenes because of the focus that's demanded. There needs to be complete commitment on the part of the Master and submissive. Total focus from me. Absolute trust from her. Bondage is a way to signify that, even to help it. That can include ropes, cuffs, blindfolds—"

"Okay, got it." She squirmed for a second but knew David didn't miss the way she finished by flicking her tongue over her lips. He probably saw other things too—like how hearing him talk like that, then imagining him using all those things on her, and asking her to be open to him like that...

It suddenly didn't seem so much like the stuff of a horror movie.

It turned into the fabric of fantasy.

Ohhh, crap.

The pulses between her thighs became a drum circle. She cleared her throat, commanding herself to refocus. She had to address the rest. The other words. The more frightening ones.

"What about..." She took a deep breath. "You said... sadism. And masochism. So there's...parts of the 'scenes' that sometimes—"

"Hurt." He supplied it as a simple fact, with brutal calm. *Like a glassy lagoon hiding a water snake.* "I won't lie to you about that either, D. Or about me. I'm a sadist, sweetheart. But a fun one. I play hard. I love the high of watching a lovely submissive writhe under me and for me. It makes my body rev and my blood sing. And I like to push limits, too, when I'm with someone who wants it and trusts me with it—because I *love* what I give her in return."

"Wait." She cocked her head, brow crunching. "Did you say someone who..."

"Wants it?"

"Errrm. Yeah."

He jutted his jaw with enough force to command an army. His one-sided smile balanced the daunting effect. "Tell me something. Raife runs you and the dancers through a new routine and shows you moves that look like torture—"

"Because they *are*?"

"Then he makes you do things over and over until you think your body's going to come apart, right? But you trust he knows where everything is going, how everything fits. And then, something happens. Everything connects, and *you* get it too." He broke out in a wide smile. It was more beautiful than any she'd seen from him before. "And it's magic."

Dasha closed her eyes for a moment. The sincerity in his voice compelled her more than the words. But she had to separate the two, if only for a moment.

"Crap," she muttered. Then shot her tone with more anger. "So, what? Did these women just lie down and say *hurt me, Davey, now*?"

His grin softened into a smirk. "In a matter of speaking, yes."

"In a matter of speaking...how?"

"Most of them came to me with previous experience in

this unique lifestyle, so we had communication about what kind of things they enjoyed. And, of course, the lines they trusted me not to cross."

"Really?" She slid it out with sarcasm but couldn't hide her surprise. So, even though submissives were...well...submissive, they got a vote about the conditions of their experience? "You mean there are choices? There's a...variety?"

If it was possible, his sexual heat intensified. And like before, it permeated her too. It turned his response into something that seemed an invitation to a deep, entrancing wonderland.

"Variety would be the understatement, sweetheart. Imagine all the flavors of chocolate and cheese you love, turned into toys for sensation and pleasure."

"And pain," she reminded.

"Part of the pleasure." He issued it as practically an order, forcing her to look up again. The wolfish smile lingered at his elegant lips. "Marceline used to cry and beg me for riding crop welts. Katy liked rope bondage and fucking swings."

TMI, buddy.

Only...it wasn't. Somehow, standing there locked in his hold and bathed in his gaze, it wasn't too much information. Because now, it wasn't *enough* information. Every nerve ending in her body wanted to know more. Craved more of the feelings he'd introduced to her muscles, her skin, her very breath...

"I suppose Jasmine loved handcuffs and ankle shackles?" It escaped before she could help it. And sounded totally dorky.

"Only if we were into cop and criminal that night." He looked almost pleased with himself. "Jaz did love her costumes. But yeah, that was probably her favorite. Probably because I withheld her orgasm for hours."

Dasha shifted again—but not to resist or squirm. She returned the pressure from his hold, curling her fingers around his thumbs. "So you...handcuffed her?"

"Oh yeah."

"And then...told her she couldn't..."

"Ohhhh yeah."

"And what did *she* do?"

"She said, *Thank you, Sir.*"

Okay, bypass dorky. *Barrel straight to* what-the-hell. "She *thanked* you?"

"In more ways than one."

For a second, Dasha couldn't identify her reaction to that. When she did, it hit hard.

She was jealous.

Thoroughly envious she hadn't been in Jasmine's skin, pleading with David.

Pleasing David...

The ache bloomed again between her breasts. She didn't hide her tears from him this time. "All right, then. Let me thank you in the same ways." Before he got in another protest, she rushed on. "I want to try it. I want *you*, David."

"Dasha—"

"Test me. Show me. How do you know I won't like it too?"

He chuffed. "By the way you had to practically choke that out?"

"You haven't even given me a chance."

"Oh yes, I have." Suddenly, his grip went from tight to unyielding. His stare bore into her with feral honesty, turning the pain in her chest into chaos. "I've done exactly that, sweetheart. About a thousand times, in my imagination."

She didn't hide her reaction to that either. Just let him take in the new desire surely consuming her face to go with the thunder of her blood. This new knowledge about him, about this secret world to which he belonged...it shifted an important axis. This was no longer about her disappointment in Dad's no-show. It was about confronting her need for David, acknowledging how she wanted to please him, in every way possible. Even if it meant trying it his way. Even if it scared the crap out of her. Maybe *because* it scared the crap out of her.

She pressed nearer to him. Clean, luxurious scents surrounded her. His sandalwood soap. The bleach in his shirt. A trace of aftershave. "And in your imagination," she murmured, "what did I do?"

His breathing stilled. His stance stiffened. He pulled away by several inches but didn't relax his grip. "You did nothing," he answered. "At first."

"Why?"

"Because you were on your knees."

Dasha swallowed. She couldn't tell if the words were comment or challenge. It didn't matter. She accepted them as the latter. Using his hands for balance, she slowly lowered to the floor. She looked up, hesitant but achingly aware of his whole body...including the distinct ridge in his pants at her eye level. "Like this?"

David released one of her hands. Stroked the hair from her eyes. His own gaze was hooded and molten...and consumed with her. Everything about the moment moved her in a deep, inexplicable way.

"Not quite," he replied.

The meaning of that came loud and clear. Definitely a challenge. And she never backed down from challenges, especially now. Taking a deep breath, she pulled her other hand from his and shirked off her shimmering tank top. A bra had been built into the costume, so there was nothing more barring his eyes from her exposed, full breasts. His eyes went from gray to kohl, their embers stoked into dark fire. The look hit her like a physical move. Her womb quivered. Her nipples puckered and throbbed.

"Like this, maybe?" she managed to rasp.

"Yes." He drew the "s" out, making it into soft praise. "Better. And beautiful." He stroked her cheek. "So beautiful."

Dasha's skin flowed with warmth. Her mind soared with happiness. She smiled up at him. "So where did your imagination take it from here?"

She didn't expect his answer. He hauled her back to her feet in a sudden, fierce surge. She didn't get a chance to gain balance, toppling into him, gripping him for simple purchase. He handled her weight without stopping his own action, locking her against him and then kissing her without a second of hesitation or an ounce of mercy.

She opened for him because he gave her no choice; his possession was brutal and absolute, a consuming command. She whimpered, loving the thorough shock of it. He groaned hard in return. The sound vibrated through her as well. She thought he'd let her go then, but no. He tunneled a hand into her hair, seizing the roots and yanking back her head so he spread her wider. He went at her without reservation, thrusting his tongue rhythmically, making no secret about other acts on his mind. Dasha reveled in every second. This was what it felt like to be consumed, desired, devoured.

It was exactly what she needed—yet she craved more.

Much more.

He pulled away. But not by far. He still held her, cradling her head. His stare was almost black. His jaw was the texture of dark marble. His lips, slightly parted, dragged in air. Raw heat shot through her bloodstream.

"Before I give you the answer," he said, "I need to hear that you trust where I'm going to take this now."

She forced her reeling head to nod. "Yes," she answered. "Oh yes."

"I mean it, D." His fingers dug deeper against her scalp. "We've been through a lot in the last five years. Across the globe and back together. But tonight...this is going to be a different destination. Our roles won't be the same, and you might not like it. I won't go grabbing you a bottle of water or an extra hairpin. I won't have time to worry about stashing your lip gloss." He raked his tongue along his teeth, looking hungry and hot as his gaze dipped to her mouth. "Actually, I'd prefer no gloss, with what I'm dying to do to those lips."

Desire deepened her dizziness. He was so close, his breath laced with a little imported beer and a lot of arousal. It was all she could do to dip an eager nod.

"You'll have a way to tell me no," he assured. "It's called a safe word, something specific and definite between us. I expect you to use it if you need to."

"Uh...huh." She tried to slam some coherence onto her tongue. "Ruh-ruh-right." Oh, *that* was a real big win.

"But make no mistake about it, I'll be the one in charge." He framed her face with his hands as he issued it. "Are we clear? This is a different playing field. I can't concentrate on reading your body *and* playing verbal ping-pong with you, so even the way we communicate will be regulated. Direct questions from me. Honest answers from you. No using your safe word to control things either—not that you'd get away with it anyway."

Dasha vacillated between fear and way-turned-on. He was right; he'd always been able to read her like a butterfly under a magnifying glass. It was one of the reasons they made a successful business team. But now, confronting the reality of getting naked with him and then some...

Oh, God.

He'd have the most direct route to her lust. And the biggest window into her soul.

The recognition made her tremble. In good ways...and in not-so-good ways.

She nodded again, more evenly this time. "All right," she said. "I—I understand."

"Are you sure? The rules aren't flexible. It's your safety at stake." He wryly hiked a brow. "And likely my sanity."

"I trust you, David." She pressed her soul into each word, wanting him to know she truly meant them. "I do."

He tilted her face up once more and took her lips again. This time, he lingered with it, tasting her deeply and sweeping her mouth with his tongue. But when he pulled away, every elegant line of his face was stamped with command.

"I'm going to give you another second to think about that while I lock the door," he stated. "I'm also going to tell the limo to wait and put my phone on DND. If your answer's the same, I want you kneeling on the floor next to the couch, naked and ready, when I get back."

"All right."

She gave back the words with eager speed, almost needing to please him—only to have him tug her chin up in the forceps of his thumb and forefinger.

"When we're together like this, the proper response to

that is *Yes, Sir.*" The glittering light in his eyes took away the sting of the words. "It's a sign of your respect for me, but how you say it also lets me know where your head is at, what you're feeling. Are we clear?"

"Yes," Dasha whispered and swallowed hard. "Sir."

David gave a little nod, so resolved and so *hot*, before releasing her and then turning without another word or touch—sweeping confusion over her once again.

The orders and details from any other man would've had her fuming like a soaked cat. Instead, she trembled with anticipation. David always knew what—and whom—he wanted and went after it at Mach five. In that regard, discovering his private "appetites" hadn't been the biggest jaw-dropper. But now that he'd mandated total honesty in all this and set the example with his open answers to her questions, Dasha confronted the same in her heart. His authoritative ways were part of why she desired him. Okay, a *really* big part. His strength, intensity, and vision had carried her through many a hellish day and just as many nights.

Now, she yearned to have that passion unleashed on her.

With shaking hands, she doffed her stage heels and pants. Padded to the couch clad only in her tight panties, trying to ignore how the air conditioning chilled her exposed skin. The floor, though carpeted, covered a plane of concrete. The hardness only heightened her awareness of being so open, so exposed, so utterly out of her element. Just thirty minutes ago, she and David had bantered like schoolyard pals as he guided her back here after the post-show press conference. And now...

She glanced down at her nearly nude body and shivered again.

Ohhhh boy.

She heard him come back in, lock the door, shed his

jacket, and turn back toward the couch. His steps were steady, determined—until he came around the couch and saw her. He halted. A huff rolled out of him, almost as deep and dangerous as his next charge.

"Dasha, I thought I said naked."

"Sorry!" She scrambled fingers for her lace thong. But before she could get a grip on the band, he caught her by the wrist and pulled her back up.

"No." He pivoted her around, away from him. "Now you do it my way. Kneel on the couch, legs apart. Lean forward a little. Spread your arms and then dip your head between them. Good girl. Very good. Christ, you're gorgeous."

His voice... God, it was so damn different now, infused with sensual smoke. Those tendrils swirled through her with such magical force, her body seemed to melt—though everything exploded into rocket fuel again as he grabbed her panties at one hip and ripped them in half. He trailed the backs of her legs with his fingertips as he shoved the lace all the way off, igniting more streaks of sensation straight between her legs...the legs he urged apart by pushing thumbs against her inner thighs.

Dasha bit her lip. Tried, unsuccessfully, to keep a groan in.

"Lovely," David murmured. "Keep those coming, sweetheart. I want to hear every reaction you've got for me. The louder, the better."

Dasha frowned. Loud? He wanted her to be loud, here in the middle of the Garden's backstage? "But—"

He pinched both her ass cheeks. "Doubting me already, sweetheart?"

"N-No. Of course not. But...what if someone—oh!"

The protest fled as he pinched her again, more gently this

time but digging closer to her intimate center. She'd never felt a man's fingers on her *there,* like that—but her own reaction stunned her the most. Against all logic or thought, another moan erupted. Adrenaline spiked her bloodstream. She arched and shoved her hips back, almost daring him to do it again. *Wanting* him to do it again. Oh God, especially now, as he brushed the skin he'd just inflamed, turning every cell into honey-warm heat.

"David," she cried. "Oh God, David!"

"Who?" he prompted as he trailed those fingers deeper. Lower.

"S-Sir," she managed, shuddering as he scraped his fingernails up and down her rear cheeks.

"Beautiful." He kept teasing her with his touch. "Oh, sweetheart, you're more beautiful than I'd hoped or imagined."

This was insane. This was magical.

And got even more so the next second, when he dipped a hand again and entered her in one sweep of a long finger.

"Your pussy likes this, Dasha. It's pulsing around my finger. And you're wet, my dear. Very, very wet."

"Yes." It was more a plea than concurrence. "Yes!" She threw back her head as he pushed a second finger in.

"Head down, please." Steel returned to his tone. He dived a hand into her hair and then realigned her head between her shoulders. "I love the way you look right now, Dasha. So ready and submissive. I'm going to enjoy the view for a minute. Maybe a couple. Get comfy."

He pulled his hand from her scalp and then trailed it down her back, digging at her skin. His touch savored her, desired her, consumed her. Her knees started to weaken. Her nerve endings sparkled. He cupped his other hand over her mound while he kept those two fingers so deep inside her pussy. Circled them rhythmically, branding her intimate walls with his touch.

She struggled to think about what was happening. This was *David*—her manager, her friend, her confidante—but right now, it wasn't. This person, sheathed in the physical shell of him, was an unknown entity to her. A leader in a new world. A commander in a dark, beautiful battlefield between her logic and her senses.

He raked her spine again, burning tracks of possession with his fingers. She felt his desire with every fresh inch he marked and lost another piece of her senses with every searing sweep.

Until he flipped the world again.

He did it with a fluid sweep, pulling her upright with one jerk, spinning her to face him the next. His grip, now on her elbows, was an anaconda squeeze. Against her naked skin, every thread of his clothes pressed and teased, a silken assault on her senses. His gaze delved into her, equally penetrating.

"Crossroads time." The jagged edge of his voice stunned her for a second. "Our direction from here is your choice, but I'm going to be clear about what happens if we go on. I want you so badly, my full Dom is coming out to play. We'll set up the rules. You'll have a safety net, but there's going to be a lot of me you haven't seen before. So if the little taste you've had so far isn't *your* dream, I understand. You just need to say so, and you can get dressed and walk away. No harm, no foul."

A stretch of silence—though David relented on nothing else. Not his stare, his grip, or the sexual heat penetrating to her very marrow.

Dasha blinked. Pulled in a breath.

Here it was.

The crossroads.

Your choice.

Crap, crap, crap.

In a way, she thought they'd already gone past this—and realized she'd been relieved because of it. Hadn't David already *taken* the choice? Wasn't that what dominance implied? But shit, the decision was still hers, and it had to be made for the right reasons. Because of David and this new man inside him she'd only peeked at—and longed to see more of. Not because of Dad and the man in *him* she no longer knew.

Could she really do it? These few minutes had been just a taste. Hell, what was the whole meal like?

Honest response? The answer terrified her.

But honest response, part two: it also thrilled her.

And in the moment of reaching that realization, she compelled herself to reply.

"I'm not leaving," she told him. "I want this. I want *you*. Please, David...Sir...I want this."

CHAPTER TWO

David stared into Dasha's upturned face, selfishly absorbing the golden perfection of her features.

He'd been her manager for five years. He'd witnessed her passion in the throes of performances, her charm with reporters, her joy in meeting her fans...all incredible moments, but none compared to this. None matched the heated desire in her caramel eyes, the longing in her parted lips, the tentative tremble of her chin. Seeing this from other subs had always been a heady intoxicant, but this...

Christ.

This was the best drug on the planet.

She was still afraid of what she'd just agreed to. Maybe more than afraid. But he vowed to take that trepidation and turn it into the most shattering satisfaction she'd had with a man. Her trust really did work like a drug, jacking his bloodstream, turning his brain into an erotic space shuttle— because he finally had the chance to take out one of his most secret yearnings.

The chance to have this with Dasha. *For* her.

He never thought he'd realize the dream. He'd learned not to air such things when they contained the sexual fantasies even avant-garde TV producers wouldn't touch. He'd fast discovered, upon finding his kink gene in college, that girls called him "Prince Charming" at first base but bolted like he'd become Cyclops at third. Even after discovering the full beauty of D/s ten years later, he found those girls grown into women who still loved crying "Cyclops" if he even hinted at a little Power Exchange. So he'd shoved his truth into a compartment, hiding it from most of the world—even the woman with whom he longed to share it the most.

Now here she was, his breathtaking, submissive dream come true.

No. Not yet.

She still had no idea what she'd just signed on for.

The enormity of it didn't escape him. He needed to do this right. To give her this in all the right ways. That was going to take two acts of God. First, he had to control the wildfire he'd once known as his cock. And second, there'd be teaching Dasha to connect the opposite way, guiding her to disconnect the mental defaults and let her lust take the driver's seat of her body for a while.

He couldn't wait.

He was scared shitless.

"Again," he directed, though his tone was now a buzz saw, conveying his need as much as his command. "Say it again."

Without a beat, she spoke. "I want you. I want this. Show me. Please. Tonight. Now."

He couldn't help but smile, running a thumb along her lips, treasuring her conviction and adoration. It doubled his confidence as well as the satisfaction of murmuring his next words.

"Then on your knees again, darling."

Only then did her nervousness show again. She hesitated a tiny second, conflict skittering across her face. David watched, fascinated anew by the pause between her reason and her need, and he wondered—prayed—which would win.

The triumph was heady when she descended for him once more, a shaky gesture signifying that she too seemed to get what her act meant and what a gift it was to him. He had no idea how she knew; to his knowledge, she hadn't been boning up on Submission 101.

Christ. That left the hope, however obscene, that she had the deviant gene too. *Impossible. Don't go there, you dumb fuck. Way too impossible.*

He drove the thought out completely by setting his sights back on the fantasy of a woman in front of him. "Thank you," he murmured, running a hand across the top of her head. "You please me already. And you honor me."

Dasha peered back up at him. No smile now, though she whispered, "I'm glad."

Two simple words, yet they made him gulp. Yeah, damn it, he *gulped*. He almost wished she'd start back again with the sass, because he had no idea what to do with the wild need her sweetness flung open inside him. How much longer could his composure stand this? He longed to go ahead with his original plan, to start his domination by getting his hands deeper into her hair and his cock at the back of her throat. God knew, every cell in his balls and shaft screamed for it too. But this wasn't a situation for the usual routines.

Nothing about being with Dasha would ever be routine, ever again.

He knew that with instinctual surety, even now.

"David?" Insecurity laced her brow and matched the insecurity in her prod. "Sir? Is—"

"Hush." The command came gently, but he emphasized by tugging at her scalp. The action pulled her face back and turned her stare up to meet his. Another thrill shot through his blood. Jesus, she was gorgeous like this. A little scared, a lot naked...completely his. "I'm just fine, sweetheart. All *you* worry about is how to please me with this incredible body. Listen carefully and obey sweetly. Understood?"

Again, she blinked a few times, ginger lashes fluttering, clearly acclimating herself to this different version of him. But she quickly smiled and whispered, "Yes, Sir."

He couldn't resist rolling his hand a little, letting her thick, golden waves surround his fingers...the way he yearned for other parts of her to cushion him too. "It'll take some getting used to," he said, again tethering the part of him craving to bust out a command and get her all the way under him. "This isn't a familiar dynamic for you. But you're a good learner. And I'm a *very* good teacher. Tough but good."

To emphasize just that, he increased his hold by another degree. He expected an oath to explode off her delicious lips, but she moaned instead. The sound was filled with feral force, pure sensual awakening.

"Oh yeah," David said. "Let that stuff fly, sweetheart. Give me as much of your *non*verbal magic as you want. Groan it. Scream it. Sing it." He shifted his other hand to the side of her neck. "I love every sound that comes out of this throat, especially when it's for me."

"Oh." The response fell out of her on a sigh this time. Her eyes drifted shut, like she'd fallen into a dream. "Yes...Sir."

"Good girl." He stressed it by dipping an open kiss to her mouth. When he finally released her, he circled to stand behind her. She shivered again as he slipped his hands to her shoulders, pressing her skin with steady care, using nonverbal language of his own. *Mine. For tonight, you're finally all mine.* He himself kneeled now, cupping her breasts, pressing his chest against her spine. Her shiver became a tremor. She arched as he explored her nipples, coaxing their sweet erections, her body begging him for more.

"I love the way you bead up for me." He said it into her neck as he gazed over her shoulder, watching his fingers trace her puckered areolas. "Look at these hard little buds. So rosy and red." He took one harder, rolled it from side to side, and then pulled. Her sharp cry filled his psyche, feeding deeper into so many caverns of his dominant need. "Hmm, and sensitive too. We'll have more fun with that discovery later."

As he took a turn at the other breast, she writhed. "David! *Damn it!*"

He let out a low growl—right before dropping that hand to swat the side of her thigh. "Where's my eager student? Don't prove me wrong, darling." Beneath his lips, her throat flexed as she took a deep breath. He felt her pulse quicken as he slid fingers back up to her breast. Drawing out every syllable, slow as the circles he traced around her areola, he whispered into her ear, "Give yourself over to it. Give yourself to *me*. Don't try to control it all. Just welcome it."

"Okay."

David bit back a laugh. She'd ripped the word out like sandpaper. Acting on pure instinct, he scraped the back of her neck with his teeth, answering her ferocity with the savage honesty of his need.

"Okay, what?" he prompted.

"Okay...Sir."

"Very good. Now let's make sure the lesson takes this time." He parted his legs a little more and anchored his arm around her waist, turning his body into a frame around hers. "I think a little repetition exercise would be useful."

Dasha snorted. "Repetition *what?*"

He ignored her little outburst. "Say the words after me. 'I will not speak unless Sir asks me a direct question.'"

She stiffened even more. Rebellion, barbed and cold, rolled tangibly from her, despite how heady and warm her aroused scent was on the air.

Finally, stammering the syllables out, she offered, "I—I will not—" Her discomfited squirms broke the words up, until she breathed deep and finally finished all at once, "I will not speak unless Sir asks me a direct question."

"And if I need something, I will use the phrase 'permission, please.'"

She didn't wrestle this time. Could've been because he'd lowered his hand to her hip, claiming her there with steady, wide strokes.

"If I—I need something, I will use the phrase *permission, please.*"

"'I trust Sir never to deliberately hurt me or give me more pain than I can handle.'"

"I trust Sir never to deliberately hurt me...or give me more pain than I can handle."

The words came with more calm—and beautiful conviction. David thanked her with a soft kiss behind her ear. He hoped she couldn't hear how his heartbeat had doubled.

He pressed on. "'And if any play or punishment becomes too much for me, I'll let Sir know with a safe word, which will be 'sound check.'"

She squirmed again, as he'd expected. "I hate sound checks."

"That's why you won't forget the word." It was sheer hell to maintain his composure. Her soft, naked curves pressed this way against him... Christ, even his darkest fantasies hadn't prepped him for this torture. He waged the battle harder by gritting his teeth and toughening his tone. "Now the repetition."

As Dasha recited the promise back, David relished the next words he'd demand from her. In the moment before he did, he ran a wet, nipping trail of kisses along her carotid. "'I will let Sir take my body in any way he pleases.'"

A delighted sigh escaped her. "Yes..."

He turned his last kiss into a bite. "A beautiful sound. But that's not the right repetition, darling."

"'I will let—*ow!*'"

He hadn't been able to resist. And pinching both her nipples gave him the reward of her cute little outcry too. "That's not correct," he reprimanded, keeping his fingertips centered on those incredible buds. "Try again."

"The reason it wasn't correct is because you—*owww!*"

The plea in her tone sang to him sweeter than any ballad she'd taken platinum. He smiled, rejoicing in the feel of her bottom against his groin. He gripped her hips tighter between his own as he ramped up the pressure on her breasts a little.

"The repetition?"

"How am I supposed to—"

"Find a way. Breathe through it, my darling. For every moment you wait, I squeeze a little harder."

"Oh God."

"No." He tightened his fingers again. "My name is *Sir*. Try again."

Her chest quivered beneath his forearms as she struggled to obey his order. "I will...let Sir...take my body...in any way he pleases."

He released his hold. She rasped in gratitude, though he

sure as hell looked forward to the next moment. To the breaths she sucked in, with lips trembling and eyes hazy, as the stings gave way to the warmth and the endorphins washed away her agony. "Good girl." He emphasized the praise by raking fingers down her rib, intending to intensify her pleasure. "Very good."

He turned her again, now searching for his own breath. Her breasts were inflamed with the marks of his use, red and bold and breathtaking.

Mine.

Fuck, yes.

He longed to repeat the treatment, simply to seal his claim further. But he'd taken her as far as she could handle in that department, at least tonight. Next time, perhaps he wouldn't risk her slapping him if he did push—because next time, he'd tie her back well. Maybe he'd secure her with his padded cuffs, wrists over her head, so her breasts stayed high and hard for him. Maybe he'd get her into a blindfold too...

The trip into fantasyland carried repercussions—up the whole length of his cock. Even his balls throbbed, helping the shaft punch at his pants, self-inflicted sadism at its finest.

Dasha's own expression didn't help things. Though her eyes still hid beneath dreamy hoods, she waited with lips moist and parted, skin dewy and glistening, body expectant... and oh-so-ready. He explored those incredible curves with fervent need, playing the luscious string of her spine before dipping into the crevice of her ass. Her breaths quickened as he went lower, turning his fingers into claws against the swells of her buttocks, pulling the flesh apart, indirectly kneading the sensitive tissues of her back hole. Dasha lifted her hands, instantly clutching his shoulders, but her teeth gripped hard on her lower lip. She fought back a verbal reaction with everything she had.

Her effort for him again hit like sexual crack, turning his blood to fire. "Sweet thing." He bracketed his hold to her hips. "You're so ready to be taken, aren't you?"

"Yes, Sir," she answered on a gasp. "Yes!"

"Then lie back for me," he instructed. "Keep your knees bent but press your ass and shoulders on the floor."

As she complied, David relished the view, her trimmed bush parting a little as she went down, giving him a glimpse of the gorgeous pink flesh beneath. "Spread your legs farther." He assisted by pushing with his hands. He couldn't keep his touch far from her now. "Perfect." He stroked her thighs from knees to pussy. "This is called kneel-back, darling. I know it's not really kneeling, but that's part of the fun. It's one of my favorite submissive positions, so I'll likely be asking it of you again." He moved his knuckles inward, brushing directly across her sex. "Would you like that?"

She nodded, making her hair into a more wonderful mess along the floor. "Yes. Yes, Sir."

"And do you like it when I touch you like this?"

"Very much, Sir. *Ohhh...*"

The moan continued as he slipped a finger into the folds he'd been craving. He almost groaned when her wet, hot walls welcomed him, but he managed to stave the craving. Instead, he focused on finding the exact slit of flesh to make her—

"Ohhh! Sir!"

Scream like that.

She cried out louder as he turned his caress into a swat. "Naughty," he scolded. "No words unless I demand them from you." He gave her mound another light smack, loving how that made her arch and squirm, before leaning back on his heels. "To keep yourself distracted, why don't you use your fingers.

Slide them up. Spread yourself for me." While he issued the direction, he got to work on his belt and then his fly. "Excellent, sweetheart. Nice and wide. Keep making those little sounds in your throat too. It tells me how much you like this. Now unbend your knees. I want your legs in the air, open for me. Unless you're *not* ready?"

"No!" Her voice was drenched in need. "I mean yes! I'm ready, Sir. Please!"

He fisted his erection, though the move was a huge risk. Pre-come hovered at his tip; a breeze from the air conditioning would send him over the edge. Nevertheless, he got out, "Give me the exact words. 'I'm ready for you to fuck me, Sir.'"

"Yes, please. I—I'm ready for you to fuck me, Sir."

"Fuck you with what?"

"Goddamn it!" she protested.

"Wasn't what I asked." He hovered over her, his length poised near the folds blooming for him. So dewy. So delectable. Such a perfect bloom, he'd never order flowers again without a smile. "I should punish you for that, you know. Roll you over and spank your ass until you're too delirious to think of swearing at me again." Her little shiver was payment enough for now. He wasn't sure he'd last through another assault on her ass. "So what do you want me to fuck you with, Dasha?"

"Your cock. Please. Oh please..."

Her voice climbed higher, inching toward desperation. He couldn't hold out any more either. He'd pocketed a condom from his bag when he'd called to delay the limo and got the thing out as fast as he could now. After sliding it on, he positioned his tip at her entrance—but paused long enough to issue one more command.

"Put your hands on the floor. Dig in deep and brace

yourself. We're going for a good ride, sweetheart."

One more small push to truly test her readiness, and then the hot core of her body sucked him in. Lust drove him into her like a battering ram, and David worried that he'd hurt her like one, until he saw the sheer ecstasy on her face, the strains of her neck, the rock-hard points of her nipples. Damn it if that didn't make him yearn to hold on a little longer. *Make it last, asshole. Hold it in.* He didn't just want to detonate; he wanted to share the release with her.

He clenched his ass. Stretched his strokes out. Slid and then retreated, teased and denied, watching and feeling her spiraling pressure. The sheen coating her face and then her whole body. The breath on her lips, faster and faster, pumped from a heart that pounded beneath his touch. And best of all, the quivers of her walls around his erection, kneading him like drenched velvet. *Needing* him.

Every inch of him...

Her surrender moved him. Gripped him to his core. And compelled him to give an order he'd never issued to a submissive before.

"Open your eyes," he commanded. "Open them. Look at me. I want you looking at me when you come."

Her lush mouth curved as she complied. But he could tell she longed to squeeze those copper depths closed again.

Until her impending orgasm began taking over.

"David!"

"It's okay," he grated. "Let it take you. Let me watch it take you. Come for me, Dasha. *Come.*"

CHAPTER THREE

How the hell Dasha obeyed, she had no idea—but she did, locking her gaze to the storms in his as the orgasm hit.

It was flood and fire, ice and ignition, conflict yet resolution. And all David. Just David. Only him, filling her, devouring her, possessing her—spinning her into a universe of blinding sensation. As she shattered, she reveled in how his cock felt inside her, pushing the limits of her throbbing walls just before he burst too. He bellowed, and the sound filled her head. His beauty consumed her sight: the sweat on his inky brows, the clench of his elegant jaw, the focused strain in his body.

It was beyond what she'd expected, in her body and especially in her heart.

Oh, crap.

She shoved that thought into a spare duffel in her brain and zipped the thing shut. She'd take it out and look at it later. Right now, she wanted only to absorb the magic of the man who still rocked inside her. She wanted to run her hands up the thighs she'd ogled from afar for all these years, to feel the tendons still bunching with each long thrust.

She had no idea she'd actually acted on that impulse until he let out a hum. "That feels good. Touch me more."

His voice washed her with warmth. She smiled, though a massive case of bashful set in. Pretty hilarious, considering their current state. "Really?"

David smiled back, but his tone remained at full command. "Don't make me ask again. Touch me. Anywhere. Everywhere."

He emphasized by giving her a slow, deep kiss. His tongue didn't let an inch of hers go unexplored, as if instructing her what to do to his body too. Dasha set herself to eagerly obey him. She finished gliding her hands up his legs and then continued across the hard swells of his ass. Another growl rumbled from him, vibrating through them both. She took her time raking his back, wanting to memorize that muscled landscape, and then glided her touch along the slopes of his nape and shoulders, loving the deeper moan she got from him because of it. As she spidered her hands at the crests of his arms, he sucked her tongue deeper.

Finally, David let her mouth go. He pressed his forehead to hers, letting their breaths continue to entwine. Without a word, he slid a hand up and then clamped it over her wrist. Seconds later, he completed the action with his other arm. Before he finished, his erection pulsed against her womb again.

"Christ." It came from him on a rough rasp. "Feel what you've done to me again already?"

She sighed, loving the feel of being trapped by him. "Yes..."

He cut her breath short by biting her lip. "Yes what?"

That command.

That was all it took.

Before he was even finished, Dasha discerned a subtle shift in her brain. A release into a place filled with anticipation...and adoration. "Yes, Sir."

"Good." He pressed the word into her ear. "Very good."

Then he showed her his pleasure, revving the pace of his body inside hers again, deliberately pressing her clit with his upstrokes. Within a few minutes, she became a shuddering, needing ball of sensation, a creature she hardly knew, trembling and struggling to increase the friction between them. But the task was easier said than done. With his hands locking her wrists and his torso pinning her, Dasha could only shift her hips, trying to lift herself higher into him. She hoped a pleading sigh would earn a faster pace, but David kept his strokes at one torturous rhythm. He was doing a seven-veil tease on her pussy—now at its seventeenth veil.

She cried out, certain she was going insane.

"Hold it back." The bastard ordered it into her ear the second he glided harder.

Dasha gasped and arched her head back. Frustration slashed her bloodstream. "I—I don't think I—"

"You can. And you will." He gripped her wrists tighter. His fingers dug into her palms, a pain she welcomed as distraction from the pulsing need at the center of her body.

"I...want to please you." She panted. "But it's so hard. It's so—"

"What?" His voice was a husky, mesmeric cadence in her head. She loved it. She hated it. She wanted the one command he wouldn't give. "What is it, Dasha?" he pressed. "Tell me what you feel. Tell me what I do to you."

She swallowed. "T-tah-tingles," she stammered. *Form the words. You can do this. Probably. Hopefully.* "And...tremors. Even my skin is shaking. Tiny earthquakes, everywhere."

"Good," he praised. "Good, baby. What else?"

"You—you make me need it. God, David, please!"

"I make you need what?" He slowed by just a half beat, purposely waiting. Then commanding with deep deliberation, "Say it. Give me the words. All of it, Dasha."

His emphasis dipped only a little. But that tiny scoop delved into a giant pool of meaning. *All of it, Dasha.* He was asking—no, ordering—something different with this second union of their bodies. Something deeper than what he did to her physically. He wanted to know what was going on in her head, her heart. And that was a white flag she couldn't give.

She rolled her face to the side, avoiding his gaze. "Please— can't we just—"

At once, he went still. "Just what?"

Maybe a coy come-on would distract him from the scary stuff. She playfully bit her lip. "Please, Sir. Let's just have a little fun."

She always knew he wasn't like other men. He proved it by pulling out of her and rocking back on his knees. She gasped in shock, but he leveled a stare as silken as one of his Italian ties. "I want to give you what you need, sweetheart, but we're not going any further without the words."

Dasha blinked, even more amazed as he peeled the condom away—despite a cock clearly ready for more. She almost laughed but realized there wasn't a chance in hell David would join her. Instead, he gave her the stare she always referred to as "sharpened murder dagger"—before rising with more sinewy grace than a computer-game knight finishing off a kill. Only she didn't recall any CG hero reaching back to offer a hand of assistance to his prey. Not that she was calling him a hero. A few terms came to mind, but definitely not hero. She drove that point home by giving him nothing but her glower.

"Let me get this straight," she snapped. "You'll help me get to my feet, but you won't help me when I'm pinned on the floor underneath you, begging you to...to—"

"To what?" It was a sincere request, given in that new

voice she'd never heard before tonight.

New voice.

A new addition on a fast-growing list...

Still with that maddening calm, David stepped to the waste can, throwing in the condom and her ruined panties. He slid his pants back on and zipped up in silence. And yeah, he still stole her breath with every confident movement. Damn him.

As he got back into his shirt, he tilted a softer regard toward her. "I didn't make the request to torment you, Dasha."

"Request?" She huffed. "Is that what you call it?" She balled up, pulling her knees to her chin. But he wasn't going to let her get away with such an easy retreat. He crouched in front of her, lifting her chin beneath his finger once more.

"I didn't make you answer me, did I?"

She nailed him a nice, are-you-fucking-serious glare. "You didn't make it that easy to take the pass!"

To her deepening fury, he dropped his hand, rested his elbows on both knees, and chuckled. "If I'd wanted to make you dread your reticence, I would've done so. Have no doubt about that."

Dasha didn't give a peep of retort to that. His promise, given with such knowing confidence, actually stopped her heart for a moment, which did the strangest things to the juices still making acquaintance in her pussy. *Death by arousal, anyone?*

"Fine," she finally said. "So you granted me mercy—"

"Damn straight I did."

"But from what?" Now she did look away. "Deliberately pushing me like that... What were you trying to accomplish? We were having a wonderful time—well, at least I thought we were—but then you pushed with the mind-fuck, and—all right, what?" She snapped it when half a snicker spilled from him. "What's so funny? Is that part of the domination thing too? Screwing a girl's thoughts as you're screwing other things?"

David mellowed his humor to a smile, though his stare became a cutlass. When he reached and thumbed some hair off her cheek, she started wishing for his arrogance again. She knew that part of him. Could predict it. And yeah, could somewhat control it.

"Keep talking," he encouraged. "I couldn't be making the point better myself."

"Huh?"

He slid his hand to her nape. "Most women—most people—wouldn't have considered that a mind-fuck."

"What?"

She tried to jerk away, but he held tighter. "As a matter of fact, most people enjoy getting asked to unveil their desires, to voice what they want without restraint. And you?" He tilted his head again. "You, my beautiful thing, are amazing at listening to needs, to fulfilling desires..."

"But?" She filled in the implied word.

"But when it comes time to ask for something *you* want..." His face tightened. "There's a disconnect button."

"Disconnect button?" Again she fought to get free. No damn use. "My ass!"

"Your ass is one of my new obsessions, but let's leave my plans for it out of the discussion until we talk about your head."

"There's nothing wrong with my—"

"Oh yeah? Dasha, you almost fell off the stage in the first set of shoes Valentina designed for the tour, and yet you didn't tell her to alter them for fear of hurting her feelings. You let the dancers have the better suites at hotels. While we're on that subject, you'd rather freeze in your own room than make a simple call for an extra blanket. Two nights ago, the restaurant brought you salmon instead of chicken, and you refused to send it back."

He finally pulled back, once more looking like a damn CG hero. Cocky. Sexy. Infuriating. Dasha clung to the last tag to fire her comeback. "Valentina spent three weeks working on those shoes. There are eight dancers on this tour and *one* of me; do the math on the room assignments. As far as the blanket, I haven't caught pneumonia yet, right? And the salmon was delicious, so it was win-win."

"Win-win."

"Yeah. And you're supposed to be happier about it than that."

"I'm not happy."

"No shit."

"I'm confused."

"Why?"

"Win. Win." He stomped on both syllables with tight lips. "So that's what you call it, every time you smile through one of your dad's classic flake-outs?"

Dasha huddled against the pain in her chest. If she scrunched tight enough, maybe the horrid, hot agony would leave her alone. "That's not fair."

"Right. And what the senator does to you is fair?"

"My father has nothing to do with this."

"Your father has everything to do with this."

"Why?"

"Because you're lying to him, Dasha. Every time you swallow down your hurt at his no-shows and tell him everything's fine and make up excuses for his neglect, when it's secretly tearing you up...those are lies. To him and to you."

She had no luck on blocking out the pain. It invaded with its usual, ruthless vigor. "You can't know what it's like for him! Mom died right after he got into the Senate. There was nobody there for him—"

"There was nobody there for you either!"

He had more than that to fire off, she was sure of it. But David locked it back so hard, she heard his teeth smash together.

Finally, he let out a hard huff. "Look, I'm not denying how tough it's been for him. But the loss was also yours."

"But I had my music to help me through—and a lot of friends. Dad...he had a shitload of bills to vote on and a state full of people relying on him."

"So you weren't allowed to rely on him too?"

"That's not what I'm saying."

His jaw scissored. "And there's our issue."

She managed a frustrated frown. "Excuse me?"

"It's what you're *not* saying that's gotten us here." He said it as he brushed her cheek again, the movement so tender...and sad. And scaring her. "And it's what will stop us cold from going any further too."

It sounded very much like a good-bye.

Now she was *really* scared.

"David, what are you saying?"

"I'm not going to keep playing therapist here," he stated. "But I also can't be with someone who thinks she has to edit her truth for fear of it being wrong. D/s is also sometimes called Total Power Exchange—and there's a reason I seek it in my sexual relationships, Dasha. It's not just about a great fuck."

"And you think that's all I'm after?"

"I *know* it's not." His anger was oddly comforting. Maybe this wasn't good-bye. "But listen to what I said. Total. Power. Exchange. D, I'm going to ask you to give your body to me in ways you never imagined. And I know you'll rely on me to keep you safe. But how can I rely on you in return?"

"I...don't understand."

"I have to know when I'm pushing a limit for you, when I've gone too far. I can't doubt for a second that you're holding back, or afraid of ruining things, or thinking about the hard day I might have had and just want to please me..." He stopped then, probably noting how her face continued to tighten. "Any of this sound familiar?"

Dasha looked away for a second. "All right," she admitted. "Yes, you're right."

"I don't want to be right. I want to be real. I want *us* to be real. The success of D/s relies on honesty, even when it's hard. Even when it's not a perfect political sound bite. You have to trust that your Other brings their full truth to the table all the time, every time."

She looked back up. Was instantly lost in his gaze, his radiating intensity. "And I will," she told him. "I *will*, David."

He leaned in, relentless with his closeness now. "Really?" His brows went tight, his gaze a dark silver lake. "I barely tapped on the walls of your limits tonight, and you started flinging bricks at me." He shifted his hands to encircle both of hers. "If we're going to go any further, then the bricks have to become dust, Dasha, not weapons. I'm not the enemy."

To her shock, the backs of her eyes started to sting. "I know."

"I think part of you does." He gently pulled her into his lap. "You just have to convince the rest to join the party."

She nodded, slipping her hand beneath his half-buttoned shirt, feeling the steady throb of his heart—and trying to calm the torment of hers. The last time she'd experienced this, she'd been waiting in the wings at Lincoln Center, waiting to perform for Dad, the president, and three thousand invited dignitaries and VIPs. Translation: she'd been terrified out of her mind.

Still, she swallowed and forced her next words out. "I'm going to try. I promise."

One side of his mouth curled upward, giving him the look of a sweet but devious satyr. "I think that's a wonderful promise." Then he brought that mouth to hers in a kiss that stole her senses...and held a million promises of its own.

★ ★ ★

Two weeks later, she downsized that expectation. By about a million.

It wasn't that numbers weren't on her mind. They'd finished the next seven cities of the tour. She'd done twice as many photo shoots, given four times that many interviews, had lost track of the number of corporate sponsors she'd schmoozed. Her head was a basket of lottery balls, it was so filled with numbers.

Which made the "zero" she'd been getting from David a more torturous mystery by the day.

Zero: the number of times he'd touched her after they'd left her dressing room at the Garden.

Zero: the number of glances he'd given her beyond his typical, encouraging winks.

Zero: the amount of interest he'd expressed, even when she e-researched a hundred BDSM articles and blogs in front of him.

Zero: the thoughts she was barely able to give anything else after getting all that knowledge and aching to talk about it with him. And aching in other parts of herself too...to make it all happen with him.

Five hundred: the number of occasions she thought about wringing his beautiful, horrible neck.

She fought, unsuccessfully, not to entertain such thoughts as she entered the Viceroy Miami Hotel suite they'd deemed the tour crew office. Okay, she barged more than entered—whatever; semantics—while tossing down her key card and all but one of her shopping bags before whipping a glare around the room.

The *empty* room.

Ugh. One splashy entrance of fury, now wasted. She was actually late for the four p.m. meet-up David had requested, but a bunch of fans had recognized her during the shopping trip in Bal Harbour, and she couldn't refuse their autograph requests. But the driver had told her David was okay with the delay...

And maybe you should stop trying to read his mind, since that's been so successful the last two weeks.

Nevertheless, she did exactly that during the sudden solitude. Once more she hit the mental Back button, replaying those last moments from New York, trying to see how they'd gotten from her heartfelt promise and that tender kiss—to this.

Whatever *this* was.

Ivory Berber cushioned her steps across the suite's spacious living room. She'd told him she'd try to open her heart, and she'd meant it. She'd accepted his kiss and treasured it. She'd thought they'd work together on her emotional "bricks," though she had less than half a clue what David had meant. But she'd been willing to work at it—for him. She still was. At least she *thought* so...

A serrated sigh fell out. She wrapped her arms close as she stopped at the suite's huge windows. Forty-eight floors down, the lights of Biscayne Boulevard sparkled in the twilight, a silver-and-chartreuse strand winding along the water. One of the sliders to the balcony was opened by a couple feet, adding a sultry touch of late July warmth to the Arctic blasts of the hotel's air conditioner.

A tiny smile bloomed. David had done that for her, knowing how much she hated icebox hotel air.

"You're back. Good."

She spun even though his statement came on a silken tone. She tried to stash her emotions, but just the sight of him tore at her self-control. His classic mouth was bordered by a fringe of dark stubble. His hair, slightly damp from sweat, spiked in a bunch of sexy directions. The rest of him, encased in a snug black tank and matching training pants, looked pretty freaking fine too.

She frantically tried to get the barricades back up. Down they crashed again as he flipped his exercise towel over a shoulder and closed the door with a backward kick. He did both without looking away from her.

"Really?" she finally got out. "And why is that?"

"There's a stack of glossies for the radio station promos tomorrow. I need your sig on them."

"Oh." Only by sheer force did she keep her disappointment from bleeding on her flippancy. "Fine. Cool. Whatever." She thrust the bag into his hand on her way to the desk. "Hand me a Sharpie while you open your present."

"Present?" The Composure King cracked a little. His

tone warmed like honey in the sun. "What's the occasion? Did I forget my own birthday?"

"No." She sat down at the desk. *Eyes on the pictures. Eyes on the pictures.* "Not your birthday."

"Wow. It's beautiful. Italian silk in red. These are my favorite ties."

She concentrated on regulating her breath. And restraining her retort to her head. *You think I don't know that?*

"So if not my birthday...why?"

Because maybe it'll pull open whatever door I slammed in you?

The arctic air conditioning kicked on again. Cars honked on the boulevard. All that noise filled the atmosphere—paling in comparison to the tension between them.

David dug into that pause with a muttered oath. Then gritted, "Fine. I'm not going to drag it out of you, Dasha. Let me get your pen, and you can be on your way—"

"Fuck you."

At once, she longed to pull back the words, never uttered in the five years between them. Until she saw the glints in David's eyes, stabbing her from across the room, almost as if *congratulating* her.

"Fuck you," she repeated, fighting for an even keel to her voice. "Okay, David? Are you happy? I'm pissed as hell at you. How's that for a reason? How dare you! Haven't you noticed a second of my confusion these last two weeks? My agony? How I've been trying to understand things better, to learn what you need from me as a submissive and a lover?"

His gaze gleamed silver bright now. "I've noticed every second."

"Then what the hell? You've just chosen to...what...wait

me out on this?"

He took a long breath—but damn him, that maddening poise stayed intact. Until Dasha looked closer and spotted the vein pulsing in his jaw. Heard the tight string in his voice as he spoke again.

"Hadn't been my first choice. But a lot of times, the right one isn't."

"Is that supposed to make me feel better?" She bolted up, needing to pace. To give him a physical demonstration of her fury and frustration. "I don't get this bullshit, David. And nowhere, in anything I've read, does it say I have to put up with it."

The twitch disappeared as he tilted his head. "You're completely right," he said with steely calm. "But that's been your choice to make."

For a strange second, she wondered if his hard stare was due to the bruise she certainly sported across her forehead by now—the one from beating her head against his wall of cryptic crap. "Damn it, David!"

As fast as the words left her, he vise-gripped a hand around her arm. "You want to cut through the shit? Then let's do that, Dasha."

Suddenly, the workout towel was no longer on his shoulder. In a second, he'd whisked it around her nape. He twisted it, locking her in place. Their faces moved just inches apart. "The choice *is* yours, Dasha. But you're going to make it right here, right now. I've been waiting for you to finally come to me, freely and on your own, and it's been a goddamn torture session. So yeah, *I'm* sick and tired of this bullshit too."

A shiver coursed through her. "You've been waiting for me? Why? After what happened in New York?"

"What happened in New York was amazing. But it was also new and emotional and a huge change, especially for you." His nostrils flared on a harsh breath. "If I initiated anything with you after that, I knew it would unravel everything we talked about. I'd never know if this was something you really wanted."

Her mouth fell open. Closed. Dropped again. "Something...I really..."

"You think I didn't want to talk things through with you? To pull you into some dark corner, suck the air from your lungs with my mouth, and ask how you're doing? To make you repeat everything you've been reading to me, feeling your pussy pulse around my finger while you do?"

Frantic gulp. "Oh."

"Yeah," he countered. "Oh fucking oh. That's what I've been up against, about a hundred times a day—all the while dealing with the crew, the dancers, the press, and the *world,* talking about you every minute as if I can't stop thinking about you submitting to me once again, opening for me...*fuck.*"

His grip on her nape felt like feathers when compared to his stare. His eyes held her captive, a pair of relentless shackles. "So," he said through locked teeth, "you know exactly what the choice is, don't you?"

Dasha managed a tiny dip of her head. Another sparse swallow. "Yes. I do."

"Good. And now you're going to make it, one way or the other. You've danced around this bush for two weeks." He pressed a thumb up into the bottom of her jaw, digging just deep enough to keep her captive, his touch a steady burn. After a moment, he slid it to her mouth and pressed in, prodding her lips apart. "So open this delicious mouth of yours and give me the words."

She tried to shift her mouth around sound, but her heartbeat throbbed in her throat. Her arms and legs had turned to yarn. And her whole womb pulsed, dancing to the beat set by his animal tone. Yearning for him more with every passing second. God help her, needing his total control.

"I want to give you a world of magic, Dasha. A place where you'll be set free, your body and your mind pleasured like you've never known." He stroked the corner of her mouth, the pad of his thumb capturing the tears rolling there. "But you know there's a price. You know I'll demand more from you than you've ever given to a lover before. Because I'll be more than your lover."

"I—I know."

He leaned closer. He smelled amazing, full of musk and man. "Then say it. What will I be, Dasha?"

"My Dominant." She wasn't ashamed of the rasp. She longed to say it again...yet wondered how she ever could. Her body was falling into an abyss, but her mind clung stubbornly to the cliff. "My...my Sir," she managed to finish.

Though his gaze glittered in pleasure, his tone remained granite. "Is that what you really want? Or...would you prefer a Sharpie?"

She struggled to breathe. But basic actions felt a thing of the past. Oh, who was she kidding? Life as she knew it had started to change two weeks ago, on that backstage floor in Madison Square Garden. The match struck. The fire ignited.

And yet...she'd only just been singed a little, hadn't she?

If she did this, what else would the fire burn away inside her? And how much of it?

But if she didn't, could she live in the cold again?

That contrast never seemed clearer as he ran his thumb

across her lower lip. The contact was a branding iron, its wake a trail of ice.

"I'm scared," she admitted.

"I know." His mouth hardened. "And I can't promise that'll go away."

"I...know." Again, the admission felt terrible. And exhilarating.

"But I won't give you any more time to think about it either."

"I don't need any." She inhaled deeply and then smiled as she let out the breath. "I've decided."

★ ★ ★

She reminded herself of those words—more specifically, the conviction with which she'd given them—just a half dozen hours later. She'd meant every word then. And yes, no matter how loud the thunder in her heart, she did now too. She just had to keep reminding herself of that. She wanted this with David, and she trusted him.

The mental sticky note was a necessary measure, thanks to how he'd responded to her next action. She'd given him a gentle kiss, pulled the towel from him, and then dropped it to the floor, using it as a cushion upon which to kneel. According to all the BDSM manuals, for lack of a better thing to call them, that should've been enough for him to order her to the bedroom.

Instead, David had gone back to being His Majesty of Inscrutable, telling her he wanted to give her a "surprise." He'd also said it would take a few hours for the proper "setup." Her instructions would follow during the afternoon, he'd said.

They'd consisted of a single note of four lines, arriving in a plain, sealed envelope to her suite. She now held that note in one slightly shaky hand.

In the other hand, she held on to the sole item he'd directed her to come with—besides her naked body. Dasha let the floor-length cloak hang against her fingers, the garment feeling as weighted as the tension in her stomach.

She'd made a promise. She intended to keep it. Even if her nerves chomped through every inch of her bloodstream—which, right now, seemed entirely possible.

CHAPTER FOUR

He wasn't nervous.

He wasn't going to call it that.

As he stepped off the VIP elevator at the Viceroy's spa level, David mentally wadded up the word and tossed it behind the compartment's closing doors.

Like that did any good.

He'd just meditated for ninety minutes. He'd summoned every fucking Zen technique to calm the Daytona 500 of his bloodstream and still came up with the one result he didn't want.

A memory.

That memory.

Dasha, tearful and beautiful before him, showing him she was ready to begin a journey that scared the shit out of her. And, in the process, never filling him with more pride, desire, and adoration.

The feelings hit again, three times more intense, as the elevator chimed and she appeared beyond the doors. Her hair formed a golden cloud around her face, a luminous contrast against the long, black velvet cloak in which he'd told her to arrive.

Down, he ordered the cock now slamming against his black leathers.

Aloud, he said a simple, "Good evening." He smiled and crooked one finger at her. *Come here.*

Despite an obvious gulp, his valiant little submissive obeyed. Her bare feet didn't make a sound on the shiny marble floor of the spa's main lobby.

David gently pried her fingers from where they locked the cloak around her. "Let me see." He gave it a hint of threat. "Arms at your sides."

She flushed but complied.

He nudged the fabric aside with the backs of his fingers, revealing her complete nudity.

Holy. Fuck.

Pert breasts and coral nipples. Tapered waist and slender hips. Long thighs and delicate feet.

He was the luckiest goddamn bastard on the planet.

"Absolutely gorgeous." He pressed a long kiss to her lips. "Thank you for coming as I instructed."

She tried to smile. Tried. "David—"

"Excuse me?" he interrupted.

"Sir," she corrected. "Um...we're—" Her stare scurried from him, scouring every corner. "This is...uh...really public."

He gritted once more against the pain in his groin. Her frantic rasp got him harder than the silkiest come-on lines he'd ever gotten.

"Breathe, sweetheart. I've made appropriate arrangements, so the three of us won't be bothered. But, D, a note for the future..." He reached and stripped the cloak completely off her. "You'll get naked for me whenever I tell you, wherever I tell you. And you'll know that I'll always make your safety, as well as your anonymity, my first priorities. Are we clear about that?"

She swallowed again—but along with the trepidation in her eyes, he now saw unmistakable arousal.

"Yes, Sir." She parted her lips as if to utter something else but bit them instead.

"What?" David asked. "What do you need to say?"

"You said...the three of us?"

As if the question were her cue, a figure appeared in the doorway leading from the spa's treatment rooms. He turned and smiled at the woman standing there. He'd never noticed it until now, but she looked like a dark-haired version of Dasha. Long, curly, dark-cocoa waves framed a heart-shaped face of expressive features. She held her gorgeous figure with perfect posture. He would likely have fallen hard for Laurelle at one time, but one most dominant aspect of her personality stopped him. Make that *Dominant,* capital *D*.

"*Ma chere!*" the woman greeted, striding over in her tailored white medical smock, matching pencil skirt, and white high-heeled Mary Janes. If it wasn't for her dramatic eye makeup and dark-red lips, she could've passed for an efficient assistant in any medical building in the city.

"Good evening, Mistress," David said in return, dutifully kissing both her outstretched hands. Out of the corner of his eye, he didn't miss Dasha's furtive glance, filled with curiosity and jealousy in the same little move. He tried to ease both— as much as one could to their newbie, naked submissive—by pulling her close. "It's great to see you again. Business has been good?"

Laurelle returned Dasha's scrutiny with an appraising stare of her own. "*Oui,*" she said. "But better tonight, I think. She is stunning, David." She said his name with the exotic flair of the French Polynesian isle from which she came. *Dahhh-veed.* "And you two are beautiful together."

"*Merci,*" he returned.

"You say she is...new to things?"

"Yes," he answered, smiling down at D as he did. "She's very new, though the two of us have been friends for a while. I care for her...very much. So naturally, I wanted this to be memorable for her."

"Ah, *magnifique*. And she is called..."

"D," he supplied, returning Dasha's glare with a firm look of his own. Her outrage was understandable; she stood in the middle of a five-star spa reception area, exposed to a complete stranger who might be hiding devices that could instantly export images to the paparazzi or worse. "Just D," he emphasized, pressing a kiss to her forehead, "when she's with me like this." He squeezed her shoulder. "And she understands that trust is going to be a huge factor in tonight's proceedings."

Despite his efforts at reassurance, Dasha's posture stayed stiff as starch. She still felt amazing against him, her body soft, smooth, tiny, lovely. He pushed on, hoping some regular niceties would relax her, "Darling, I'd like to introduce Madame Laurelle Miri, a dear friend who is going to assist us this evening."

"Assist us with what?"

So much for niceties. He gave her thigh a small swat. "Manners," he murmured when she jerked in reaction. "I know you're nervous, but be nice. I trust Laurelle implicitly. Her discretion is solid; you don't have to worry. She also happens to be the best at what she does."

At last, Dasha extended a hand. "Nice to meet you, Laurelle."

"*Enchanté,*" his friend responded. As they shook, Laurelle also took the chance to openly admire Dasha's figure.

The extra attention didn't escape his sub. D pressed back

against him in a hurry.

"And what is it...that you're the best at?"

A thick pause fell. Laurelle jingled a little laugh, and Dasha trembled harder next to him. He admitted a few conflicted sensations of his own. What he'd planned for the next hour... it was definitely going to be one of his more creative fantasies come true; the scene he'd been saving for Dasha alone. But it would also be the litmus test of whether he and D were meant to follow a path into the D/s realm together. If the test failed, he had to be willing to deal with the repercussions, no matter what form they took.

But if it was successful...

Yeah, focus on that. Focus on the submissive you unveiled in New York. Concentrate on that awakening you beheld in her eyes, on how gorgeous she was when she climaxed for you. Focus on letting that creature fly free tonight.

It was *so* time to get started.

He took a steadying breath before smiling at Laurelle. "Go ahead," he told his friend. "It's all right to give our girl a little preview."

Laurelle returned the look with sly feline intent. "Let us just say...I like to play with shiny, sharp things."

D's reaction was exquisite. Other than the extra tension to her spine, she maintained her decorum better than a queen. "With—" She cleared her throat. "I'm not sure I follow. Wh-What do you mean?"

Laurelle took a measured step forward. "Little D," she charged from between her teeth, "stop the stuttering and answer me a question." She nodded at him. "Do you trust your Sir?"

Dasha squirmed in his hold, almost as if trying to throw

him off. But after just seconds, she snapped, "Yes. Of course."

David dipped his lips to her nape. "Thank you."

Laurelle wasn't so impressed. "*Bien,*" she stated coolly. "Then prove it. Heed his word. Mind your manners. Trust that he has arranged a unique surprise for you. Come along now."

She cut a model-perfect pivot on her heels and then started down the hallway to the treatment rooms. David already knew D wasn't "coming along" anywhere with anyone at the moment. But this reaction he could deal with. To be honest, it was better than he expected. That gave him justification to give her a patient regard instead of a reprimanding scowl.

"You have concerns."

Dasha's gaze flashed with bronze fire. "Damn right I have concerns."

"Such as?"

"Are you kidding?" Her lips twisted. "When I got your invitation, I thought we were meeting here *alone.*"

Her blush continued down to the center of both breasts. He let his gaze linger there as he began his response.

"You thought you were coming to begin your journey as my submissive."

She stared up at him. "Well, yeah."

He cupped her gorgeous little chin. And couldn't help a small smile. "That's exactly what's going on, sweetheart."

She didn't return his smile. That, he *did* expect—along with the little bite she gave one side of her lip, as well as the tormented glance she flashed. What he didn't anticipate was his body's roar of reaction to all of it, especially as she looked down the hall to where Laurelle waited. Her dilemma, wrestling with what she'd promised this afternoon versus the payback tonight, was gorgeous. Captivating. It earned her his unending patience, simply because he couldn't take his gaze off her.

And wondered how he ever would again.

Hell.

He'd called it conflict a few minutes ago. Now the truth was like a hit from a Hummer. This wasn't conflict. It was plain, simple, cart-before-the-horse stupidity.

Turn it off, asshole.

Tonight was about showing Dasha where they were going from here. *If* they were going from here. It was about her submission *and* her satisfaction, but it was also about showing her the clear rules of this deal. Going Barry Manilow now, being anything other than her Dominant, feeling anything except the desire to control her and the mission to pleasure her, wasn't part of that deal. Not now. Not ever.

She bit the other end of her lip. "I don't understand."

"There's an...appearance that I require in my playmates." He lowered his hand, cupping it over the little curls of her mound. "No offense, you understand. This is gorgeous, but I demand direct access to your sweet clit at all times."

"Oh."

The word flowed with more warmth than the V in which he lingered his touch. He dipped his own voice to a possessive growl. "I don't want anything in the way of touching you in the deepest ways possible. Of feeling you, all of you, quiver for me."

Three more seconds passed before their reverie got sliced by D's comprehension. "Sh-Shiny and sharp things," she blurted. "Oh. *Oh.* So...you're going to... *Laurelle* is going to..."

"Shave your pussy for me." Saying the words did nothing to improve his composure. He fought the craving to just slide his fingers into her now. He'd find her wet too; he was sure of it. He could feel the moisture, teasing his fingers even through her pubic hair.

"Wh-Why don't you just do it yourself?"

"Because I want to watch you. I want to see every beautiful inch of you...as you enjoy things."

She didn't miss his stress on enjoy. "You sound damn sure of that."

"Because I am." He met her gaze directly. He wanted her to know how deeply he meant it. Most importantly, he needed her attention for what he said next. "I've also requested Laurelle's expertise...for a second procedure."

As carefully as he'd couched it, he still couldn't predict her response to that. All things considered, he thanked fate for her fondness of the royal family impressions tonight. Her step back, seeming to forget her nudity in the wake of indignation, was both adorable and gorgeous.

"Procedure?" She gave the word air quotes. "Listen, mister. The girl-kissing thing jumped the shark last year. And I'm not sticking around for a pap smear either."

He let her see the arousal in his face as he lunged and pulled her close again. Like he'd be able to hide it. "No mouth touches yours but mine tonight." He palmed both her ass cheeks. "And believe me, Laurelle doesn't do speculums."

A tiny smile touched her lips too as she wriggled in his hold. His cock lurched in reaction. Fuck. She was so vulnerable, so warm, so naked. It was going to take a miracle for him to last until Laurelle finished the shave, let alone the rest of what he had planned.

"All right, then. What's your devious plan?"

He forced himself to step back and shifted his hold to her hips. If he stood a chance of making it to the end of this thing, it started with reestablishing roles. On the other hand, a full disclosure would derail the plans before they'd chugged out of the station. Tact was in order. And he sucked at the stuff in the best of situations.

"It pleases me to hear you asking questions and speaking up." He let his hands slide up her rib cage. "As a matter of fact, you're fucking gorgeous when you do. Thank you."

Dasha arched both brows. "That's your answer?"

He leaned and bit her bottom lip this time. "Let your Dom finish." By now, his grip reached her breasts. He reveled in the sweet little intake of her breath as he tugged at both nipples. "I love these," he said against her mouth. "And I've got plans for them. A way of branding them as mine."

She pushed her face up, begging for deeper contact. "Sounds wonderful."

"Even if there's a little pain?"

Her features trembled anew. But she looked him in the eyes with ferocious intent. "If you'll be there, I'm ready for anything."

The Manilow tune threatened his blood again, specifically in the region of his heart. For a second, just one, he gave in enough to drop a kiss to her nose. "I'm not going anywhere."

After that, it was time to shut off the tenderness faucet once more. David slipped a firm hand into hers and guided her down the hallway. Once they got to the doorway where Laurelle waited, he shifted his hold to Dasha's waist—conscious preparation for her next reaction.

He was glad he had that forethought.

Dasha stopped cold in the doorway. Went stiff. Then backed up by two steps.

The room was clearly one of the spa's cosmologic

procedure areas, with an adjustable treatment table and bright gooseneck lights instead of a candlelit massage setup. The table looked almost medical—except for the straps along its length, the fresh plastic sheets, and the modified gynecologist stirrups at its base. Each steel bracket sported a set of padded ankle cuffs. When Laurelle told him she had connections in the city, she wasn't kidding. He had no idea how she'd gotten the thing in here, but he was damn grateful. Just looking at it ramped his blood again. And his cock? Erection came nowhere near describing the torment.

He couldn't wait to see Dasha mounted in it.

He just had to melt her down again.

"Uh...okay..." She tried backing up again, but David had already closed the door—and retightened his hold. "The straps will help hold you," he explained, "so Laurelle gets exactly what she's aiming for." He raised his other hand to her face and pulled her gaze to his again. "You're going to be beautiful. And you're ready for anything, remember?"

Laurelle, however, wasn't synching with him in the patience department any more. "*Cherie,* I am accredited and licensed for this procedure in seven countries." She sharpened the edge on her voice with the dual smacks of her medical gloves, fitting them against her wrists. "You are going to be fine, D. Come on now. Up into your place."

She patted the table, but Dasha didn't move. Laurelle arched an elegant brow. David caught the message as if she'd sprayed it on the wall.

He released a sigh. Then looked at his sub. "You need a little motivation, don't you?"

As he expected, she lifted a hopeful gaze, lips already half pursed.

He didn't give her that kiss.

Instead, he turned his grip into a full arm-wrap to her waist. He turned her in that grip, shoving her over for a good stare at his foot, her ass high and unhindered for him. He used that access at once, dropping one hard *thwack* to each cheek. She matched two startled yelps at the openhanded spanks, and the sounds tugged at him in all the right places. That and the twin blooms he'd created on her delectable, creamy swells.

"Hmm," Laurelle crooned. "You have gotten better at that."

"Better target," he returned, taking full advantage of the chance to smooth out the pain for D, slowly stroking her skin.

The Domina directed her next comment at his sub. "Have you learned your manners, *peu soumis*? Or would you like your to Sir deliver a bit more motivation?"

All David's senses tuned themselves to Dasha's reaction. He'd seen her bristle at reporters for less attitude than Laurelle's, but this was a different time and a very different place. She'd already floored him so much with her courage tonight and did again now. Though her breaths came shallow, she went slack in his hold, silently acknowledging his leadership. When he brought her back up, her eyes hung at half-mast. She stepped obediently to the table. As she slid onto it, he watched a multitude of emotions cross her face. There was still the fear, of course. But he also saw the beginnings of a submissive's deep peace...and the light of adoration. She even lifted a tentative smile.

He returned the smile as Laurelle positioned each of D's feet into the stirrups. The ankle straps came next, clinking as the Domina locked down on each side. Laurelle moved up, strapping in each of Dasha's thighs, followed by a strap across her waist. A pair of thinner restraints went above and below her breasts, making those incredible mounds push up more. His own chest constricted, clamped again by those sensations he'd had out in the foyer. Those goddamn emotions, taking new pickaxes at the caverns of his heart. He swore inwardly and then dynamited the fuckers again.

"Would you like to have the last honor?" Laurelle held out a pair of leather handcuffs joined by a double-sided latch. She finished by pulling another extension from the table, directly over Dasha's head, a hearty steel rod with a fastener hook on top.

David grinned. Now this was familiar territory. Dasha's muscles trembled as he brought up one of her arms and then the other. She wanted to resist. Badly.

He soothed out her rebellion by trailing kisses across her face as he snapped the bonds around her slender wrists. Holding her gaze, he finished by hooking her into place... exacting her final piece of trust.

Words swelled in his heart. Surged up his throat. He let them spill out.

"Thank you."

He brushed her breasts with his knuckles.

"Thank you."

He ran an open palm down her stomach.

"Thank you." As he gave it to her the last time, he stepped between the stirrups, spread them wide, and locked them into place.

From just outside the vortex of their bond, Laurelle hummed her approval. Then issued the words that officially began their flight as Dominant and submissive.

"*Trés bien, mon ami.* Shall we begin?"

He looked again to the tremulous face of the most special, incredible pet he'd ever known...or had. And watched the golden depths of her eyes go wide as Laurelle stepped between them with a long, gleaming shaving razor in her hand. And once more, forced his cock not to burst from need for the sweet grotto at his fingertips.

CHAPTER FIVE

Dasha had been on the brink of protesting how they treated her like a pinned butterfly. That was before she felt like one.

She'd barely been able to believe what she'd done already, but David had been at her side the whole time, his presence so different in his domination yet so *him* at the same time. That perception was quickly obliterated, thanks to Laurelle and her long steel blade.

Holy shit.

Now the straps made sense.

Every cell in her body screamed at her to take flight. All right, damn it—not every cell.

The exception to her terror was, horrifyingly, confined to one set of nerves. The ones now spread beneath the stares of the people who *could* move.

"She has a lovely little pussy." Laurelle said it with a surprising note of reverence. "So sweet and petite."

"Agreed." David's tone was tight. So was his face. No. Not tight. Restrained. The look on his face was mesmerizing... because he was mesmerized with her. In giving him complete power, it was like he turned around and gave it right back to her. His eyes glittered with silver intensity, and his jaw was etched in stark beauty. He took a breath, long and labored, as he knifed his gaze up her body, deliberately lingering over every inch.

Yep. Pinned butterfly.

But suddenly, the most beautiful one on earth.

If she was even on earth anymore.

For now, the restraints on her body felt like hoists to heaven. *Look at me like that forever, please.*

"All right," Laurelle instructed, shoving at him. "Back with you now. Go sit and enjoy the show, *Monsieur Dominante.*"

"David." The protest spilled before she could stop it. She lurched against the straps for the first time—and truly discovered how little she could move. Her pulse calmed a little when he rose over her, sliding a hand to her cheek. She pressed her face into his touch, not caring how awkward she looked. "You're not going far?"

He stroked her cheek with a thumb. But his reply came with low control. "I'm going to let you answer that." When she winced, he shifted his hold to her nape. "D, answer me. Do you really think I'd let you come to any harm?"

She answered without hesitation. "No."

"All right, then. Do you wish to please me?"

That slammed her eyes shut. She had to, in her battle to fight the encroaching sting behind them. *Don't do it. Not now. Don't turn into a sprinkler ad.* "Yes," she got out. *More than anything.*

"Then are you going to speak or act out again, unless Laurelle or I ask you a question or give you permission?"

Just like that, he morphed the sting. It dissolved and turned into mental mist instead, that strange, soft haze he could bring just by threading the perfect strand of command to his voice. Her pussy completed the circuit, trembling and trickling in its need for him. Damn it, how was this possible? How could she be the picture of turned on, when to any fly on the wall, she was the epitome of bare and helpless? Apparently, she'd earned the trophy for Completely-Smitten-with-Sir too.

"No," she finally replied. "I won't."

David pressed closer. He drew breath as if to kiss her, but instead, she felt a moist stroke at the corner of her eye. His tongue, warm and sure, licked her tears away. "Good girl. You honor me so much."

Then he was gone.

Dasha willed her eyes to stay closed, her mouth to stay silent, and her heart not to pull an *Alien*. Laurelle didn't speak again, though the woman sang a soft tune in French as she shifted to where David had just stood, between Dasha's legs.

There was a gentle clinking sound from the same vicinity, like something being mixed in a bowl, and Dasha detected the smells of eucalyptus and mint. After that, a soft swishing...and then a cool, wet brush across the top of her pussy.

Her nerves flared to life. Even the deepest parts of her womb reacted, clenching with tension. Thick, creamy suds were spread along her skin and into her tight curls.

Before she could stop it, a low moan trickled out.

"Relax, *chere*." Laurelle stroked her gloved fingertips along the insides of Dasha's thighs. "Open to me."

Right. Relax. Because the possibility of becoming a Clue game answer was so soothing. "She was gutted with the razor in the spa, by the kinky French nurse."

Her sarcasm fled the moment Laurelle began her grooming.

The experience...

Was exquisite.

Laurelle took brief, light strokes, an impeccable combination of purpose and stimulation. The eucalyptus in the cream brought on endless tingles. Right after the hair was gone, the woman's velvety, slender fingers soothed and stroked Dasha's intimate lips, transforming the terror into a cloud of pure arousal. Her thoughts tunneled and focused on every moment. It was like a spa massage, only better...so much better. She silently begged the woman not to stop.

Please don't ever stop...

She came seriously close to yelling it out as the strokes on her clit got warmer. Longer. More incessant. Dasha writhed, squirming against her bonds as the gloved fingers explored, opening her pussy like she'd never been exposed before.

"Fuck." The guttural exclamation belonged to David. It was beautiful.

"*Oui*," came Laurelle's concurrence. "She is stunning, *monsieur*. Such a lusty little thing. Look how pink and soft and wet she is."

"Yeah. I see. *Damn*."

"Shall I spread her more for you? I have brought my pussy clamps."

Tension gripped anew. Clamps? On her? Down there? But David's harsh moan stripped the protest from her. To make him feel that way, to elicit such a sound from him again, she'd agree to damn near anything.

She wouldn't have to cross that bridge tonight, though.

"No," David returned, his voice an unwavering growl. "My turn. I want to taste."

"Ah. *Magnifique*. Have a go while I prepare for the next step."

Dasha's mind reeled again. The next step. The second procedure he'd mentioned and she'd forgotten about, thanks to the incredible turn of the last twenty minutes. Fear bit again but gained no purchase. Her body wouldn't let her brain take that dive. Her muscles, nerves, and skin quivered together as Laurelle stepped aside and she felt David's presence between her legs again.

His touch descended upon her bare flesh. His fingers, long and sure, claimed her more boldly than Laurelle's soft strokes. Taking her as if to possess her. He pinched one side of her clit and then the other, tugging the folds until she shuddered. Dasha hissed, fighting her outcries, until he ordered, "It's okay, sweetheart. Scream for me."

She did, wailing as he squeezed her core, kneading her without compunction. He focused the pressure low, drawing her clit out, exposing the hard, needy ridge to his stare and his gritted, "Fuck, *yes.*"

She screamed again, the sound born of both pain and pleasure, as he sank his mouth to her flesh with hungry abandon. His tongue gave her no mercy, no tenderness, no cessation. She couldn't fight, had no choice but to let him ravage her. She'd never felt more desirable or needed in her life, and though he ate at her like a savage, he draped her soul in swaths of silken joy. She was bound to him. Connected with him. She sighed in surrender as his mouth broke open the chrysalis of her awakened senses.

But suddenly, he tore away. No, she realized, was whacked away.

"Naughty man," Laurelle scoffed. "*Cesser,* Greedy. You are going to cause our darling to come. You know we cannot have that yet."

Why the hell not? For all the magic the woman worked on her body, this micromanagement was exasperating.

Which made David's follow-up more than a stunner. "Right," he stated. "You're right. Let's get on with it."

Dasha opened her eyes. She kept her commitment not to speak but hurled a questioning stare at him. The bastard actually grinned, thumbing her juice off his lip and then licking that finger again, as if sucking her pussy was better than digging into a chocolate bar.

"G-Get on with...what?" She'd meant it to be more Lara Croft and less Snow White, but his attitude was her undoing. The look he delivered, continuing the heat from his sexy-as-freak thumb-suck, warmed every inch of her all over again. He ran his hands up her skin in its wake, even savoring the buckles that bound her, before cupping both sides of her face.

"How are you doing?"

She got down a dry swallow. She had no idea how he'd turned four simple words into sexual crack. Or how she absorbed every one of them like a desperate junkie.

"Not...bad." It wasn't a lie.

"You're the most breathtaking thing I've ever seen."

She knew he meant every word too. Her skin flared hotter. "Thank you, Sir."

"You've been so amazing." He pressed a kiss on the corner of her mouth. "Now I want you to be a little more so." He did the same to the other corner. "And I think you can do it too."

She should've felt it coming, even without the new edge to his voice. All she'd had to do was breathe. A distinct smell entered the air, coming from the counter where Laurelle now prepared the second procedure. It was alcohol. Not a nice Pinot either.

Shit, shit, shit. What was up the man's beautifully filled sleeve? She knew it involved her breasts in some way. He'd prepared her. But somehow, that didn't stop her heartbeat from making its way into both her jutting mounds.

But he's kept his word. You're still safe. More than safe. Floating on a cloud of endorphins and lust, as a matter of fact.

But still cuffed in. Still being asked to give up her trust again.

She finally got a reply out. "What kind of...'a little more so'?"

He cocked his head, teething his bottom lip. All he missed were a pair of horns to look like a rogue from a Renaissance painting about to tie down a princess and have his way with her. The look deepened as his gaze dropped to her breasts. No surprise there. He'd given her notice.

"I always ask my submissives to wear a little piece of bling with my initials, to remember me by when we're apart."

Dasha almost laughed in relief. Until she got a whiff of the alcohol again. "Oh kaaay..."

"But you're no ordinary submissive," he qualified. "In many ways." An arch of his black brows amped the whole rogue thing, especially as he rubbed a thumb over her right nipple. "If you suddenly appear in public with *DP* on a necklace or a bracelet, the media will swoop like vultures. So I got a little creative." He scraped his nail over that erect nub, making her quiver whether she wanted it or not. "Damn. I was right. Your nipples *do* like being played with." He paused, openly admiring the flesh between his fingers. "Yes. They're the perfect choice."

The arousal cloud officially evaporated. Dasha ground her wrists into the cuffs. "The perfect choice? Okay...David... what—"

"Hold her still." Laurelle turned and braced against the table in a commanding stance. She'd ditched the razor, though—for something that iced Dasha's blood. A long piercing needle. "The less you fight, *chere,* the better this will go."

She shot the woman a glare. Her heart hammered. "The *better* this will go? I don't see anything better about—"

"Pinch it a little harder, *monsieur.* I enjoy decorating a nice hard nipple."

Dasha glared back to David. His expression arrested her for a second. She'd never seen him so magnificent, the demon in him melding with the beautiful man, eyes molten silver, tongue against his lips, openly desiring her. "David, I—"

"Yes?" His voice coiled through her with its rough, possessive arousal. Crap. To elicit such a sound in him... Couldn't she do this? How bad could it be?

"I'm not a damn cake!" she cried. "I'm not going to be decorated like—"

She would've screamed in shock if the sharp seizure on her breast didn't hurt so much. She looked at the odd silver clamp David now attached to her throbbing nipple.

"They were invented by the Japanese," he explained just before his lips quirked in a sideways chuckle. "Who apparently know how to turn subbies into gorgeous cakes." He dipped his head and took a playful nip at the side of her breast, right below the clamp. "Oh, yeah. Delicious."

"I hope it gives you diabetes."

The words were satisfying, but she should've known they'd have repercussions. David exchanged a nod with Laurelle just before he tugged a string that dangled from the contraption at Dasha's breast. The pressure instantly doubled. Dasha keened.

"Very delicious," he repeated and then let the string go slack. She gasped in relief but refused to show anything else she felt. Certainly not how his tug-of-war with her breast added a little tingle to the pain...and absolutely not how that tingle danced its way down her body, courting even her toes. Would he even believe her? How could pain make one's bloodstream feel so magical?

"All right," he stated. "Now that I have your attention again, I'm going to ask, once more... Would I ever do anything to jeopardize your physical safety?"

She responded with nothing but a glower, refusing to give him an instant victory. The pause cost her another pull on the string. "Fuck!" she cried—while half her mind thought of the tingles. They would come soon; she had to remember that...

"Answer my question, D." He brushed the skin around the grip of the Japanese torture device.

She fought through the fog of torment. "No," she got out. "No, Sir."

"No, what?" he directed.

"No...you would never do anything to jeopardize my physical safety."

"Good." His raised his touch to her cheek. "So good, darling."

His words, church-soft now, unleashed the final dam on her tears—especially as he pulled off the clamp completely, sending the tingles everywhere. The flood cleansed her to emotional depths she'd thought long-buried. Depths she'd thought sealed forever after the loss that had ripped apart her world. But her heart wasn't ripped anymore. It was filled. Engorged with feeling and color and intensity. For the first time in a long time, she was lost to the wonder of a single moment. She didn't think back or ahead. All that existed was this singular moment—filled with David. His gaze on her. His touch on her. His focus on her.

Dasha bent her head toward his palm, silently begging him for more of that amazing spiritual sustenance.

He didn't heed. Instead, lowered his fingers back to her nipple, holding it for Laurelle to sanitize. Dasha's skin went frosty with the cold contact, but her senses froze worse—especially when he stared straight at her and then ordered, "Do it. Now."

CHAPTER SIX

She screamed.

David smothered the sound with his mouth, gripping her face between his hands and forcing her to give him every decibel of her pain. Though Laurelle put the jewelry in with skillful speed, he couldn't let his writhing little sub free. Not yet. He was a fucking fireball, needing to feel more of this, craving the intensity from her body, the fever of her struggling muscles. He finally released her, only to run his tongue up the wild heartbeat in her neck and brace his fingers against her lips, savoring every hot, heaving gasp she emitted. She was taking it, all of it, for him. For him.

She catapulted him to a new stratosphere. Dasha, his gorgeous and amazing Dasha, let him inside her experience like none before.

He didn't want to ever pull away. But he finally forced himself to do so, raising a few inches from her.

He braced for the backlash. Prepped his eyes for her forest fire of a glare. Steeled himself for another scream, perhaps using the safe word that would end this incredible night for good.

Instead, she gave him something more decimating. Her tears. She'd been fighting them with valiance, but now they spilled, heavy and hard, from eyes that held feelings he couldn't decipher...emotions that were soul-deep and perhaps on display for the very first time.

Holy shit.

What was happening inside her?

He'd locked up her body, but in her mind had freed...

What?

He didn't know the answer to that and was damn sure D didn't either.

Without hesitating, David reached for her wrist cuffs.

"Don't." Her charge came with forced strength. "Sir," she corrected and took a ragged breath. "Please don't." He watched her fingers actually curl and stroke at the cuffs. "Finish it," she snapped. "There's another one, right? So finish it."

Laurelle's chuff confirmed he wasn't the only one just thrown into a pit of shock. "Well, well, well. Look who has found himself a brave little girl. Lucky you, *mon chou.*"

"Yeah." He gave that reply readily, gaping at the tawny glory of his amazing little sub. He hoped she saw how she blew him away with her courage and fortitude...and her off-the-Richter fuckable factor, with his first initial in diamonds locked on her right nipple.

Laurelle tossed a suggestive smile. "Perhaps you should make her the lucky one too?"

Thank fuck *someone* in the room was still thinking. "Great. Idea." He was already in position, probably out of hope that D would really endure the depths of his little initiation fantasy then let him "make it up" by filling her in a way she'd never forget. But she'd earned the trophy. He yearned to give her that brass ring and turn the thing gold in the process.

Dasha clearly didn't read his mind on that one—fully justifying her petrified gaze. That made it all the sweeter to secure his hips between hers and then give her pussy a gentle rub. Her glare gave way to a sigh as he explored deeper, swiping her moist clit with his thumb.

"Are you anxious to finish things up, sweetheart?"

"I...ohhh..." Another tease of his fingers. Another sweet, wonderful gasp.

He pressed his crotch against hers, letting her feel each motion as he unbuttoned his pants and took down his fly. His cock busted free of the soft leather, pounding and ready, diving at her slit like a heat-seeking missile.

"I have a new lesson for you." He stated it while sliding on a condom in record seconds. "It's called *Agony and Ecstasy*." He had to lock his jaw as he rocked against her, fighting his body's demand to get inside her oh, about ten minutes ago. "Think you're interested?"

"Yes, Sir!"

He smirked. She was getting the idea.

"Excellent." He started teasing her entrance, pushing in enough so his head was buried, instantly grabbed by her tight muscles. As she whimpered with high-pitched abandon, he again fought against driving into her. This took care of the "agony" part of the deal. God *damn* it.

"Mmm." Laurelle eyed the juncture of their bodies with glittering interest. "Just as I always thought. You are well-built, *monsieur*. Your *fille* is lucky, indeed." She reached and pulled the Japanese nipple clamps from David's pocket. "Shall I make the lesson more interesting now?"

"No!"

"Oh yes." David grinned through the countermand. Still, he delivered discipline on her throbbing pussy. "Unless you do want to end things now, darling?"

He damn near regretted the words, as well as the implication he backed to them, retreating from her a little.

Dasha's gasp paid back the effort. "Okay!" she cried. "Just please...don't..."

Her body finished that with involuntary cunning, sucking him back with excruciating pressure. His grin fell. His dick screamed. For years, he'd been dreaming of having Dasha like this. The fantasies were pale ghosts to the reality.

"I'm not going anywhere." The authority in his tone was possible only from years of practice. To Laurelle, he commanded, "Clamp her. But I'm feeling merciful. Use only one, but use it well. I want to see that pretty tit go nice and hard."

Laurelle released something between a purr and a growl. Dasha whimpered but said nothing else. He adored her for the surrender, for the increasing chunks of trust she gave him...and more. He wasn't sure what that "more" could be described as, not yet, but he was determined to show her how much it meant to him.

He pressed forward again, giving her another inch of his erection. Raw ecstasy filled her face. He savored every second. Her walls pulsed around him, sucking harder at him. He hovered both thumbs over the dark-pink folds just above the juncture of their bodies. As Laurelle began to pinch Dasha's breast, prepping her second nipple, he lowered his fingers into fluttering caresses on her slick flesh. Dasha winced and then gasped. When Laurelle secured the clamp beneath her stiff bud, he slid everything in to full hilt. His thighs slammed to hers. His cock was a solid stick of fire, plunged deep inside her body. He drove his fingers along her clit.

For a moment, he simply soaked in everything about Dasha's energy. The clench of her teeth, countered by the arousal in her eyes. Her moan of pain, mixed with gasps of pleasure. Suffering and succor. Penalty and payback.

Agony and ecstasy.

"You're doing so well." He was mesmerized with how that lifted her mouth—though it was replaced by her grimace as Laurelle tugged on the clamp string.

"Shit! Ohhh..."

"So well," he repeated. "Take it, sweetheart. You can do it."

Her brow furrowed, but she nodded. "I can. I *can.*"

Fuck. Just...fuck.

She drove him insane. He had to claim her. Right now. Dominate her womb as the final seal of his ownership, as the second symbol of his name got driven into her nipple. And feel her accepting him too.

Completion tore close to his surface. Come raced up his cock. That was a good thing, because Laurelle was nearly ready too. Under his fingers, D's juices seeped like tears. Her clit pulsed, hard and ready. Thank God.

"You're going to come with me, D," he ordered. "Do you understand?"

"Y-Yes, Sir."

"You're going to come now. You're going to come hard."

"Yes, Sir!"

He nodded at Laurelle. "Pierce it."

His groan slammed with Dasha's scream as Laurelle drove the needle in. His climax was a mixture of soaring heaven and decadent hell. It rocked him, drained him. He felt D's orgasm consume her too, even as her face contorted from the torture to her breast. He kept up his strokes as a second orgasm shook her, and he signaled to Laurelle to release the clamps along with her wrists. As soon as she did, Dasha pulled him down, clinging hard. She gulped and shook, gripping him like a life ring.

"Careful, sweetheart," he murmured. "Slow, take it slow."

She rebelled by clutching harder. "I—"

"What?" He stroked the dip of her waist. "What is it?" he pressed. "No holding back. I need your complete honesty, D."

Her tears soaked the crook of his neck. "Confused," she finally whispered. "Just...confused. I didn't..."

"What?"

"Expect that. Expect this. All of this."

David smiled and kissed her forehead. "Okay, that's honest. And acceptable."

She burrowed deeper against him before speaking again. "David?"

"Yes?"

"Thank you for my new jewelry."

He pulled away enough to take in the delicate features of his beautiful little sub. No. Beautiful didn't begin to describe her. He hadn't given her a subtle experience tonight, a decision he'd first written off to impatience, for he'd dreamed of doing this with her, *only* her, for years. But as he'd prepared for the scene and looked hard at his motives, he realized that somewhere, somehow, the vision had blossomed with D's desires in consideration too. Dasha Melodia Moore wasn't a "halfway" person. The woman had raced bicycles with Matt Bellamy, Zumba'ed with Rihanna, even skydived with Bono. A beginner's scene wasn't going to hit shit with her. After all the reading she'd done, she would've called him on it too. So, he'd taken a huge chance. In a bunch of ways, he'd ventured onto his own limb of terror tonight.

And to his not-so-small shock, the limb had...grown. It'd grown into a tree, majestic and magnificent, bolstering them to this moment. To a height so incredible, he couldn't find any words to give back to D.

He worked his jaw, hoping it would help him get coherent, but nothing came.

He opted for leaning in again and tenderly taking her mouth. She tasted sexy and sweet and warm; he let every flavor flow through him. Words would come soon enough. They always did. He had a knack of picking something appropriate too, a glib combination of humor and appreciation that brought on bashful laughter from his submissives, easing everyone back behind their walls where they all belonged.

Realization broadsided him.

He didn't want the goddamn words. Didn't want to waste a second chasing them. He wanted the walls to stay a million feet away. He yearned for the power to freeze this instant, to lock himself inside D, and—

And then what? Buy her a collar and ride away into the sunset together?

You gave up on collars a long time ago, buddy.

And sunsets? Best enjoyed with margaritas and a lively discussion about limits for the night's kink. Nothing but that. Nobody who wants more *than that.*

He swallowed hard. It was sage advice, given from a tried-and-true friend: his soul. Getting the buy-in from the rest of him, *that* would be the trick.

And the necessity.

CHAPTER SEVEN

They exited the spa, still empty of any staff or clients, once more via the hotel's VIP elevator—though Dasha wondered why the ride was necessary. She likely could've flown up the side of the building, since her brain had turned into a cloud. It floated atop the ball of sensations she somehow still called her body; such a stupid and plain label for the limbs and nerves and muscles that'd been transformed in the last hour. She'd been run through the full spectrum, from low to high and then back again, an e-ticket journey she still replayed in her mind's eye. Yes, all of it. Yes, even the pain—perhaps especially that, since her nipples already screamed at her for acetaminophen—and even the bondage...

But absolutely all of the pleasure.

Pleasure she never imagined she'd know. All because of David.

David. She cried out for him silently, yet somehow he heard. He turned, his gaze strong as pewter, captivating her as he had after their climaxes.

Ohhh, that look.

Taut yet searching, like he had something to say but couldn't find the words. No way would they be enough to describe this anyway. She knew it as he stepped to her. As the elevator doors slid shut, David slid his arms under the cloak, gently pulling her against him. She sighed, breathing him in. Sweat. Spice. Skin. Sex.

David. Sir. Home.

His murmur warmed the top of her head. "Thank you for being so sweet to Laurelle. Offering her tickets to the show in Baltimore was a lovely gesture."

Dasha smiled into his shoulder. "She's your friend. And she was part of a wonderful night for us."

He tugged her head back enough so they looked at each other again. "Wonderful?" he echoed, unleashing the power-to-a-hundred version of his stare. An equally dazzling smile bloomed on his elegant lips. "You...mean that, don't you?"

She was certain she poured more of her soul out all over his face. He didn't look like he cared. "Yes," she told him, holding her chin high with surety. "I do."

She hated to interrupt herself with a frown, but her gaze fell on the floor call buttons then. Only one number had been punched. "Sir, my room's on forty-eight."

"Not anymore." He amped the force of his proximity, bringing his legs beneath the cloak, bracing her with them. "I want you next to me tonight," he said, bracing a hand against the elevator wall next to her head. "Right next to me. I know you. You'll want to play with your new bling, and that can't happen. Your piercings need to heal, and I need to monitor that."

"Every second?" she teased, trailing a finger up to a breast. "Isn't that like watching paint dry?"

David yanked her hand back. "I'm serious. No playing with your piercings." He turned her palm over and gave it a rough kiss. "Or I'll create diversions."

The possessive move made Dasha bold. She ran her other hand up the front of his black shirt, loving the rock-hard pecs and delts under her fingers. "Does that mean the dancers can have my suite now?"

"That means I'll think about it. You may have to earn that privilege...on their behalf."

She bit her lower lip and smiled. "Starting now?"

The elevator doors shooshed open to his floor. A laugh started on his lips, but he growled, "Absolutely not now. You've given your fair share of dues to the cause tonight. Food for you and then right to bed."

"Party pooper."

"You're taping with *Wake Up World* tomorrow. You want to be spouting 'Sorry I look like shit on a stick, but my Sir was fucking me silly till four this morning'?"

"Hmmm. Not a bad opener."

"Shut up and come eat your cheese."

Shock eclipsed her lust. "Cheese?" She never got to have cheese. Stopping at one bite was impossible for her, but stopping at twenty wasn't an acceptable option. Lycra stage outfits were unforgiving.

"I can have them take it away." His shrug was a maddening combo of commanding and adorable. "I'm sure somebody in the hotel will love a taste of stuff that's been sitting in a French cave for fifty years..."

"Don't. You. Dare."

His chuckle was magical music. It assured her that even though they'd come so far together tonight, they were still *them,* circling back to the home of their sarcasm and banter.

The feeling followed into her dreams that night...at least for a few hours. At precisely twelve minutes after three, a different version of David roused her from that slumber. She knew this because, at two minutes after four, that same David still assaulted her mind. He smiled at her from the realms of memory, that devious, mysterious smile thickening into adoration as he bound her wrists and caressed her body. Then the smile melted away as he claimed her...conquered her by breaking her down completely before he lifted her back up on wings of desire and ecstasy. She remembered his fingers, warm and demanding, spread across her bare pussy. And *oh yes,* his body, preparing to enter her there. Yet he waited, not letting her have him until the piercing hit her breast...

She ran a tentative finger over that little diamond P. The loop of the letter was filled by her sore, tender nipple. Her flesh throbbed even more as she touched it. She clenched her teeth and rolled to her side, away from David, but continued to rub. David had given her more directions about caring for the piercings. No touching or playing for a month. But the pain...

The pain was the most exhilarating thing she'd ever felt.

It arrested her. Called to her. Reminded her of the path she'd taken to earn his jewelry. Of how it had felt to please him so completely...

In the silence of the bedroom, interrupted only by David's steady slumber, she heard her heart racing, even her blood pulsing, to catch up with her coursing adrenaline.

"Well, well, well. Look who has found himself a brave little girl."

She grimaced. The words had both taunted and infuriated, but David's rough growl had transformed them to intimate praise, making her feel as precious as the diamonds embedded in her skin. Her core had gone white-hot, wanting him more than she'd ever craved a man.

It's four in the morning. You're not coherent. Count sheep and get back to sleep!

She took a deep breath. It only succeeded in surging more

arousal to the crevice between her thighs. Hot, heavy, pulsing torture.

She slid tentative fingers down her body. Her pussy seeped in happy greeting to her touch. With her other hand, she gave an experimental pinch to the flesh beneath her piercing. It surged with pain, and she bit her lip. Her pussy trickled again. Her juices seeped over her fingers. Her clit pulsed and expanded too, begging her for more.

Yes. More.

David grunted and shifted. Dasha looked over at him. Her new lover...her incredible Dom. He'd passed out the second his head hit the pillow. He'd worked hard to make that event happen in the spa, she had no doubt of it, on top of his regular juggling act in handling the daily demands of her career. She didn't have the heart or guts to wake him up just to refuel her rocket ship of a libido.

She slipped back the covers as gently as she could and then eased from the bed. David didn't stir. She breathed easier as she padded to the bathroom. Though it would be more comfortable to get herself off on the lounger in the suite's next room, David would be likely to go back to sleep if he did wake up, figuring she was taking a bathroom break.

She lay down right on the bathroom's marble floor, welcoming the shock of chilled marble against her naked body. The stone gave her skin no mercy, like she'd been thrown on a slab by a strict master. In her mind, that master morphed into David. She slid her eyes shut, tracing her fingers around his initials in her flesh again as the fantasy took over.

Very good, her master praised, standing bare-chested over her. *Yes. Touch those letters and think of my name as you do. The name of the man who possesses you...* He braced his hands on his hips, which were sheathed in the same black leather pants from their time in the spa. Her mind eagerly created the same fierce bulge at their fly. *Spread your legs wide,* he repeated, *and let me look at your pretty cunt.*

Slowly, Dasha opened her legs. She slipped her fingers down, into the damp petals at her core, and started rubbing herself. The tangy scent of her arousal filled the air. Her fingers felt so good against the wet nerves, which came alive with her strokes.

A small cry erupted before she could help it. She winced, battling to hold back a sob. She was so wet, so ready, so needing the climax she could practically taste. Damn, *damn,* she wanted it to last longer! Though she longed to fill out the scene in her head, she was quite certain if Dream-David uttered one more thing, she'd—

"Dasha?"

Her eyes flared open. She sat up with a jolt and clutched her knees to her chest. The action bumped both her piercings. She hissed in pain, weirdly grateful for the distraction. It was something to focus on other than the very real David, who opened the bathroom door all the way. And, damn him, looking even more gorgeous even in his stubble-jawed, messy-haired, half sleep.

"What are you doing?" he mumbled.

"I—I uh—"

"Answer me." So much for the mumble. His demand drilled like a crucifixion nail.

Her response was a pathetic gargle. "I didn't want to wake you."

"Are you saying that to your toes or to me? Look at me."

She bowed her head, unable to obey. Because he was

naked too. Magnificently so. His erection had started jerking to life the second he'd walked in on her, and it was likely more incredible now. If she looked up, she knew where her eyes would go, and he'd know exactly what she was thinking. Worse, he'd know exactly how much she hadn't been able to control her stupid urges, even after he'd given her the orgasm-to-end-all-orgasms earlier.

"I just...didn't want to bother you," she repeated. *Dumb. Ass. Dumb. Ass.*

"Bother me with what?" But his tone already began to shade with the answer to that. The answer he'd already surmised. "D," he commanded—*D,* not Dasha—as he took a step closer. "Stand up."

When she complied, he captured her chin with his fingers. His gaze overtook her with its thunder-dark scrutiny. His lips barely moved as he asked, "What's the most important thing I require of you?"

"C-Complete honesty."

"Then give it to me." His features didn't flinch. "What were you doing in here?"

She wanted to heed him. God, she needed to; he'd earned that and more. But shame filled her throat with nothing but parched air. She gulped, riveting her gaze on the wall. "David—I was afraid—"

"Of bothering me. We've had that recap already. Afraid of bothering me about what?"

"You were so tired," she protested. "You were sleeping so peacefully. So when I woke up and started...well..."

"Playing with your piercing." His voice was brutal as the thumb he pushed into the same breasts she'd been stroking, lifting her nipples for his inspection. "If I ran fingerprint dust on this, you'd be guilty as hell, sweetheart. Don't really need to, though. The skin irritation says it all." A long moment passed as he raked the rest of her body with his stare, giving her no mercy with the scrutiny. Dasha shivered. His glare hit her like knives.

"Yes...Sir," she finally said in a rasp. Maybe he'd recognize the effort it took to at least do that.

No such luck.

"So, against my instructions," he continued, "you woke up and started stroking your new piercings." He let out a long breath. "I'm guessing that led you to stroke other things too." He finished that by dipping two fingers into the apex of her thighs. Dasha gasped as he shoved two fingers up inside her. "Yep. Soaking wet." His voice dipped too, descending to harsh disapproval. "Like I expected."

She bit her lip, unable to feel even a burst of arousal at his touch. "I'm sorry," she whispered. "I feel like—"

"What?" he inserted into her self-interruption.

She gazed at him, confused by the words that came. "Like...I've let you down. But about more than the piercing. That's weird...right?"

"No." There wasn't a beat of hesitation to it. His hands braced her hips, those strong, long fingers locking her in place in front of him. "You feel that way because we opened a huge door in our relationship last night. We shared ourselves in a real, raw, and open way. But then you felt the need, however well-intentioned, to pleasure yourself without me getting to control the fun."

New feelings flooded her. Frustration. Confusion. A little fury. "Without you getting to—what the h—"

Smack.

He brought his hand down on her right ass cheek, a firecracker of sound in the bathroom, jolting her to attention.

"Before you say something you're going to regret," he said, "let me enlighten you about a key part of this new commitment to which you've agreed." He'd kept his hand on her bottom and now brought his other hand around, doubling that possessive hold. "You're my submissive. That means everything about your sexual experiences, good and bad, painful and pleasurable, completely and totally, is mine." He tightened his grip.

If they weren't standing inches apart, his cock pressing against her stomach, Dasha would've laughed. "You're kidding me, right?" But his stare said he wasn't. Perfect time for the memory of the first conversation they'd had about his preferences...about how he'd denied Jaz her orgasms for hours. "So...what... I need you to sign a permission slip now or something?"

The slight tilt of his head didn't ease the thuds starting in her stomach.

"A signature won't be necessary."

"But your consent is?"

He didn't move, which served as a resounding confirmation. Her mind fought that truth, though a forbidden little thrill trumped it. She'd have to consult with him...about when she orgasmed? "That—that is just—"

"Going to need a touch of enforcement." David's face hardened into commanding angles again. "That much is clear. Yet a perfect dovetail into the discipline I've got to give you for slathering your filthy fingers across new piercings, darling."

She shot him a glare. She longed to give him the perfect follow-up too, by slapping his arrogant jaw and then getting the hell out of here. But everything about him tethered her.

The hard dominion in his voice. The harder control in his eyes. Dasha openly admitted her fixation with both... God help her, perhaps her bizarre need for both. With days that demanded a constant stream of decisions and strength from her, relinquishing herself to David felt like...

Freedom.

She dropped her glare into a frown as the thought hit her. But the only words that came were just as inane. "I'm not filthy," she snapped and jerked as he shifted his hold to her arms.

"Filthy isn't always bad," he countered softly. That tugged her gaze back up, curious about the look he accompanied it with. But she found his eyes fixed to something behind her. With *a lot* of interest. "But the theme gives us a perfect place to start."

"Start...what?" She flung the retort as he stepped around her, threw open the glass shower door, and pulled the nozzle on.

"Get in."

The order wasn't negotiable—but he didn't compel her physically. He just stood at the stall door, looking like a Greek god incarnate against the marble-lined bathroom, his body honed and perfect, his sex half flexed, his stare as potent as that of Zeus. Against all the pride still left in her body, Dasha complied—for exactly two steps. She stopped as soon as the spray hit her.

"It's freezing!"

"All the better to extinguish that fire in your pussy." He arched a brow at her new gawk. "It'll be hot again, don't worry, but it'll be me who gets you that way." He dipped a nod at the stall again. "I gave you an instruction, sweetheart."

His tone changed with that, deepening as if he accessed a

secret well of wickedness. A well she'd started to recognize as the sole property of "Domination David." From the moment he'd first used it on her, a thrill of anticipation came as well... until now.

Dasha folded her arms and pushed out a determined huff. "No!"

"Are you refusing a direct order of your Sir?"

"It's—" She fumed. "It's a ridiculous order."

He looked like she'd simply told him the day's weather. "Get in," he repeated, "or get out. Your choice. I'm not going to bodily force you; however, your trust of me has to extend to disciplinary actions too."

Her arms dropped, weighted by disbelief. "You *are* really kidding, right?"

"I kid with bell hops and reporters, sweetheart. Not disobedient little subbies."

"But—"

"That isn't a word you're allowed right now. It's either 'Yes, Sir' or 'Good night, Sir.'" His brows rose. "I'm running out of patience. Get in the shower, or throw on a robe and go back to your own room."

The urge to slap him burned worse than ever. The fear of doing it wrestled back.

She didn't want to do this.

But the thought of having to leave him was a worse alternative.

Especially because she only had to glance down to see how much his body clearly wanted hers again. He grew harder, a sensual promise she couldn't resist. And beyond that...damn it, she'd asked for this. When he'd asked her to dive into the D/s rabbit hole, she'd freely accepted. And she did want to go further...to discover more of the new creature inside herself... even if getting there meant subjecting herself to a Neptune-worthy ice shower.

She glared once more, if only to save face, though she didn't have the guts to lift her gaze all the way to his face.

Then got in under the freezing spray.

"Ssshhhhiiiit!"

"Lovely," he stated. "But the commentary isn't necessary. You're there to wash clean. Get busy, baby. Soap and water everywhere. But be careful around your piercings."

The faster she complied, the faster she'd be free from the torture. So she did, scrubbing with frenzied speed between chilled breaths. She tried to shove the discomfort from her mind, focusing instead on the lean, dark beauty of the man watching every inch of her movements. She didn't miss a single detail. The way David's mouth parted, as if craving to take a nibble on her. The newer jerks in his cock. Looking at him spurred her to just get the hell done and re-earn a place in his arms.

"Done." She whooshed it with relief while reaching for the door handle.

And got pushed back from the other side.

"You're clean," David asserted, his hand still shoved on the glass, "but you're not done. That happens when I tell you."

Frustration sluiced colder than the water, but she muttered, "Yes, Sir." And yeah, damn straight she boosted the misery factor. Was that a pleased growl she heard in return?

Bastard.

"I'm going to prepare the next phase of your punishment. It won't take long. I'll get you out when I return."

"Goody." She grumbled it as he rounded the corner into

the bedroom. But her mind whirled. *Next phase? Prepare? What the hell was his devious mind concocting next?*

Despite that mental roller coaster, flashes of sanity returned. What the hell was she doing here? Why the hell was she subjecting herself to this? She'd auditioned for assholes, undressed for crazy costumers, and sung for millions. There was no good reason to be standing here like an ice sculpture at a record-exec soiree, feeling foolish and nervous and...

More aroused than you've been in a very, very long time.

Before she could generate a proper rebuttal for that, David reappeared. A smile ghosted his lips as he gazed at her from head to toe, though she couldn't fathom why. She caught a brief glance of herself in the vanity mirror: huddled, shivering, soaked, pathetic.

"Perfect." His drawl seemed to taunt those miserable thoughts. "All right, go ahead and get out. But no drying off, so be careful walking on the tile."

She was so grateful for the reprieve from the water, she didn't care about the ban on the towel—until she followed him back into the bedroom and the blast of air that almost made her look around for a penguin or two. Part of the bastard's "preparations" had included dropping the temp by at least ten degrees. Her nipples squeezed into tighter pinpoints—a sight not lost on the man who turned on her, arms crossed, eyes twin lightning bolts.

"How do those piercings feel now?" he asked.

Fuck you. "They hurt like hell, Sir."

His chuckle dug like a spur. Had she thought that sound magical a few hours ago? "Good girl. That's honest and a real turn-on." He reached back, pulling the room's spare blanket off the bed and then spreading it wide. "Come here."

So maybe she'd forgive him for the laugh. Maybe. Or maybe not, considering he kept the blanket at bay while watching what her hurried hops did to her breasts. She glared. He smiled like she hadn't. Finally, though, he folded her against him, wrapping her completely.

At once, her glower dissolved into a blissful moan. The broad plane of his chest supported her head; his arms were a solid circle around her. Best of all, she was cushioned in luxurious Sferra, making her feel like a soaked nymph who'd finally gotten into a down-lined burrow. Correction: a burrow with a Master who welcomed her with warmth, shrouded her in strength, and then sought her mouth to dominate it with the thorough press of his.

Coherent thought fled. She sighed her thanks while wiggling to get even closer. Hmmm. If this was what Domination David described as "punishment," she'd make plans to pull the sassy act more often.

"Don't get settled, brat."

Crap.

"Sir?"

David shifted his hands to her face, which caused the blanket to drop. He kissed her once more, demanding deeper access to her mouth, before stepping back and giving her body a long, assessing study. That, along with the fresh flare of air conditioning on her skin, caused a top-to-toe shiver.

Only this time, strangely, the chill wasn't entirely awful.

The mixture of icy and expectation got even worse as he tilted his head with purpose.

"Step into my parlor, darling. Then present yourself on all fours for your spanking."

She followed his direction around to the other side of the

bed. There, he'd spread several towels, which glowed brighter than the sand on the beach outside due to the unrelenting light from a couple of readjusted floor lamps.

"Into the spotlight," he ordered. "I'm not a hide-in-the-dark Dom. I want to see every stripe of my handiwork on your skin."

As if to give her a preview, he smacked her firmly across both ass cheeks, giving her body another one-two punch of flames and icicles. The sensations kept up their duel as she stepped to the towels. David followed, staying right behind.

"Down on the floor," he directed. "Hands and knees. Point your gaze down and spread your legs a little farther than your shoulders. Are my instructions clear, my dear?"

"Yes, Sir." This time, she gave the answer without hesitation. As she lowered to the floor, she tried to dissect why. Going through that crap in the shower had been humiliating and hard, but she began to understand David's purpose for it. She'd been a solid brick of defiance—but he needed her to be putty, ready to place her soft core in his strong hands. Ready to show him she really *was* sorry for defying his directions...and ready to atone for it.

Putty. Good word for what she felt like now. And if her pussy had been ignited in the process...well, that wasn't so bad, was it?

"Excellent." He raked a hand down her back and then dipped it lower. Dasha's breaths pumped in her chest as his touch moved in, exploring her intimate parts, until he pushed a finger inside her again. "Hmmm. Soaking wet again."

"Yes." She panted it. "God *yes,* Sir."

Her heart thudded harder as his voice went low and gruff. "Oh, Little D, taming the fire in your clit is going to be fun."

He punctuated that by landing two more swats on her ass. The take-no-prisoners blows made her gasp with shock. A couple more followed. Two more after that. The entire time he kept thrusting his finger, a steady rhythm causing her walls to tremble and her core to ache.

By the time he stopped the beating and pulled out his finger, she was shaking and sweaty. Only by force of will did she maintain her position, though she was pulled from it by David's hand at her scalp, bringing her head up. Something hovered in her vision. His finger, soaked with her juices.

"Open up. Suck it. Taste the honey of your sweet little cunt."

As she took his finger, the tangy taste of her arousal filled her mouth. Her very senses.

"Good girl." He shoved three more fingers in.

She closed her eyes, letting her head shut off as her body sparked brighter, servicing his invasion. He never altered his pace. Just kept on thrusting in a perfect emulation of the next thing she yearned for him to put there. Sure enough, she felt him sliding into position in front of her. She breathed in the musk of his lust, could practically taste his erect length on her tongue, beaded with the salt of his sweat and the—

Something flat, cold, and earthy replaced his fingers in her mouth.

She jerked open her jaw. And her eyes. She blinked, stunned, at the tapered end of his black Prada belt.

"Don't stop now." It was an unequivocal order; he backed it by digging his free hand into her hair. "And lick it good, darling. I want to see it wet with your spit before I use it on your ass."

The words coated her brain like sensual magma. Black.

Dark. Inescapable. Dasha didn't even stop to question the sanity of his command this time, just realized the vortex was no longer a choice—because every inch of her body trembled in need for it. She sucked in as much of the belt as she could, laving the luxurious leather, helping him prepare the instrument he'd be using on her flesh. That connection almost made her worship necessary...a consecration of her penance. And, in the doing, her salvation.

At last, he withdrew the belt from her mouth. As he glided the strip down her back, he braced one leg against her waist. His other thigh stayed in front of her, which brought his erection to her lips.

"You know what to do, sweetheart. Take a deep breath, because I'm going to fill you up."

Dasha dragged in air. In that moment, she opened her eyes and, for the first time, realized the size of the flesh she was about to suck. David's penis was like the rest of him. Firm, lengthy, commanding. The veins stood out against the taut skin, all leading to the shiny head now pulsing at her lips. He was right. He would fill her mouth and more.

As she opened and he slid in, she expected a shudder, a groan, normal "guy" stuff that happened in the position he was in. Instead, David only grunted once and then coolly delivered the first *whack* of the belt. The lash shocked like live fire, branding her skin. The blow was worse than any pain she'd ever felt from just his hand, and she choked from the surprise. She lost her grip on his cock, and he fired a sharp growl.

"We're not getting off to a good start, are we?" His fingers coiled tighter in her hair. "You'll take my cock and you'll take your punishment, both right now, both with no more protests."

The world spiraled away as he sealed his domination. The

belt turned her ass to throbbing heat. His cock seared the back of her throat. And she did take both for him, submitting in a silent haze, every moment worth it as delicious male rumbles emanated from him.

His hand set her head into a forceful rhythm, ramming her mouth around his flesh in time to the slaps on her ass. Thought disappeared. Logic fled. Every desire became his, turned over to pulling more satisfied sounds from him with each brutal thrust and whack. It was indeed punishment, primeval, ruthless, and raw. Her mouth had never been more sore. Her ass had never been more inflamed. And her pussy had never been more ready to be filled.

Suddenly, he flung the belt to the bed. He joined that hand to the other on her head and used it to jam himself deep down into her throat.

"Swallow."

He spasmed, filling the air with his bellow and then her throat with his climax. His come seared her, completed her, made her feel as powerful as standing on a stage before thousands. She was so wet now, shaking from the need for her own release. David knew that too. He slipped one hand from her scalp and ran it down her back, making several long swipes across the marks on her ass before sliding those fingers to her sex from behind.

Dasha groaned from sheer pleasure. So did he. The invasion of his fingers made her body tighten, including her mouth around his cock. "Yes. Oh yes, sweet girl. You're so beautiful like this."

Dasha could only moan. Her pussy throbbed so badly for his touch, it echoed through her whole being. Within seconds, the entire world seemed to pound.

Wait.

The pounding was real. It came from beyond the bedroom, at the suite's front door. Somebody was apparently trying to beat the door in. Strident shouts followed.

"David! David, dude, are you in there?"

David stiffened. "What the hell?" His mutter reflected Dasha's bafflement. It was Raife, the tour's dance lead. But he was the clean-living, early-morning-run-on-the-beach type. Why was he laying into David's suite door two hours before his alarm clock was set to chime?

David sat back with a heavy sigh. Dasha did the same, flashing him a rueful stare. He leaned to her, on all fours himself now, and lifted gentle fingers to her chin. "Better stay here," he instructed, pulling her forward for a lingering kiss. "This isn't over. I promise."

Dasha smiled against his lips. "Thank you, Sir."

"Thank *you*, pet."

She dealt with the half dozen stomach flips that gave her while he rose and grabbed a black robe from a chair. He threw it on and cinched it and then disappeared into the suite's living room. A few seconds later, Raife did another drum solo on the door, though she heard David interrupt the performance by wrenching the thing open.

"Raife, what the f—"

"Is Dasha with you?" A stampede of footsteps ensued. Raife didn't arrive alone, not by a long shot. The stress in his voice was multiplied by the mini cavalcade into the suite. Shit. It sounded like the whole dance crew was with him.

"Why would she be—"

"Just tell us she's with you!" The interjection came from Raife's second in command, Mary. The girl was a diminutive blonde with a face that belonged in a Louisa May Alcott novel and a conquer-the-world attitude to match. "She's not in her room, and she's not with any of us, and—"

"This isn't good," said Raife.

"Crap!" Mary cried. "Dasha. Oh God!"

An outbreak of panic followed.

"Whoa," David yelled. "Everybody calm the hell down. What's going on?"

Long silence. Past the thudding of her heart, Dasha sensed them handing something to David. He let out a heavy grunt, shifted, and then repeated the sound with harder emphasis. The room dipped to such stillness, he barely had to raise his voice when he spoke again.

"Dasha, you'd better get out here."

She popped to her feet, despite the two weights of emotion that slammed. Panic came first. His summons had outed their relationship to the tour's whole crew. The fear came fast after that. Whatever had caused him to take the risk was serious. Very serious.

She frantically searched the bedroom. David's tone hadn't left room for dawdling, but she'd arrived here in nothing more than the cloak, which had no closures or fastenings. There wasn't a second robe in the closet either. That left his open suitcase. She dived in, finally finding a clean pair of boxer briefs and a dark-blue workout shirt. Without thinking about the sanity, or lack of, in the action, she threw them on. Then she took one steadying breath and left the bedroom.

The breath was a wasted step. It got knocked out of her the next second.

"Oh, thank God!" shrieked Mary, launching a full Wayne Gretzky on her. She'd barely finished the body check before the other dancers swarmed her.

"Are you all right, Dasha?"

"Did you get the message too?"

"Who the hell is doing this?"

"What if it's one of *us*?"

"Should we call the police?"

The din got sliced by another arrival to the room. It was George, the show's tech lead. The tension beneath his gray-tinged beard softened a little when he laid eyes on her, but only a little. He scanned the rest of the room, seeking David. When the two men locked gazes, their expressions darkened from intense to ominous.

George glanced to the smart phone in David's hand. Only then did Dasha realize everyone else had their phones out as well. Whatever the displays carried, it was critical to the point of dire. No one had noticed, let alone commented, on her David Pennington designer attire.

"You got it too?" George asked.

"Yeah," David said, his voice tight. "I got it too."

"Got what?" She forced her mind out of its cocoon of blissful submission, back into the take-charge star everyone expected. "For God's sake, David, what's going on?"

He answered by holding up his phone's window. As soon as she read the message there and then gasped in shock, everyone else in the room held up their devices too.

Every phone had been sent the same text.

Dasha dies and delivers us all.

CHAPTER EIGHT

"Miss Moore, are you certain you don't know of anyone who'd want you dead?"

"For the thousandth time, no."

David clenched his teeth and his fists, also for the thousandth time. Special Agent Phelps, with his polished loafer braced on the table between him and Dasha, had David mentally reassigning the initials FBI to *Fucking Batshit Idiots*.

The moron stood here treating her like the suspect instead of hunting down the lunatic who'd sent texts to all sixty members of the show's cast and crew. Damn it, the psych-job was still free somewhere out there, no doubt dreaming up his next scheme to get close enough to—

He had to force-feed the rest of that into his brain.

Close enough to kill Dasha.

It definitely wasn't where he'd thought the morning would go. Not when he'd answered the door four hours ago, expecting to get rid of Raife fast as possible and return to rewarding his girl for taking her punishment so well. A back-burnered plan for now...but absolutely still on the stove.

"No pissed-off ex-lovers? A reporter or blogger you might have offended? Maybe some fan who's been showing up at your stage door, begging for extra attention?"

"That's enough." David pushed off the wall where he'd been standing sentry. "She's told you everything she can."

"Which is a hell of a lot of nothing," countered Phelps.

"Which is where you guys come in to do your goddamn job." He surged forward, sending the strongest back-off-fucker vibe of his life. "She's been through enough already with this, and you assholes keep prodding her like a science experiment. You're not gonna get a different answer, no matter how you rephrase the question. So lay off."

Wisely, Phelps eased his pose. That brought a modicum of satisfaction. But no more. For the last two hours, since making the call to the police and then watching them hook in the FBI due to Dasha's high profile, he'd felt like a piece of the room's wallpaper. Just *there*. Useless. Purposeless. And worst of all, powerless. This time, it wasn't just about his recurring, brother-on-brother world war with Josh. Maybe because this time, it wasn't just about their past personal baggage or future Pennington stock standings. This power suck had to do with Dasha. Silence wasn't going to solve it. He had to do something. *They* had to do something.

"Listen," Phelps said, hands held up. "I'm just trying to be thorough."

"Great." David didn't waste effort on inflecting it with anything but rage. "Glad to hear it. *Thorough* would be tracking down the source phone of those texts. *Thorough* would be learning if there's any credence to this shit or if we're just dealing with some fanboy whack job. Leave *her* the hell alone."

"Well said."

The commendation didn't come from Phelps. David snapped his attention to the suite's doorway and the stranger standing there. Everything in the guy's tone said he was just another FBI jack-off, but everything in his appearance defied that. From the neck up, he looked like a casting shot for some Knights Templar epic. His dark-brown hair tumbled well past his nape, and his formidable jaw sprouted a small forest of stubble. But from the top of his leather-jacketed shoulders to his Bauhaus T-shirt, black cargo pants, and heavy boots, he was complete modern Goth. The guy wouldn't be making the cover of *GQ* but probably didn't give a fuck. Where he did narrow his focus made David victorious and furious at once.

The guy honed his brilliant green eyes on Dasha.

And locked his gaze there.

"We tracked the cell that sent the texts," he said, again in that no-bullshit tone. Despite that very good update, David's tension hovered right where it was, thanks to the way the guy didn't waver his stare from D. Who the hell was he? Were they really letting G-men do the scraggly knight look these days?

"All right, so who is the scumbag?" David sat as he issued it and then scooped a fast, possessive arm around D's shoulders. The guy tangled stares with him again, though he cranked down the temperature in those laser irises.

"Untraceable so far," he replied. "We found the device in a trash can at Miami International, in the Central Terminal. The number is registered as a corporate phone for an exports business out of Buenos Aires."

"Which tells us what?" Dasha asked. "Agent...ah..."

"Moridian," he supplied. "Special Agent Kress Moridian, undercover operations. I'm the lead on your case, Miss Moore. We're not usually brought in for a case like this, but Miami PD made the call, based on your high profile."

"It's *our* case," David injected. "I'm Miss Moore's manager." *And a lot more,* he said via the tight handshake he gave the agent. *Moridian, huh? Hell, you really are a holy crusades rehash.* "David," he stated aloud. "David Pennington."

Moridian held his own on the handshake, but the bastard's

face took another bath in tenderness as he looked back to Dasha. "I apologize for taking so long to get here. I know you've been waiting to get back to your suite and your things, but we felt it important to track the source phone first."

"Of course." Dasha colored a little at Moridian's reference to her state. She was barefoot, disheveled, and still dressed only in David's shirt and boxers—not that David complained one damn bit. He'd actually indulged a mental fist-pump when she'd emerged in the stuff, sex-flushed and gorgeous, wrapped in the clothes of who'd made her that way. If it were up to him, she'd stay like that all day—but she needed the comfort of her own things on her and around her. These pissants weren't helping the cause. For three hours, she'd been answering all their runaround questions. That was two and a half hours too long.

"Can we get on with it?" He rose, pulling Dasha up too. "She can at least get into her suite for a few minutes now, right?"

"Of course." Moridian was the picture of forced decorum. "And...refresh my memory...why wasn't she in it to begin with?"

Dasha stiffened. "I was with Mr. Pennington. And that information needs to remain exclusive to your team, Agent Moridian."

"She'll be remaining with me too." David dropped his hand around her waist. "I'm not leaving her side until this bastard is found."

Moridian's scrutiny swept over both of them, the period irises missing nothing. *Take your time, Lancelot. I'm connected to her, and I'm staying that way.* "Details of all our cases are kept confidential. So don't worry about that, Miss Moore."

Another agent waited in the hallway and accompanied

the three of them into the VIP elevator. Though the ride up the next thirty floors took only a minute, David captured Dasha's stare and then nodded toward the wall, silently inviting her to join him in a shared memory. Her eyes, molten copper, told him she'd gladly take him up on that. For a few seconds, they remembered those magical moments they'd shared during their last journey in this space...a welcome break from this surreal day.

"The hotel moved the other guests from this wing," Moridian explained as they got off at the forty-eighth floor, and Dasha shot a furtive stare down the hall. "Like I said, confidentiality is key to a case like yours. If this ass wipe is motivated by publicity, then lack of it will smoke him out."

David grunted approval at that. He hadn't wanted to. And that made him grimace. All right, fuck it, he wasn't a fan of how Mr. M eyeballed his woman, but he appreciated the respect Moridian gave this case and this criminal—and the determination he already showed in chasing down the cocksucker.

They arrived at Dasha's suite. A handful of agents still swarmed the rooms, FBI bees looking for any evidence to cross-pollinate to their lab for clues.

"I just need a few minutes to pull my stuff together," she told him quietly, daring a small kiss to his lips. As he expected, Moridian joined him in watching her disappear into the bedroom.

"She's nice," the guy commented.

"Mmm-hmm." It was all he could do not to growl it.

"Not the stuck-up pop princess I expected."

"Nope." He drew out the vowel in it, hoping his territorial subtext seeped through.

"How long have you two been together?"

David arched a brow. "Professionally or personally?"

Moridian didn't flinch. "Both."

"And is my answer relative to your investigation?"

Those nearly neon green eyes finally darkened. For once, the guy looked normal. Yet pissed off too. "When I'm brought in to secure the personal safety of a beautiful woman it is."

David almost smiled. *Hell.* Under different circumstances, he'd enjoy having Moridian as a friend. He could easily envision them shooting some pool, maybe downing some beers. But as the man had phrased it, the safety of a beautiful woman was at stake. A beauty that had taken on new dimensions for him since she'd knelt at his feet two weeks ago...and deepened dramatically for him over the last twenty-four hours.

There was nothing beautiful about the scream shattering the air then.

Dasha's scream.

"Oh God!" she cried out. "Oh my God!"

"Fuck." David blurted it as he and Moridian raced to the bedroom. The other agents joined them. They careened through the doorway but froze once they got there—except for David, who rammed them all aside to get to her.

He gripped her shaking shoulders. Like that did any good; her whole body quaked. Her stare didn't veer from her toiletries case. There, lying on top of her makeup and tampons and deodorant and toothpaste, was a white dove with its neck sliced open. The mirror embedded into the lid reflected the creature's murdered eyes. Around the bird's neck hung a note, printed and taped to a piece of cardboard:

Bleed, Sweet Dasha, and Save Us All.

"Who the *hell* missed this?" Moridian bellowed.

David raised his hold to the back of D's head and turned her face into his shoulder.

"Get her out of here," Moridian told him. As David gave him a concurring nod, he muttered one more thing. "This changes the game, Pennington. Whether you like it or not, I'm not leaving her side now either."

CHAPTER NINE

Eight hours and several hundred miles later, Kress took a long-overdue drag on a beer and finally shifted his brain out of overdrive.

Nobody was happy about the situation, least of all him. The last thing he'd joined the FBI for was pop-star babysitting duty. He knew Pennington wouldn't believe it, though, so he didn't bother saying it. But it was clear they had a sick fuck on their hands, one who'd had access to Dasha Moore's suite, expanding their possible suspects to the army of people who worked in and around the Viceroy.

They'd flown her out of Miami right away. Pennington ordered reschedules on the next two weeks' worth of concert dates, and CNN was called about a backup plan for the Piers Morgan gig. Kress had backed him without hesitation, earning them both a fuming silence from Dasha. Kress could protect her in a lot of places, but the middle of an arena concert stage wasn't one of them. So here they'd landed, hiding out in Atlanta in an opulent rent-a-mansion, which had clearly taken some major string-pulling prowess from Pennington. On the other hand, he was a Pennington. One of *those* Penningtons. David hadn't believed it when Phelps handed the guy's file over after checking out everyone on Dasha's tour staff, but there it had been, in black and white:

David Tristan Pennington. Primary residence: Rancho

Palos Verdes, California. (Secondary residences: Paris, France, and Barahona Coast, Dominican Republic.)

Parents: Maddox and Sarah "Sissy" Pennington. Primary residence: Scottsdale, Arizona. Relationship: cordial.

Brother: Joshua Kerrian Pennington. Primary residence: New York, New York. Relationship: estranged. (*Flag as possible suspect?)

The file had gone on with details piled on details. He'd discarded most of the facts right after reading them, except having the brother checked out, of course. But it explained David's hat trick in scoring this place so fast. And as a venue for playing the lay-low game for a week...well, it sure didn't suck. The mansion was pure Margaret Mitchell on the outside, all shnoo-shnoo Designer-Snob on the inside. Marble floors, wool carpets, leather wallpaper, designer chandeliers. The couch on which he'd just parked his ass probably cost more than his annual pay.

He rolled his eyes and bit into more of his dinner, a roast beef sandwich brought to him by a friendly maid who, God bless her, had read the "I'm starving" part of his mind when they'd arrived. At least he didn't have to sleep on the couch, which felt as comfortable as a prison bunk. A plush king-size bed waited for him across the room, which in turn lay leaping distance to the room's other door: the connecting portal to the bedroom Dasha and David would share during their "vacation" here.

The adjoining rooms sitch didn't sit well with Pennington at all—but Kress hadn't backed down on that part either. His sworn duty was to protect Dasha Moore, and that didn't change even if she had turned out to be the bitch-princess, hidden-warts, pop-priss he'd expected. Which was actually the furthest thing from the truth—but which, damn it, he almost wished had been the case.

The woman was...special. Her beauty wasn't just a gold veneer. Kress had watched her insist on paying her dancers through the show's unexpected hiatus. She'd even asked him to ensure the dove received a proper burial. And warts? None so far, in the looks he'd been able to sneak in at her gorgeous, honey-colored skin, but shit, he couldn't help fantasizing about looking for more. Preferably starting with her ass, at the end of his best cowhide flogger...

He shoved aside that thought as Pennington swept in, holding hands with Dasha. It was a good thing he took another bite of his sandwich at the same second; the action hid his gulp as soon as he saw the woman. *Amendment.* The goddess. Dressed in a shimmery gold chemise, black bolero jacket, and black jeans, every curve of her petite figure was highlighted to perfection. She leaned on David, looking ready to fall over in her strappy gold shoes. Her hair, hanging loose and shiny and curly, framed her weary face.

"Hey. How'd it go with *Wake Up World*?"

"Good," Pennington answered. "Real good."

He directed his gaze at Dasha. "You look fantastic."

"Thank God for experienced makeup girls." She laughed at that. The sound was soft but musical, yanking another gulp from him.

Before he could help it, Kress grinned—and for one perilous second, envisioned getting to push that hair from her eyes and then gorge his gaze on her sweet pixie features. "The paint's only as good as the canvas, sugar."

Pennington's tension hit like an invisible anvil. "It's time for the canvas to rest," he directed, sliding his hand to the side of Dasha's neck.

Kress watched every nuance of the move. Steady. Squeezing. And not a place a normal boyfriend would hold his girl.

It *was* a typical move for a Dom to his submissive.

"Yes, Sir," Dasha replied with that same wind-chime laugh.

Kress fixed his stare back down to his sandwich. And took a long, desperate drag on his beer.

"Good night, Agent Moridian," Dasha said.

"Night," David seconded.

"Uh-huh," Kress mumbled. "Yeah, okay."

The moment they shut the bedroom door, Kress rushed to it. Self-disgust flooded him as he pressed his ear to the heavy wood portal, but Pennington hadn't even bothered to lock the thing anyway. With a mouse-quiet turn of the knob, Kress saw why. The couple had barely entered the room before attacking each other. David rammed Dasha up against one of the bedposts, locking both her hands over her head with one of his, kissing her like it was the last taste they'd get of each other.

"Thank you," she said, breathless and sexy, when they broke apart. "Thank you, Sir. I've needed that so much."

Her utterance woke Kress's dick the rest of the way up—as well as every other caveman instinct in his body. *Fuck.* Could it be that Dasha Moore, feisty and headstrong pop goddess, was secretly a gorgeous submissive?

He dreaded it was true. He prayed for it to be true.

Hold the phone, fucker. Just because she tossed a couple of "Sirs" into the mix doesn't mean—

"Yes," David replied. "Yes, you *have* needed it, haven't

you?" He took her lips again, even nipping at her bottom lip. "Thank you for your honesty. It's beautiful."

She settled deeper against him, sighing softly. "See? I'm working on it."

"Mmm-hmm."

Pennington's tone carried an all-too-recognizable edge.

"I see. Okay, then. Now tell me what else you need."

Her smile gave way to uncertainty. It was a tiny click of time yet a telling moment of truth. Forget the caveman; the Dom in Kress roared to life. He craved being the one to unearth her, unglue her, unravel her completely...

Pennington's indictment sliced into his fantasy.

"Stop thinking, D."

Raw steel roughened the guy's voice. With a hard tug, David unzipped Dasha's jeans and then shoved them past her ass. He dipped his hands, scooping both sides of her honey-colored ass, unyielding in his intent.

"Just tell me what you *feel*. What you need. We didn't finish your pleasure this morning. Have parts of you been aching for what they didn't get?"

Dasha mewled as he cupped her bottom tighter, yanking her forward and molding their pelvises. *Hell.* Kress went rock hard. He hated Pennington for being the one to mark that golden flesh with his touch, to coax that look on her face...the lust in her eyes yet the trepidation in her mouth...

Back off. You're a disgusting voyeur, intruding where you haven't been asked. Just shut the damn door and go find a nice episode of Golden Girls *to deflate your johnson...*

Pennington's next words superglued him in place.

"Speak up, or I'll pinch."

The guy had shifted his hand to the front, lowering it under her panties.

"Right here, on your tender little clit. I'll pinch it hard; you know I will."

She gasped, trying not to squirm. "Please...Sir..."

"Then don't hold back. I'll see it in your face if you do."

His forearm flexed; if Kress interpreted the move right, the sonofabitch had started spreading out the folds at his fingertips.

"Tell me what you need, sweetheart. In detail."

Kress almost moaned himself. *In detail? You're good, Pennington. Hell's fucking hounds, you're good.*

"I—" Dasha stammered. "I want—"

"I don't care what you want. What do you need? I'll get you started. 'Please, sir, I need...'"

"Please, Sir..." Her ginger eyelashes closed on her cheeks. "I need...your fingers...on me. And inside me." She drew in a sharp breath as he worked his hand deeper, pushing into the flesh beneath her black lacy underwear. "I need your fingers inside me," she said with more urgency.

David leaned and jammed his tongue into her mouth before ordering her, "Then get these pants all the way off. Now."

Fuck, yes. Right now.

The jeans were practically painted onto her. Dasha had to bend over to wrest them off. Kress called Pennington five kinds of a bastard for crouching as she did, enjoying the view from behind—and blocking the same sight from Kress's vantage point. Damn it, he almost blew his cover in straining to see a little of the treasure between her thighs. His imagination took flight with the possibilities. She was petite, so her clit was likely in equal proportion, tight and lovely, the blonde curls there probably trimmed into a neat strip...

"Back against the bedpost." David said it when she was bare from the waist down. "Grip it over your head with both hands and spread your legs. Yes, perfect. You're getting used to this. I love it, pet."

Kress watched her face as Pennington pressed in for another kiss, mesmerized by the way it had changed. The poised pop starlet was gone. And in her place...*oh, yeah*... All his previous uncertainties about her true nature got obliterated by the expression taking over her face. The hooded gaze. The slightly parted lips. The rosy sheen of her skin. He gazed at a submissive in the first, dreamy stages of giving herself to her Master.

A woman who made his body a forest fire of need.

Especially when David stepped back for a moment and gave Kress a full view of her from the bottom down.

Forget the forest fire.

He was blowtorched.

Her pussy was totally shaved. And more beautiful than his fantasies had conjured. The slick pink folds gleamed with her arousal, barely hiding the small fissure leading to her core. Striations of coral flesh blended with the pink, turning her into an unfolding rose, though likely smelling twice as sweet. Staring at the muscles there, pulsing and quivering beneath David's study, was the closest thing to torture Kress had ever experienced. His fly was a barbed cage against his dick. He couldn't think about the time bombs calling themselves his balls.

Pennington twisted the agony deeper. He sat on the bed, next to where Dasha stood. After tormenting her for another long, aching moment, he started spreading her sex like the layers of a flower. Slowly. Excruciatingly. He smacked her thighs back if she so much as twitched in reaction.

Screw concerns about the pair discovering him now. Like that would happen, since he'd given up breathing. The sacrifice was worth it, a small price for the privilege of watching Dasha's senses come apart as her pussy was given the same treatment. With fingers more steady than a surgeon, Pennington taunted until only her hard, red clit remained for his touch.

He tapped her there lightly at first, making Dasha keen with gorgeous arousal. "Hush," he reprimanded. "Hold it back. Breathe it down."

She exposed the cover-girl perfection of her gritted teeth. "Holy shit! David!"

"*Who?*"

"Sir! Damn it! Please—I don't know if I can hold it in!"

"Yes, you can. No coming, D. Who owns your orgasms now?"

"You do."

Her resigned whimper had Kress tossing props and hatred at David in the same second. Props for the way the guy drew out that precious acquiescence from her. Hatred for being the Dom at the receiving end of it. *Fucking lucky bastard.*

"You own my orgasms, Sir," she clarified.

"Good girl. So you're going to get your body under control for me and let me get these fingers inside you..." He went to work on her clit again, kneading, tormenting. "All right?"

The mesmerizing little sub was anything but all right. Within seconds, Dasha panted hard again, wincing and trembling. "Sir," she pleaded, nearly sobbing with it, "I can't! I—owww!"

He rained a trio of swats right on the area he'd been caressing. Her flesh instantly bloomed red. She shook with arousal and desperation.

Kress tried to swallow. She was breathtaking, her teeth turning her bottom lip as red as her pussy. He fantasized about being the one close enough to watch her mouth doing all that... and then the one guiding those sweet lips onto his extended cock...

"So tell me now what you need, sweetheart." David stood but shifted back from her now, not laying a finger on her, simply gazing with a firm face. He raised a black brow. "You know the trembling won't earn you mercy. Only your honesty will."

"This *is* my honesty!" She forced in a couple of deep breaths and then continued in a desperate rasp, "P-Please, Sir. I just..."

"Just what?"

"I want—I need—to be fucked." Like a Greek chorus lending its support, all the inflamed tissues of her pussy trembled. "Please, David. I've waited all day!"

"But what about my fingers inside you?"

"Your fingers. Your cock. Anything. I need it. Please!"

In the long moment that followed, David swung a few hundred rungs higher on Kress's ladder of respect. The guy gave her enough of a smile to let her know he'd heard, loud and clear, but simply looked her up and down once again.

"So you need me to fuck you," the guy repeated. "With anything?"

"Yes!"

"All right," he finally murmured. "On the bed with you, beautiful." He emphasized that by grabbing her wrist and guiding her toward the mattress. "Arms spread, legs spread. Sweet and wide. Very nice. Keep your top on. Let's keep those tits clean tonight."

Kress wanted to be pissed at the decision to keep her

half-clothed. But it was hard to be anything but rock hard as he watched that breathtaking woman go spread-eagle for her Dom. He was dying to know what "pleasure" of hers had gotten cut short this morning, what Pennington could've possibly been doing to her. To have been a fly on that wall too...

Her face popped into apprehension as Pennington disappeared for a second and then came back to tug at one of her wrists.

"I managed to secure some special deliveries this afternoon," he said with a slow smile, lifting one of her wrists. He wrapped a padded cuff around it and then locked it closed, securing her to the headboard.

"Wh-Why cuffs again?" Dasha stammered.

"Shhh." He gentled his tone to balance the shock of his actions. "Take a breath for me, pet. And another." After he clicked the second cuff shut, he smiled down at her. "They're lined with velvet. Do they hurt at all?"

Dasha averted her eyes. "No. But—"

"And your Sir won't do anything to harm you, right?"

"R-Right. But...why..."

"Number one, it pleases me to see you tied up and at my mercy." He grinned before bending over to give her a long kiss. "And second...let's call it a precautionary measure."

"Precautionary?" This time, her voice shook. "Why?"

"No more questions." Pennington pivoted and made his way to the foot of the bed, his pace smooth and controlled. "Time to meet your needs." He pushed her legs wider, showing off the real evidence of what the bondage did to her. The lips on Dasha's mouth might have protested the treatment, but the lips of her pussy dripped with glistening new juices.

"Oh yeah," David praised. "You're ready to be fucked, little sub."

What he said. Goddamnit, please—

"Yes."

With her breathy surrender, Kress couldn't take the pressure anymore. He unzipped his pants with painstaking silence. His dick burst free, boulder hard, covered in pre-come. He fisted himself, grinding off three layers of tooth enamel to keep his groan in check, battling shame and ecstasy at once. Christ, he had no idea how long he'd last this way.

Pennington stepped out of his view for a second. He heard the guy unzip a suitcase and rummage through it. When David reappeared in Kress's sightline, he carried a long, silver tube. The handle of it was attached to a lengthy black cord, which he plugged into a nearby socket.

Crap, yelled the part of his brain that could still think. *Holy crap, is that a—*

"Wh-What's that?" Dasha's gaze went wider as she too focused on the thing.

"Wizards have their magic wands," he replied, "and I've brought mine." He paused as if expecting her to fire a smart-ass-ism then. When she didn't, he nodded his approval. "You need to be fucked," he went on. "We've established that. And this is what you'll be fucked with. I'd planned to introduce you to this in Miami. Good news is, it packs light." He flipped the switch on the handle, and the rod emitted a sumptuous, erotic hum. "You'll enjoy electro-stim, D; I promise."

"Electro—*what?*"

For the first time, she battled her wrist bonds. But she kept her legs open, belying two things. One, she really did trust Pennington. Two, a secret part of her was fascinated by the sensual promise his statement had carried...by the dark magic of the instrument he hovered above her core.

Pennington batted her inner thighs with his free hand. "I expect these legs to stay nice and wide, or there'll be some more restraints invited to come play. I brought those too. Got that?"

It took Dasha a long moment and a deep breath to answer. "Yes, Sir."

"Very good. You *are* my good girl, aren't you?"

"Y-Yes, Sir." It squeaked out as David slid the stim wand into her body. Heat roared through Kress as he watched her pussy grip the silver stick, her thighs quivering from the foreign shock of it. He flicked a glance at her face. She'd closed her eyes and worked at turning her bottom lip into hamburger with her teeth. So scared. So nervous. But so trusting, so wanting to please. So—

"Perfect." The Dom in the next room finished his thought. The Dom he'd give his left nut to trade places with. But, pitiful as it was, both his nuts were fine remaining where they were, torturing the hell out of him and aching for release.

"Oh yeah, perfect," David repeated. "You're so gorgeous, sweetheart. Just an inch more..." He gave the wand a little twist, ignoring her cry of protest. "Now the fun begins."

He clicked another switch on the stim wand.

Dasha's shriek was one of the sweetest sounds Kress had ever heard.

She clearly cycled fast through shock, pain, rebellion...but then ascended to arousal. Deep. Sexual. Raw. Guttural.

Pennington zapped her again.

Her shriek filled the air once more. Kress couldn't look away from the sight of her, abandoned to the moment. The muscles in her arms were defined with her strain. Her head jacked back on the mattress. Her lungs heaved, and her beautiful legs shook...struggling to remain spread for her Dom.

Pennington, Kress decided, must be half robot. *He* was a dozen pumps away from shooting a Nile-sized climax, and he wasn't standing inches away from that whimpering submissive...that lush body...that shivering pussy...

Which seized again as David pressed the wand—and left the charge going this time.

"Ohhhh!" she whimpered, collapsing her legs inward. Her fingertips gripped the cuffs. Her body contorted, shivering in time to the current that fucked her from the inside out. "Please, Sir! I can't take it!"

David ran a thumb the length of her clit. Then back down again. "Are you safe wording, sweetheart?"

"Ohhh. I don't know..."

"Then you'll keep taking the wand." His voice was an iron drill. With dexterity that stunned even Kress, the guy sprang onto the bed and locked Dasha's torso back into place. He straddled one of her legs, securing it into position. Dragged his free hand off her clit and up her leg, pressing it firmly too. He went to work on securing the wand again, tormenting her by making the thing into a makeshift cock for a few deep thrusts. "It's going to make you come, D. Is that understood?" When she gave him nothing but a groan, he pumped the wand again. "Can't hear you, sweetheart."

"Yes," she cried. "Yes, Sir!"

Kress prayed that moment was destined for sooner than later. Indeed, less than two tormented minutes later, Dasha Moore orgasmed for her master in a rush of screams and gasps that not only clawed at Kress's dick but sucked at the fibers deep inside his chest, his heart, his being. And as he wrested the climax from his own body, one thought took over, filled with more sick certainty than a Marilyn Manson lyric.

You're in trouble, Moridian. The big, dangerous, objectivity-fucking kind. Which doesn't leave your job, your credibility, and other important shit very far behind.

Damn it. His jeans weren't the only thing in a mess now.

CHAPTER TEN

Three days later, David prayed they weren't tempting fate for a cluster fuck.

After that first incredible night in the mansion, he'd purposely laid low on the D/s dynamic with Dasha, letting her get settled while he and Moridian transformed the library into a Let's-Find-the-Lunatic command center. He made it a point to carve out "normal" couple time too. They'd slept in every morning after staying up late on the couch, catching up on movies. They'd swum in the pool and taken walks along the little creek behind the house—shadowed by someone from Kress's team, of course.

He only had to pull out the Dom mode for a few select occasions. Nearly all of them had involved requests from D for off-property excursions—and his subsequent vetoes. A farmer's market visit with the mansion chef? *No.* Shoe shopping with Mary and the girls? *No.* A haircut at Atlanta's newest hot salon? *In the heart of the city's hottest shopping area? Surrounded by a few thousand strangers? Definitely no.*

He put up with the bratty silences that followed because he understood them. Cabin fever sucked ass—but damn it, she was still alive to be pissed about it. For that payoff, he'd gladly be her nemesis a few times a day.

He'd given in to only one of her requests—and now regretted the decision for the hundredth time. Make that the hundred and first, especially as he looked across the crowd waiting in the central plaza of the Lenox Square shopping mall.

This scene wasn't supposed to be happening. This was supposed to be an intimate gathering to benefit Dasha's favorite cancer charity, going down inside the mall's Neiman Marcus. *"A friendly meet-and-greet,"* the planners had said, with a handful of fans who'd paid for the right by forking over the VIP price for her new perfume. But given the event's beneficiary, D told the planners not to cap the number of eligible participants.

They should've capped it.

Apparently, a lot of folks had big piggybanks and weren't afraid to break them. Only now, the VIP. group of a couple hundred was backed by the thousands more who'd come just to be in the same building as D. For her safety, mall engineers had started unfolding stage risers too.

Tempting fate.

He tried to ban the words from his mind, but every passing minute brought more mental vultures. They helped drive his stare into the crowd again. Any one of these faces could belong to their dove-killing pal. Any one of these people could be their lunatic, who could've easily learned about the event and how Dasha had insisted on going forward with it.

He turned and paced back into the Gap Kids Store. The store had offered to be their green room for an hour. Like that had been a sacrifice. The managers eagerly snapped photos of Dasha with their kids—who were dressed in GK's latest styles, of course. Hurray, fun times for everyone.

Except the woman who'd take a giant chunk of his heart if she died today.

Even the mental vultures froze. *Whoa.* When the hell did his *heart* play into any of this? Yes, he was all the way committed to Dasha—professionally. Yes, he was overjoyed to see her fulfilled—sexually. But that was where the love stopped. That was where it *had* to stop. Getting anything other than his head and his cock tangled with her would be disaster.

Hadn't he proved that already with another disaster named Sophie?

He grunted and shook his head. This wasn't the time to be dwelling on exes, especially those who took steak knives to their wrists when he suggested they have a night out with the girls and then dragged in his own brother for support on the matter. Yeah, he'd learned fast about losing objectivity for a submissive, because he'd fallen in love with his. He'd fast learned about the guilt and pain that came with that package. So he just didn't take the package anymore. Period.

He bit out an oath, dumped the memories behind a display rack of chinos, and told himself to focus on getting Dasha through the next hour intact—though as he approached Kress Moridian, he discerned the agent waging an internal fight of his own. The guy stood against a store wall, clearly yearning to yank the plug on this chaos in his own right. Thank fucking God.

That observation brought another hit of confusion. Moridian's chivalric act about Dasha had gotten worse over the last seventy-two hours, which, given all the baggage from Sophie, should've turned him into a raving commercial for *back-the-hell-off, Agent M*. But something had shifted between G-Man and him. Something significant. He'd spent a lot of time with Kress over the days, had seen the guy in a bunch of different circumstances, most in the stressed to very stressed range. In every instance, Moridian never became the FBI asshole David would've laid money on. Instead, with every new roadblock they encountered in the investigation, the agent indulged some choice cuss words, slugged another energy drink, and then went at their challenge with fresh eyes. Looking for a new angle. Peering for the chink he hadn't yet seen. Not giving up.

It got damn hard, David admitted, to hate someone who did things exactly like him.

Moridian reinforced that thought the next second. "I don't like this," the guy muttered. "I really don't like this. They're putting up a goddamn *stage* out there."

"I'm aware of the operational developments."

"So do something!" the guy snapped. "Control your s—"

David wheeled a hard stare. "Control my *what*?"

"Nothing. *Fuck*." Moridian looked away, eyes glittering. "Nothing."

David gave back a noncommittal grunt. He could afford the benevolence. He'd picked up enough veiled innuendoes this week to know he shared more than a hardcore work ethic with Kress. And though the guy had cut himself short, they both knew what statement he'd almost spilled.

Control your sub.

"Look, Pennington. She listens to you, right? Then *make her listen.* I have ten men and half of the Atlanta PD out there, but we're still piss-poor outnumbered against that mob, and—"

"They're not a mob." The verbal whip was lashed by a glaring Dasha, who'd somehow approached without them noticing. For a wonderful second, even in full brat mode with hands on her hips, she made David forget what planet he was on. She was all soft curves and flowing femininity, her cream-colored, lacy dress skimming the tops of brown hip boots in a soft, touchable leather. Matching fabric strips wrapped most of her torso, acting like a corset to her breasts, cinching them up and filling the dress's bodice in a cock-tugging combo of creamy-tease and Southern-belle-innocent.

"They're not a mob," she repeated. "They're my fans, and a lot of them have driven far to be here. A lot more have postponed concert tickets. Do either of you want to tell them we're canceling this appearance too?"

Moridian huffed and hunched his shoulders. He slanted a furious glance to David, but when swinging his regard to Dasha went mushy and intense about it.

"Fine," the guy finally muttered. "Let's get this damn thing done."

★ ★ ★

A little under an hour later, David took a relieved breath. It was only a short one, sneaked between all the clenched others, but few more were certain to follow.

Thank fuck.

He stood discreetly next to the stage, watching his girl plant the crowd firmly in the palm of her pretty hand. They enchanted her in return. Dasha Moore, the stunning senator's daughter, had worked hard to earn her fans' devotion, proving she was really an ordinary person with stories in her heart that needed to be sung. Because of that, over the last five years, she'd learned other people's stories too and never took one of them for granted. Even today, she'd listened to several tearful teenage breakup tales and right now hugged the brother of a woman who'd succumbed to the same cancer that'd killed her mom three years ago.

As the young man pulled away, David caught him stealing

a view of the valley down D's bodice. In reaction, he only smiled.

Maybe he gloated about it. A little.

Go ahead, pal. Fantasize about what they look like. Now add my initials pierced into her perfect nipples. Nice picture, eh?

The guy who did look like he'd tear off the fan's head was Kress. The agent glared while edging over but extricated the admirer with surprising diplomacy. He pulled back enough to let D throw out a few more waves to the crowd before guiding her by the elbow toward the rear stage stairs. David moved the same direction, toward the canopy-covered area where the VIP group awaited. Moridian had mandated the cover when the event turned full circus on them. *"The less time she's in openly public ground, the better,"* the agent had said. *"You all got a stage in here. Now add a tent to it and make those people go to her."*

The memory allowed David to take another relaxed breath. Moridian was a credit to the badge in his wallet. He felt a little safer, knowing Kress's focus never veered from Dasha.

He got in one more normal breath before a dozen rifle shots ripped the air.

Before figuring he'd never breathe again.

As he lunged for the stage, smothered in the eruption of screams and wails and chaos, David's stare went tunnel vision, locked on one horror alone.

Dasha was down. And covered in blood.

CHAPTER ELEVEN

She struggled to think. To process the logic of the chaos that had seemingly invaded the world. One second she'd been jubilant, high on the crowd's energy; in the next, the celebration was a war zone. Bodies falling. People shrieking. Uniformed figures sprinting everywhere.

The pops. They echoed through her mind, body, and skin. Harsh cracks, like fireworks. But no, a horrible replacement. Somebody had shot at them. At *her*.

She'd fallen down. No. Something had made her go down. No. Some*one*. Kress Moridian was still in that position, splayed atop her, his body a shell over hers. She swore she felt every tense, solid muscle in his big frame.

"Don't move!" His command was harsh in her ear. "Don't move until I tell you!"

"Ohh...kay."

Like he could hear her. Her rasp was foreign even to her ears, a pair of terrified syllables. She didn't bother repeating them due to two things. One, Kress was barking orders into his headset radio. Two, the blood. She stared at it, splashed across her forearm and hand. Bright red. Fresh. Was it hers or his? She trembled, too terrified to tell. Too numb to feel.

"Help APD secure the perimeter!" The intensity of his voice reverberated through his body and hers. "Nobody gets in or out! And notify local medical. I'm hit."

Nausea burned her trembles away. Question answered.

The blood was Kress's. He'd been shot. Because of her.

Which brought the assault of another terrible thought. *Who else had the sick bastard hit?*

★ ★ ★

It was a full forty-eight hours before she could process the memories again. But even now, sitting safely in one of the mansion's big sitting rooms, with two agents and an army of security cameras outside, the recall struck Dasha with the same rush of dread. She was back on that stage, pinned beneath Kress, consumed with the wild wondering of whether somebody in that crowd had been hurt. Or killed.

She shivered and thrust her book away. Like she'd retained any of the three sentences she'd reread over the last hour. The words were shadowed by five horrific others. *It could have been Kress.* Then four more. *Dead. Because of me.*

It was over. She forced the truth into the meat grinder of her heart.

It's over.

They'd caught the shooter minutes after the incident, in one of the mall's trash bins, getting ready to use the rifle on his own brains. He'd also been clutching the *Vanity Fair* cover she'd done last year. When the news came in, David had indulged a moment of morbid humor, something about trash going highbrow.

David wasn't rolling out any more jokes now.

He paced the garden adjoining the mansion's sitting room. It had become their secret entrance into the house, providing a handy box hedge shortcut to the carport. The guys had quickly located the garden's other perk: an ivy-lined patio with a built-in barbecue and a refrigerator that was continuously stocked, in Kress's words, by the "magical beer fairy."

And speak of the devil. Kress followed David a few steps, a delay giving David the chance to pop a bottle with an embossed gourmet label and then extend it to the agent upon arrival.

"Just what the doc ordered," Kress murmured.

"Thought so," David volleyed.

The agent implied his thanks by tilting the neck of his bottle forward. After David knocked his against it, they both took long draws on their brews.

Neither observed the sitting room's slider was open, probably because of the heavy gauze drape a maid had pulled across it in an effort to keep the afternoon heat at bay. Since Dasha sat on the chair farthest from the window, neither noticed her in here either.

She was on the brink of rising and disclosing herself, but then the men sprawled into the padded patio chairs, looking as gratified as Labradors in a mud puddle, and she didn't have the heart to interrupt their quality guy bonding. More importantly, she hadn't seen either of them more relaxed since they'd arrived here. Amazing what could happen when these two weren't stressing about every move she made—and how dazzling they could look too. Both pairs of long legs stretched out, breathtaking even beneath blue jeans. Their dark heads lolled. The late-afternoon sun etched the contours of their torsos with the beauty of an artist's brush.

David emitted a long sigh. "If I remember correctly, the doctor also ordered a week of rest and a handful of painkillers."

Kress didn't flinch. "Fuck off."

"Says you, dill weed. If you die of some exotic infection from that wound, I'm the one who has to live with Dasha. She's a mess as is it about all this crap from the mall. What you did for her—"

"I know, I know. Don't you go getting all sappy on me too. Not after today."

"Afraid I can't help you on that either. So hey...listen, Moridian—"

"Shut. Up."

"No. Let me do this."

"Yeah. Fine."

"Thank you. I mean it."

"I know. But I was just doing my job."

"If there's anything I can give you in return—"

"An hour with your subbie?"

Shockingly, David barked a laugh at that. Kress looped in his own chuckle. Dasha was glad for the sounds because they masked her gasp. *Subbie.* How did Kress know about...that? Had he simply figured it out? But how? Had he just known by looking at them? There was no way David had openly shared that information. He was the king of paranoid about personal secrecy, even before they'd turned this corner in their relationship. But she hadn't misheard Kress's joke. Nor the not-so-joking glance he'd thrown at David afterward.

Nor how her body surged with warmth as a reaction.

She shoved her hair back and downshifted her heartbeat. As for the fresh blood rush to her most intimate core... hopefully, her fast rise and determined steps across the room would help.

She pulled back the sheer with a feigned look of easy-breezy-okay-I-just-got-here. "All right you two, what's so funny?"

Her smile dropped when theirs did too. Their weary

humor evaporated as well. Okay, mutation time. Good-bye Labradors, hello pit bulls. Dasha looked to the new expressions on their faces: tension, sadness, even anger. A wave of energy blasted off them both too. With it came the next shock. Their new attitudes were less about what she'd interrupted and more to do with why they'd even taken the break, why they hadn't come into the house right away, to look for her how they normally did.

Had they deliberately lagged on seeing her? If so, then why?

A hundred answers did mosquito dives at her. None of them were good. Not when the tension levels in both men's stares ramped to DEFCON 3.

"Uh...either of you want another beer?" She nervously grabbed two bottles from the fridge, ignoring the near-full levels on their first drinks.

David smiled in the gentle, knowing way that said he understood. "Thanks, D." His murmur matched the soft brush of his fingers on hers. They exchanged a meaningful look, which thickened as he sneaked a hand along her inner thigh, under the gauzy skirt of her white sundress. She tried to compose her features during the delivery to Kress but found the man's laser-green eyes fixed on her, taking his face up another DEFCON point. She knew, beyond a doubt, that he'd not just witnessed every inch of David's caress but enjoyed it. And wanted *her* to know he had.

Her womb vibrated like an arena speaker on high bass.

She slammed it off. The mixed messages from these two were playing enough havoc with her head; her body was blacklisted from the party list for now.

To prove the point, she locked hands to her hips and glared

at Kress. "Okay, so how're you doing? Did you go for your bandage check today?" She pulled him forward so she could gingerly press the square of gauze beneath his red Ramones T-shirt. "Did they look at everything thoroughly? Did they—"

"No, *no*. I'm fine, Dasha. Flesh wound, remember? The bullet only grazed me."

"Only?" she snapped. "A five-inch laceration that turned your back into Spin Art?" Horror broadsided again. "Damn it," she snapped, feeling the strange urge to slap him for his flippancy—until the idiot himself forced her attention back down with a forceful tug on her hand.

"Dasha. I'm okay. It was my job. Cut the worry and the guilt."

"I'm not—"

A low growl from David halted her this time. Instantly, almost surprisingly, her brain clicked into that different place only he could take her to. She yanked the protocol off her feelings and forced herself to face them more honestly. "Fine." She got in one more starched scowl at Kress anyway. "I'll work on the guilt if you work on the bad cop-drama lines."

Kress matched her on the look, inch for inch. The action forced her to look deeper into his gaze and see he hadn't dropped the memory of watching David touch her. Or where his imagination had taken the sight.

So much for wishing they'd drop the mixed messages. Or thinking every cell in her body would just ignore them.

Or telling her temper not to erupt when they followed all that with a thick silence.

"Okay, what the hell's up?" She fumed as they both just took longer swigs on their drinks. "Shouldn't we be celebrating? They got him, right? The bad guy's put away, and—"

Comprehension sucked the air from her lungs. And the strength from her legs. She sagged, leaning on the barbecue ledge. "Crap. He's not put away, is he? The bastard got away?"

"He didn't get away," David emphasized.

"Then what? He says he didn't do it or some bullshit like that?"

"His name is Ambrose Smith," Kress added. "Forty-eight years old, native Atlantian, never been married, lived here with his mom his entire life." He swung out an emphasizing hand. "His *entire* life. As in, has never left the city or the state. He doesn't even own a cell phone. Mom doesn't either."

"The last two on the planet," David said.

Dasha swung her stare between them both. "So that means..."

"He's our rotten peach from Atlanta," Kress clarified. "But not our mashed pineapple from Miami. The first merely gave inspiration for the second."

David shot him a grimace. "Did you really just go there?"

"What?"

"Peaches and pineapples?"

"Hey, fruit is good for you." His dry tone dissolved into a grunt.

Dasha barely noticed it. She ground her grip on the granite ledge as acid freshly knotted her stomach. The coil had been loosening since they'd caught Smith but was back, tighter than before.

"Hey...D?" she heard Kress say, the firm highway resurfaced to his voice, though it seemed so far away, so distant. "Dasha, are you—"

"Sweetheart?" David's interjection came closer. She felt his arm around her. His muscles were as tight as his voice.

"Hey, you're shaking like a—"

She pushed away. She needed to move, or the fear would drown her in its dizzying destruction. "So he's—still out there," she stammered. "That asshole's still out there, isn't he? And now *inspiring* others?"

The men didn't get a chance to answer. A chime came from the sitting room. Her phone. Dad's ring.

David glowered. "Fucking great. Just what we need."

"What?" asked Kress while following her and David back inside. "Who's—"

"Daddy," she said into the phone, deliberately pacing away from the guys. The next room had probably been a cigar parlor when the mansion was first built; it was more masculine than the sitting room, with a circle of mahogany wingbacks. "Hey," she said, curling into one. "Thanks for calling."

Dad responded, but static drowned him out. David didn't help, growling from the doorway, "Yeah, thanks for calling— twenty-four hours after a madman shot at your daughter."

Before she could fling a glare at him, the line cleared. "Dasha? Songbird? Can you hear me now?"

She clenched back a sigh. *Songbird*. It was the pet name he used on her only when his staffers and the press were around; an endearment for making a great impression. She didn't need "impressions" right now. She needed the familiar rhythm of his voice. Needed the *Daddy* in him to sneak past the *Senator Moore*. If any situation could bust him past that divider, surely it was this one.

"Yeah," she said. "Yeah, I can hear you, Dad. I—I just need... Things have been so—"

"I know. They briefed me."

"They did?" She blinked in surprise. A lot of it. "When?"

"Yesterday morning. My security lead received the update from your Agent Moridian. Listen, I know you're scared, Dasha, but the FBI has a good man on your case, don't you worry."

Despite her agreement to the assessment of Kress, her chest tightened. "They told you...yesterday?"

An awkward pause filled the line. Dad finally said, "I would have called sooner, darling. I was worried sick. But we were over in Iraq, and I'm just on the plane back to DC now. As you know, I'm on this trade development task force. The Iraqis really want to get back on their feet. The talks have been intense."

"I didn't realize that'd started already." She got her turn with the embarrassment. There had probably been a memo on all this, and she hadn't read the damn thing.

"Yes," Daddy went on, brightening again. They were back in his sweet spot of subjects. "It's exciting. The agreements we're entering into will create thousands of new jobs, both here and there. The benefits for both countries will be incredible. We're exchanging some breakthrough ideas..."

As he launched into a string of statistics and superlatives, Dasha gulped back a softball-sized lump—and then gave up on fitting any hope around it. She forced herself to listen to Dad, to insert the proper "ooos" and "ahhs" at all the right places in his sentences...to be the ideal political daughter she so often wasn't.

What the hell was wrong with her? Did she think her ridiculous pop-princess drama was more important than the work he was doing, the lives he was changing? So she had a wingnut who'd made her his latest obsession; wasn't that practically a rite of passage for her world? *Her* world, not his.

Worse, a world outside the acceptable options for a senator's kid. She should be with him on that plane. Or if not, then in a skirt suit and pumps somewhere, opening a hospital wing or busting a bottle on a ship or...

Anywhere but here. Not here, helpless and wordless and worthless.

Again.

She tugged her hair into her face, hiding from the stare she already felt from David. He'd be able to see those thoughts on her face; she was certain of it. Right away, he'd see the doubts that sneaked back in like mooching old friends, slinking in to camp out in the kitchen of her mind and scarf a free meal of her soul, courtesy of her insecurity.

"...so what do you think about that, darling?"

The question from Dad caught her off guard. But she'd caught enough to hear about a music education program being part of their Save-the-Iraqis miracle package. "That's...great, Dad. Really. Awesome job. I mean it."

"I know you do." But his tone had turned more fake than it was in "Songbird" mode. "And your support means the world to me. I support you too, Dasha. You know that, honey."

Then make the plane bypass Dulles and come here and be with me. I need you, Daddy. I'm scared. I'm so scared.

"Yeah," she got out. But little else. The disappointment layered atop David and Kress's bombshell. Dad wasn't about to change his flight plans. He'd barely altered his schedule to get in the call. After he hung up, he'd go back to concentrating on changing lives and helping people, confident enough in Kress's credentials to know they'd find the bad guy and keep his little girl safe.

The trouble was, she felt everything except safe right now.

With a wince, she wondered if she ever would again.

"Songbird mine, we are going into landing mode and they're making me turn you off."

"Okay, Dad."

"Tell that Agent Moridian to keep his eyes on you."

She glanced up—to find Kress doing just that. His gaze, the roiling green of an early stage tornado, made a perfect match to the gray thunderclouds in David's stare as they stood together in the doorway. *Perfect. Not.*

"Right." She dipped her head away from them, indulging one last shred of hope. "Hey...Dad...I love—"

A trio of beeps blared in her ear.

For a long moment, she stared at the dark screen. *Just like always.* And just like always, she willed for the thing to light up again. She yearned to hear those wonderful words in her ear. *Darling, how could I be so silly? I love you too, Dasha...*

They didn't come.

The next words with real volume came from the doorway behind her. Kress issued them, his tone a bite of gothic sarcasm. "Was that a shit-pile of weird, or am I high?"

"No," David replied. "You're wired fine." He chuffed without humor. "That's par for the course when the senator calls."

"But it's like she gets a personality transplant. Right into the Land of No-Spine."

"Duly noted. About three years ago."

"But it's wrong! The guy's her *father*. Why doesn't somebody set the man straight?"

"You think I haven't tried?"

Dasha still didn't turn. She didn't need to. She could clearly envision David's face anyway. Tension dug into his broad forehead, and his jaw was a hard line of pissed-off. In an equally tight tone, he went on. "The regrettable news is, our girl inherited her stubborn streak from Daddy. Whenever I say anything, the man calls me an old woman, says I'm stressed about nothing. He says Dasha hasn't voiced anything to him, so all must be well in Oz."

"And that's where new-personality girl comes in and doesn't say a fucking thing."

"You're getting it, Toto."

"Shit on burned toast. That's a mess."

"Amen."

There was a long pause, but Dasha knew the guys hadn't stopped communicating. She finally put her phone down and dared a peek out from the chair, half expecting to see them gesturing in American Sign Language. Instead, those twin stormy stares still confronted her. Now they also rocked matching postures: legs planted, arms crossed over the snug shirts encasing those well-honed chests. Crap. If she wasn't drowning in fear and frustration, she might've counted herself a lucky woman just for the view.

She surged to her feet. "You both want to stop talking about 'the mess' like she's not sitting right here?"

David's jaw flexed harder in reaction. But to her surprise, half a smile played at Kress's lips. "Well. Somebody needs some discipline."

"Also duly noted." When David simply shrugged with that, she was certain her eyes bugged again. He aggravated the effect by dipping a knowing nod at her. "And as I said, working on it."

"Well, if it were me..."

The rest of the sentence hung unsaid in the air, though

Dasha wondered if that was the case. It really did feel like the two had some secret language going on, activated the second Kress had used the magic word. *Subbie.* In the minutes since then, all their actions felt different, a change she'd been willing to ignore—but no longer. Not when David stepped forward, braced his stance, and challenged, "Yeah? What *if* it were you?"

Silence stretched. But not the energy between all of them. A grinning Kress suddenly found the carpet interesting. David caught her stare and held it, as if assessing where her mind was really at right now. As if that lightbulb had flicked on for him, he smiled too.

Ohhhh, hell.

It was a smile she'd never seen on his Greek-god mouth before. If he was Zeus back in Miami, he was certainly Eros now. The broker of love and passion.

And sex.

Dark, forbidden sex.

Kress lifted his head again...channeling the exact same energy. Both of them stared at her from head to toe and then back again. Dasha, gripping the back of the chair she'd just left, forced down a breath. Like that stopped the escalation of her heartbeat. Something strange but tangible had shifted the room's atmosphere. The threads in the air were now wires, forming a new, sensual power grid. Where once there was a loop, now there was a triangle.

It terrified her.

It entranced her.

Kress finally broke the silence with a quiet question. "You said you've tried spanking?"

The ball in her throat erupted on a choke. She stared at David and voiced the unthinkable. "You...told him?"

"Hush." It carried the same strength as Kress's voice, but it wasn't a request. Not by a long shot. "Your secrecy and security are the most important things to me, D. I've been consumed with ensuring both over the last week."

"I know," she answered fast. "I do know, David. And I—I'm grateful. But—"

"So do you think I'd deliberately talk about us to another if he didn't place equal importance on your well-being?"

She lowered her gaze. Closed her eyes. And behind her lids, once again saw Kress slamming her to that stage. Throwing himself on top of her. Knowing it might've gotten him killed because of her. And then, the mind-bending kicker: she knew he'd do it again. Without hesitation.

"No, Sir."

"Hm." The injection from Kress was laced with approval, though he directed it at David.

"Kress and I have had a lot of time to talk this week." He started pacing toward her. "And since the subject was often our mutually favorite subject, your sanity and safety, we've discovered we have...similar viewpoints on some things."

It took her a few long moments to respond, mostly due to the hand he now lifted to her nape. He didn't place it there for a massage. His hold was firm and tight—and she loved it. His command rippled through her body, making her capable of giving him just one word.

"Oh."

Oh?

What was wrong with her? Misgivings whirled and attacked again. This had nothing to do with her shortfalls as Senator Mark Moore's daughter. This had everything to do with the chip in her brain that was clearly, irrevocably, *wrong*.

Because, as David coaxed up her head in time to see him motion Kress closer, all she could feel was thrilled...needed. As the agent stepped closer, the ink-dark pupils in his eyes showed nothing but desire, fixation.

Kress stepped forward and then grabbed one of her wrists, locking her in his hold. The only reaction she could scrape was a surrendering sigh. She barely held herself back from adding another monosyllable to it.

Yes.

The world and all its lunatics, insanity, guilt, and insecurities began to fall away.

If this was wrong, then maybe she didn't need to be right. Ever again.

Kress's rugged face, framed by those unruly brown waves, hardened in all the right places. "So you've been hiding your real feelings from Daddy," he stated. "Holding back from telling him what you really feel because you're afraid you'll hurt him?"

Dasha's breath caught. Okay, maybe the world wasn't going away so fast.

"I didn't ask that for my health, Dasha."

She gulped. And stammered, "N-No, Sir. I mean, y-yes, Sir."

"I'm not your Sir. You can call me Kress." His voice flowed like water from an underground pool, shadowed yet fluid. "Now answer the question again, in a complete sentence. From what your *Sir* tells me, you know those pretty well."

"Yes, Sir. I—I mean, yes, Kress. And..." She flicked a glance to David, who encouraged by squeezing her nape tighter. "Yes. I've been hiding the truth from my father."

"Even after your Sir has told you that such behavior will

harm your dynamic with him?"

Conflict raged again. David had mandated, in no uncertain terms, that honesty with Dad wasn't an opt-out choice. It was a necessity, and she knew that now. Shutting off things from Dad had forced her to compromise other parts of her life. Every time she submitted to David, she relearned that lesson in beautiful detail. Their journeys to sexual heaven had been fueled by pure honesty and trust—elements she'd openly, easily promised to him.

But she hadn't kept those promises.

Not even close.

Tonight, she hadn't even tried with Dad.

Where did that put his reciprocal trust now?

"Yes." She rasped it, yearning to hang her head. Somehow, David knew that. As he moved behind her, he shifted his hand to cup her chin. He tunneled the other one into her hair and then yanked, forcing her head to arch back—and her gaze to lock with Kress's ongoing, unfaltering stare.

"Even after he's said that complete honesty is essential for your relationship?" he charged.

"Y-Yes."

"Were you thinking about all this when you were speaking with your father?" Kress's hold became a knot around her wrist. "Were you thinking of the trust of your Sir at all?"

That broke the dam. "I—I wanted to say more." She let the tears flow down her face and neck. "I wanted to be honest! But he was on a plane, and the press was with him, and—" She tried to shake her head. David didn't give her an inch for it. "I-I'm sorry."

David tightened himself against her back. Angled her head into the crook of his neck. "I know," he said into her ear.

"Thank you," she whispered.

He pulled her against him a little more, sliding a hand to the valley between her breasts. "But you also know there must be discipline now."

"Y-Yes."

It felt right to say it. She needed to have this, to make things right again between them. She hadn't wimped on Dad on purpose, but letting David guide her, to make her better at the process next time, was a choice she *could* make—no matter how scared she was about his definition of "discipline."

She needed to give him her trust again.

So she'd earn his again.

"The punishment may take you past a few comfort points," David stated. "Maybe more than a few."

He likely felt her heartbeat react to that. But he waited, his hand a steady pressure between the swells of her breasts. "Yes, Sir," she finally replied. "I understand."

"Very good." As David issued the praise, Kress roped his hold around her other wrist. "Because we're getting to the first point now."

They both moved in again, practically crushing her. Her breathing shallowed, practically at hyperventilation.

It was good. So damn good.

She looked up, feeling tiny between their planes of power. "All right," she said, sounding timid and unsure but unable to control it. Yes, these men were obsessed with protecting every cell of her body, but the heat radiating off them was so potent, so powerful, so overwhelming...

So. Good.

"Breathe," David instructed. Easy for *him* to say, being the one nuzzling her neck with firm warmth. "And listen."

"Yes, Sir."

She fell back against him, reveling in the thrum of his pulse as well as hers, a potent energy through all his muscles...and every inch of his erection. She tilted her head back, exposing her jaw for another of his commanding kisses.

"You must have surmised some of it by now," he murmured.

Dasha fought for thought. "Some of...what?"

"I'd like Kress to assist with your punishment, sweetheart. I think he's earned that right, don't you?"

She looked up to Kress. His features held the same protective intensity with which he'd always beheld her—magnified by a thousand. As if she needed the impression reinforced, he shifted again, fitting the ridge between his legs into the apex of hers. She gasped. Dear God, even through their clothes, she felt his rough heat...and huge length.

Lust tumbled from both men, filling her senses with its raw masculine magic. The elixir acted like a drug on her tongue. "Yes," she finally answered David. "Yes, Sir, he has."

Kress moved in even closer. Without warning, he whisked her arms above her head.

"Pretty words," he drawled. "But too swift to be your truth."

He shoved her wrists, now slammed together, back by another few inches. "Hold her for me," he directed David. After her wrists were passed into her Dom's crushing grip, Kress caught her face in a commanding hold. His fingers splayed against her cheekbones.

"I haven't known you for years, sugar. There's a good chance my mercy has a lower threshold than your Sir. And a *very* good chance I'll use some creative techniques he's not brought out yet. But be confident in this: my creativity won't mark you in places you'll have to be concerned about." His mouth, just inches away, lifted into a knowing smile. He dipped his head, brushing those made-for-sin lips against hers. "We'll just make it count in other places, yeah?"

"Yeah," Dasha echoed on a sigh. She parted for him, yearning for the invasion of his kiss. When Kress didn't return the pressure, she gave a tiny buck of her hips, urging him to satisfy even a piece of her body's need. In return, he tunneled his fingers into her hair and twisted.

"Oh, no, honey. I'm not here to fuck you, remember? I'm here to help punish you. Maybe my cock will help me do that too, but you'll have to earn that as well. Dishonest girls don't get any cocks or any fucks until they've served their punishment. Perhaps together, we'll convince your Sir that you've learned your lesson and are ready for those again." By gradual degrees, he corkscrewed his hold tighter. "Are you ready to help me do that, Dasha?"

Heavy tears came, blurring her vision. But her heartbeat revved to full throttle. She swallowed again, struggling for coherent thought...

Knowing she only had one answer to give.

"Yes. I'm ready."

CHAPTER TWELVE

Christ. Now Kress knew why Pennington was such an asshole when it came to ensuring his woman's safety. Even with tears brimming in her eyes and pain contorting her face, Dasha was a breathtaking portrait of submission. And her voice... The soprano that captivated millions with an addicting pop hook was a siren's song when she whispered her brave words of surrender.

He looked up to David and took in the guy's face full of lust-mad impatience. And was so damn glad that, as they'd discovered countless times during the week, the two of them were on the same page.

"Set her free," he told his friend, "so she can get naked for us." He wasn't surprised that, as David let her arms down, the man reached around and tore back the panels of her dress bodice himself, popping buttons and ripping fabric. Since it was one of those sundress things with the bra built in, her breasts were free as soon as the bodice fell down.

The sight of them blew the air out of his body.

But before he could confirm the truth of what he'd just beheld, Pennington ordered, "Finish up, D. You heard the man. Do it fast."

Dasha bent over, peeling down the rest of the dress along with her white lacy thong. When she rose back up, the air rushed out of Kress's lungs all over again. And blood sluiced straight to his cock.

She was more gorgeous than he remembered. Her skin was the color of whipped honey, and it covered angular, muscled legs that joined in a perfect V at her bare pussy, leading up to the indent of her waist and the soft curve of her torso, shoulders draped in her golden, tumbling hair. And then...oh *Christ,* and then—

"You sly, fucking fox," he declared. At last, he had the chance to stare unhindered at her perfect, firm breasts, each centered with a dark-coral nipple that was wrapped in a distinct diamond letter. "That's the most beautiful monogram job I've ever seen."

David smiled, leaning to kiss his woman's cheek. "It starts with a beautiful toy to monogram."

"No matter what happens, she'll know exactly who she belongs to."

Not surprisingly, Dasha shot up a glare of pure copper fire. "I'd know it even without the diamonds, *sugar.* The initials might be pierced on my body, but they're already branded on my heart."

For a long second, he didn't say anything. It might've had something to do with the rubber band now cinched around his chest. At last, Kress took her face in his hands once more. This time, he did it with gentle fingers. "Then your Sir is not only sly but damn lucky."

"All right, man." David's grumble came with his new hold on Dasha. "You going soft-serve on me already?" He arched a black brow as he turned her fully to face him.

"Fuck you." Though it was part of their typical banter, he almost felt guilty about the crack. This encounter was one hell of a generous gift, especially from a guy he'd first pegged as a show-biz poser.

On the other hand, maybe David hadn't even heard him. The guy was busy giving their sub a long face-suck of a kiss. When he was done, he directed her back toward Kress. "Watch her for a few," his friend requested. "I'm going to go get some things ready."

Kress nodded, using the moment to widen his stance. His erection was already at torture status. Dasha, watching her Dom disappear with a look mixed of confusion and longing, didn't help the sitch at all. God *damn*, she was so gorgeous. And so naked. And so close...

"What *things* does he mean?" she asked him softly.

Though Kress didn't know the answer any more than she, he debated his choice of responses. Let her ruminate while he enjoyed—*really* enjoyed—the sight of her, or take advantage of the chance to see how she liked his style?

He decided within seconds.

Without preamble, he leaned over and gave her little ass a firm strike.

"Owww! What the hell, Kress?"

He pivoted to stand in front of her. "First, I've changed my mind about that. Addressing me as Kress clearly has given you the illusion you can take casual address with me tonight. So from this point, I'll be Sergeant to you. Second, initiating questions without asking permission is also not your place. Are we clear?"

He half expected her little smirk. "Sergeant?"

Before the word left her lips, he'd dropped to one knee and slammed her over it, delivering another series of whacks to her lovely, smooth backside. "My rank in the army before I left for the Bureau. Anything else you want to challenge me on, as long as we're at it?"

"No, Sergeant," came her breathless response.

"Damn shame," he countered. "Because your ass is stunning with my palm marks on it."

She writhed in a delicious way beneath the appreciative strokes he gave her cheeks. "It...feels nice too. Thank you... Sergeant."

Though she hesitated over the last word, her voice gave it to him with a dreamy cadence. Too dreamy. It was acclimation time. He'd get her too dreamy; they had a lot more ground to cover first.

With a determined sweep, he returned her to her knees and then rose to his feet.

"Stay right there," he bade when she moved to join him. "You'll assume proper submissive position while we're waiting. Ankles beneath your ass, hands atop your thighs, back straight, gaze at the floor. Do you understand the instruction?" he asked when she shot another questioning look at him.

He watched her mouth twist as if she'd just swallowed something nasty. Still, she complied with, "Yes...Sergeant," as she slowly lowered to the floor.

"Could've fooled me," he returned.

Her starchy little quip had Kress chewing back a chuckle. Ahhh, the sound of a subbie fighting her feistiness. It had been too long for him. Online lifestyle match sites were filled with a lot of loons, and he'd given up on club play at least a year ago. Even in the members-only BDSM houses, the unattached submissives were so eager to *be* attached, they'd nearly let a guy slit their wrists in exchange for the dynamic. Now he had a beautiful pixie at his feet who could barely string two civil words together for him, let alone submissive phrasing.

The challenge doubled the tension in his cock.

Jacked his senses like an addict after a dry-out.

He had to look at her again. Up close. He crouched, nearly eye to eye with her—only this time she kept her gaze dipped, as he'd instructed. Kress didn't mind. Not only was her acquiescence a thrill, he projected the new trajectory of her stare—and knowing she was getting her fill of his crotch gave him a pure, hedonistic thrill.

But he had other things to address with her. Such as the event that had gotten her like this in the first place.

He gently tugged her chin with his forefinger. She met his eyes directly, though hers surged like a bronze tempest. So many layers that compromised this fascinating creature. Some that made perfect sense. And others...that clearly didn't.

He followed just a strand of that contemplation. "I'm not here to bust out a psych-job on your issues with Daddy, at least not tonight—but I do need you to be brutally honest with me in this moment, D."

The solemnity of his tone settled over her whole face. "Okay."

Kress dipped in closer to her. "If you don't want this to happen, say so this second. Though we're here because of what you can't communicate to Dad, I'm not him. I won't take offense. I won't hang up in your ear or disappear in a sulk, and neither will David. He'll still drag you off somewhere and then have you fifteen ways till tomorrow, and I'll still be outside the door, watching out for you, still ready to go hunt the bad guy for you tomorrow. Do you understand?"

Great. *Now* she looked away. Kress ground his teeth together, willing his grip to remain gentle and his breath to stay steady. *You opened the escape hatch, lunkhead. Don't be surprised if she uses the damn thing.*

But then she turned her stare back up—and gave a smile so wide and certain, his gut turned to butter. "Sometimes, I think David knows me better than I do." She squared her jaw a little higher. "He knows...that I probably need this. And you—" Those two words tripped out fast. "He knows you—"

"Need it too."

So much for breathing right. Or controlling anything below his navel. "Christ, Dasha." He compelled his hand to stay on her face and not travel those gorgeous inches south. "Nearly since the moment I met you, I've dreamed of this. Wanted you like this."

The declarations were enough to crown him King of the Dorks—but as her smile grew, he proudly bolted the crown down. She took a long breath, lifting both her breasts higher, also ensuring he was ready to screw diplomacy, flatten her, and fuck her if Pennington didn't get his ass back here within the next minute.

Where the hell was he?

In their talks throughout the day, the guy hinted if things developed into a situation like this, he had a surprise waiting at the mansion. But for God's sake, how long did it take to set out some toys and turn down the bedroom lights?

"Well. What a nice sight."

About that long.

"What the fuck?" he snapped. "You forget your toothbrush in Miami?"

Pennington had the balls to chuckle. "Looks like you put the time to excellent use." The guy joined him in front of Dasha, crouching as well. "Very pretty, sweetheart." He pressed a kiss to her forehead. "But not my favorite presentation. Do you remember what that one is?"

Her gaze went liquid caramel, a sight almost as stunning as what the rest of her body did. Kress gave a long, low growl as she tilted into a full kneel-back: legs parted, thighs taut, pussy high and moist and inviting. The growl died in his throat when Pennington reached and parted her labia. Without hesitation, he pushed a couple of fingers up into her. She moaned, hiking the sexual heat in the room by about a million.

"Feels like this little one has been enjoying the anticipation too." Pennington extracted his fingers and then raised them to his submissive's mouth. "You know what to do, sweetheart. Get it all."

"*Fuck.*" Kress gritted it while watching her lap at her Dom's fingers, flicking between the digits before pulling each one all the way into her mouth, cheeks hollowed.

"Good girl," Pennington finally declared. He rose, pulling her with him. "You can stand up again."

Kress didn't think he'd ever get used to gazing at her totally naked. Her body was a lush collection of curves and muscles, all defined by that deep honey skin. As for those diamonds in her tits...damn. *Damn.*

"One more appetizer before our main course." A devil's glint appeared in David's eyes.

Kress noticed the guy had changed pants, going from his twill Prada *GQ* look into a heavy, custom black pair with multiple pockets down the legs. From two of those pockets, he pulled items that made Kress grin.

A pair of padded wrist cuffs. And a matching pair of ankle shackles.

"Help me out." David tossed him one of each.

"Don't have to ask twice." As they closed the clasps around their sub's slender extremities, Kress's pulse roared.

But it placed a distant second to where his mind careened. What the hell kind of setup had Pennington arranged? He didn't remember seeing any hard points for bondage or ample space for other kink equipment in the pair's antebellum-era bedroom. On the other hand, the last time he'd seen the chamber, he'd been distracted by...well...other sights.

"The main event awaits, kids." David kissed Dasha before taking her hand, courtier-style. "Are you prepared for your punishment?"

"Yes, Sir."

Once again, her layers astounded Kress. Her eyes screamed how she wanted this to be over, but the rest of her body proclaimed she never wanted it to end. One glance confirmed it: the tremor of her lips, the twin erections of her breasts, the willing way she followed her Sir. God *damn*. Pennington was indeed a lucky bastard.

That envy was eclipsed by the feelings that slammed three minutes later.

David led the way to the back of the mansion, to a plush study with bay windows and lots of leather furniture. After producing an ornate metal key, the guy walked to what looked like another panel in the wall and yanked on one of the sconces on it. The fixture turned out to be a handle, assisting David to slide back the entire panel. Behind it lay a smaller door, clearly original to the house, which looked like a portal to a simple closet.

"They used to hide moonshine in here," Pennington said as he clicked the key into the lock. "During the twenties, it was a speakeasy. More recently, the owners converted it for a different kind of fun."

Needless to say, the door didn't lead to a closet.

After about five feet, the carpeted passageway within surrendered to heavy stone steps that descended beneath the building. Each brick plane was illuminated by an oil-burning wall sconce, plunging them from the real world into a romantic, Gothic alternative. Pennington went first, still guiding Dasha, with Kress performing rear sweep as they traveled past flocked walls mounted with portraits that looked like someone had shown Scarlett O'Hara and her friends the glories of kink. At last they passed through a drape of heavy crimson velvet and the stairs were behind them.

While heaven opened up in front of them.

CHAPTER THIRTEEN

Hell.

David didn't have to look at Dasha to read the word on her mind. He felt it in the wrench of her hand against his, in the way she stopped as if suddenly glued down. She thought he'd brought her to hell, and he figured that was exactly what he'd think too—if his first trip to a BDSM dungeon had been to one like this.

He couldn't wait to prove just the opposite to her.

The room was a labyrinth of steel, velvet, machinery, and luxury. Muted lighting made certain corners more mysterious than others—these were the places where his favorite electric playthings resided next to padded platforms with selective hard points—while flesh-gelled spotlights directed the eye toward the more elaborate equipment: a St. Andrew's cross, a stand-up cage, a swing with retractable pins, a spanking bench, a spreader stockade, and other elaborate pieces, all accented with red crushed-velvet cushions. On one wall, a backlighted chest was filled with handheld tools of all kinds: floggers, paddles, Wartenberg wheels, clamps, canes, and a multitude more. In the center of the dungeon, a half dozen heavy steel rings hung from the ceiling, already prepped with red and black ropes that hung to the floor. A box of carabiner hooks waited nearby, ready to assist with the most elaborate bondage a Dom could dream up.

By the look in Kress's eyes, those dreams were already running rampant.

Past a dropped jaw, the guy stammered, "Holy mother of..."

"Mention fruit and you're a dead man," David snapped.

"I'm already dead. That's got to be the explanation for this."

"Helps to know a few people in the specialty real estate market."

"Specialty is right. When you said a surprise, I thought you meant a couple of new toys, not a whole toy *room*."

"Merry Christmas."

"Bastard."

Beside him, Dasha fidgeted. He watched her stare roam over the furniture again, stopping to notice the hooks and chains on each...knowing they were meant to hold her in place while Kress meted out a punishment far beyond what *he'd* ever done with her. Conflict raced across her face. Clearly, she wondered if she should cry her safe word—though if she did, what would she have passed up?

The question weighed just as heavily on him.

He shifted his grip from her hand to her wrist. As she looked up to him again, he hardened his face in equal proportion. "You have the option of your safe word. You know that."

Please don't use it. For fuck's sake, please don't use it.

She nodded. He tightened his hold, hoping it made her decision a bit tougher—hating himself and thanking himself for it.

Her muscles eased, a tiny yet discernible surrender.

Yessss.

"Let's get on with it," he told Moridian. "I've got a naughty girl here who's eager to pay her punishment."

Kress stepped forward, laser-beaming her with his own regard. David's chest filled with pride when she maintained her proud stance, despite flicking one more glance to the exit. "Yes," said Moridian, "you certainly do, don't you?"

"Where do you want to get creative first?" he asked.

One end of the guy's mouth curled up. "The wolves don't want to terrify Riding Hood before we can eat her up. Let's go slow."

"Good idea."

"Take her to the cross and lock her in. Warm her up while I get acquainted with the supply closet."

David arched a puzzled brow. "Warm her up?"

Kress grinned. "I noticed a TENS unit on the table next to the cross. I think you know what to do with it."

David didn't waste time with a reply. Locking his hand to Dasha's, he crossed the room to the eight-foot-high, X-shaped bondage mount in the far corner. D kept dutifully quiet during the journey, but he heard her breath coming sharper. By the time he stood her before the cross, the bling on her chest cast frantic sparkles against the cross's polished steel.

David released her hand and circled behind her. As he dragged his hands down her sides, willing his strength into her skin, he leaned in and kissed her nape.

"What are you feeling?" he asked. "Complete honesty, D."

"Terrified," came her whisper. "Sir," she amended after a gulp.

"But you're willing to do this anyway."

"Y-Yes."

"For me?"

"Yes."

He gave her neck another kiss. Then a hungry bite. "You

make your Sir very proud." As shivers raced down her body, he added, "And his cock very hard." He raked his fingers along her shoulders, the sadist in him flaring to life, needing to feel her tremble for him again. He reached down and slipped two fingers into her tight core, hoping to encounter her wetness. Oh yeah, there it was. Her walls dripped and pulsed against him. He adored her. He worshipped her.

"I can't wait to fuck you tonight, D. I'm gonna do it hard and long, until you come apart beneath me."

"Yes..."

This time, she said it with much more passion. That was his cue to bind up the balls and get to work on prepping her for Kress. He wiped her juices along her ass and then gave it a quick swat. "For now, you're up on the cross, sweetheart."

After guiding her legs onto the footrests and locking her in, David spread her arms along the upper beams, snapping the restraints on both sides there too. So much for giving the balls a take five. His sac throbbed by the time he finished even that. As he stepped to the table and fired up the TENS electrical box, his cock merrily joined the party. "Warm her up," he said, forcing his gaze past the probes and insertable attachments, settling on a set of fingertip electrodes instead. "Warm her up. That's *all*."

He attached three, to each of the middle digits of his right hand, while leaving his left free to adjust the voltage knobs on the box. After clicking the knob to a three, he returned to Dasha. Then went to work.

"No peeking." He emphasized the soft admonishment by coaxing her head onto the padded chin rest in the cross's apex. Less than a second later, he raked her from shoulder to ass with the live current.

So much for the chin rest. Her head snapped back as a high keen broke from her lips.

So much for any remaining softness in his pants either.

He swiped her three more times, covering new skin with each stroke, reveling in the intensified cries he got each time. Finally, he couldn't resist going for her backside and thighs too. Both had bunched and flexed while he'd focused on her back, and he craved to feel them flinching under his power before Moridian took over.

"Shit!" Dasha yelled as he first ran his fingers down her delectable ass crack. The way both her cheeks quivered gave him an idea for a game change. He pulled off two of the electrodes, leaving only the nodule on his index finger attached. Using his other fingers, he spread her ass cheeks, exposing the tender hole into her back passage.

"So sweet," he crooned, caressing the narrow canyon with his other hand. "You're so sweet and gorgeous here."

She trembled. "David. *Sir*—"

"Relax."

"But—"

"Breathe. Push out the muscles toward me. That's it."

The whimper she gave him pitched into a scream as he pushed the electrified finger into her ass.

She bucked, but David pushed his free hand against the small of her back, locking her in place as he worked the nodule in deeper.

"Relax, baby." He made it an order now. To be honest, the steel spine of his tone surprised even him—mostly because he barely controlled the urge to replace his finger with his cock. "Calm down and take it, D. I know you can. For me, remember? Breathe. Let me in."

Her body sagged as she finally submitted to the treatment. But after just a minute, her choked cries took on a different cadence. Her whimpers pitched more with need and fell into a sighing song he loved more than any sound on earth: a submissive learning she *liked* a new torture. David exchanged a pleased glance with Kress, who now arrived bearing a large wood tray loaded with his toys of choice. As David had suspected, the guy had a healthy taste for the BDSM smorgasbord. He wondered if the man planned on using everything he'd picked, though that certainly seemed his intent as he ran a hand across the cheeks still clenching against David's finger.

"Beautifully done," Kress stated.

"Warm enough for you?" The man's hands traveled up, assessing the fading trails along D's back. "A little pink, a little shaky, still tied up and whimpering for more. Not a bad way to start."

David grunted approval to that and then carefully pulled his finger out from Dasha. As he expected, her head jerked like she'd just been roused from a nap. Her spine stiffened again, and her fingers curled anew around the tops of the restraints. Though her trepidation sent new blood to his cock, part of him shared her anxiety. Kress had been right; his lack of history with her would let him push limits David wouldn't.

David kissed her nape while caressing the area he'd just penetrated, again willing some strength to her through touch. He had a feeling she was going to need it. But damn it, she was due for a breakthrough in this lying-by-omission game she'd been playing with the senator. It wasn't right or healthy for either of them—not to mention where things were going in his own relationship with her.

"Sir?" she asked, though dutifully keeping her head lodged in the proper place this time.

"I'm right here." He moved to the back of the cross so she could see him. "I'm not going anywhere, D." He cupped a hand around her face, lifting it so their gazes met. "I'll help you through this, but I'm also here to remind you why I'm letting Kress push boundaries with you tonight. Maybe you want to tell me why?"

Her slender lips pressed together. "Because this is a real punishment."

"And...?"

"Because I chicken-shitted on the conversation with Dad. And being more honest with him will help me be more honest with you."

"Not more honest," he returned. "*Completely* honest. This journey we're on...it involves more than your body. I need your head too, sweetheart. I can never doubt that you're telling me the total truth. I can never think, for an instant that you're holding back to spare my feelings."

She nodded a little. "You're right. Okay. Complete honesty. Thank you, Sir."

"That's an ideal reflection to begin with," said Kress from the other side of the cross. David recognized a tease in the tone, a deliberate tool to relax their girl—just before he brought on the meat of her punishment.

Kress selected a swivel flogger to start with, a pearl-handled beauty strung with thin rubber strands designed to impart a sharp, severe sting when wielded at full strength. For now, the guy only brushed her ass and back in a graceful figure eight, intending to get D used to the sensation. David wasn't sure she understood it the same way. From the first stroke, her gaze went wide, and she locked it on David as if trying to suck the strength from his body into hers. He kept holding her cheek but regulated his voice to a dominating timbre.

"Close your eyes," he ordered. "And accept it." There was no use giving her the "relax and breathe" mind-fuck again. She wouldn't heed it, and it was likely best that she expected the pain—because it was coming.

Kress cracked that fact home the next second. Though he varied his intensity for just two passes, the strokes were given at the man's full strength.

"Ohhhh!" Dasha wailed. David lost his grip on her head as she flailed back. He reconnected by raising his hands and locking them into hers instead.

She repeated the cry as Kress gave her another two strikes at full force, but those were the last words she voluntarily formed through the better part of the next half hour. She spoke only when David directly addressed her, and he did that only when Kress paused between one instrument and the next.

After the rubber-tail flogger:

"How do you feel, D?"

"Horrible, Sir."

After the riding crop:

"That wasn't so bad, was it, sweetheart?"

"Fuck you, Sir."

"Give her another ten with the crop, Kress. Then use the cowhide."

After the cowhide flogger:

"Are you ready to tell me how you really feel now, darling?"

"It's...hot. So hot. And it hurts, Sir. Please, it—"

"Who's in charge of this punishment, D?"

"You. You and Sergeant Moridian, Sir."

"That's right." He didn't know where that Sergeant bit came from, but he liked it. "Use the paddle now, Sergeant. The one with the holes. And don't give her a ramp-up on pressure."

She broke completely after three whacks with the paddle. The sobs came, shaky and sloppy, through the next three blows. David watched her closely as she slipped into tight silence after that, her ginger lashes fluttering, her face taut...yet oddly at peace. He lowered his touch back to her cheek. She leaned eagerly into his hold and readily sucked in his finger when he offered it to her lips.

He looked over to Kress, who'd stripped off his sweat-soaked shirt a few minutes back, and now cocked a confident smirk. "I take it we've achieved subspace?"

David tried not to think about how incredible her tongue felt, swirling and pulling at his finger. And Christ, her face. The sight of it intoxicated him deeper. Her skin gleamed, her eyes were glassy, her nostrils flared in cute little spurts. To less-enlightened people, she was totally wasted. To him, she'd never been more beautiful. Her body and brain were currently the property of subspace, the happy, frothy, better-than-drugs pinnacle for every submissive on the planet.

"Copy that. Give her a nice, solid finish, and we'll move on."

"Perfect. That stockade's been calling to me for the last five minutes. I have some ideas. Wiggle your sweet little ass for me, sugar. I feel like playing with a moving target for these last few swings."

★ ★ ★

Fear flashed back into her gaze after Kress got her off the cross but disappeared soon as the guy grabbed her by the nape, letting her know it was okay to let everything go again. Oh, yeah, David concluded. She was under pretty deep. The happy world of subspace had thoroughly claimed Dasha's brain, and right now, she only wanted somebody to keep her safely there. He backed Kress's move by circling behind her, bracing her waist and running soothing hands along the strikes on her backside.

In firm silence, Kress guided her to the device that looked like Ridley Scott had redesigned the colonial age. The custom stockade was like nothing David had seen in any club: a front panel had a scoop for the submissive's neck, with an option to place their wrists in the traditional stockade holes or stretch out their arms on side rails to be locked in by both the wrists and elbows.

Kress, also correctly interpreting the glaze in D's eyes, opted to use the latter restraints. After clipping in her neck and adjusting the torso pad for her petite frame, he positioned her knees in place against two pads on the floor and then deliberately slid them out to match the wide settings on the back spreader bar.

While his friend finished locking her in, David shed his own shirt, which was also damp from his efforts of helping her travel into mental delirium. He yearned to shuck the pants too, but Kress moved like an artist at work around her, double-checking restraints, running his hands along the lovely bruises he'd just inflicted, keeping her mind right where he wanted it. Their personal sexual putty.

"Are we still feeling good?" he asked, winding a hand into her hair and lifting her head. "Nice and comfy?"

Dasha gave him a dreamy smile. "Yes, Sergeant. Thank you."

"Good. Because here's the finishing touch." He slid a fitted leather blindfold over her eyes. "Surprise can be a very good thing, D."

"Yes, Sergeant." She trembled a little...though for the first time, David noticed the smile hadn't vanished from her lips. She was still afraid—still terrified, as a matter of fact, by what Kress had in store now—but now her brain was sucking in the adrenaline and cortisol of that stress and delivering it straight to the walls of her womb.

She was fucking breathtaking.

He really didn't know how much more he could take of this. Judging by the hard knot filling the front of Moridian's pants, he wondered about the resistance level in his friend too.

The guy turned to his sadism buffet plate and selected a steel-pronged pinwheel that even sent a shiver down David's spine. The prongs gleamed in the dungeon's golden light, their inch-long spines ending in wicked pinpoints.

Without hesitation, Kress pushed the thing up Dasha's back.

David tensed as she hissed and moaned, but Kress didn't let up with the zigzagging torment. Once her back was crisscrossed by gorgeous red tracks, he pulled the wheel back. "How did that feel?" he asked.

"Sharp." D got it out on a gasp. "And destructive."

"Kind of what holding back on Daddy does to your heart, right?"

"Yes." She emitted it on a sob. "Yes, Serg—owww!"

The exclamation went on as Kress rolled the wheel down her ass. David could tell he dug in a little harder across the flesh that was already tender from the impact toys, adding pain on top of pain to drive the message into her. Damn. He could almost sympathize. The sight of her struggling, helpless and submissive and reacting openly to the raw sensation, had pre-come seeping from the head of his cock.

Thank fuck for observant friends.

With a small smile, Kress interrupted his torture session to level another order. "Sugar, it's time to put that sweet little mouth to use for something productive, like atoning to your Sir for the stress you've caused him in all this. He's going to take out his cock now, and you're going to suck him deep."

"Yes," Dasha replied, clearly grateful for the chance to feel something other than pain. "Yes, thank y—"

David cut her short by sliding himself into her mouth.

"Christ!" Her mouth was hot salvation and tight torture. His erection pounded harder, lightning straining for release against his skin. He seized the chance to command her a little himself again, grabbing the corners of her jaw and pinching them wider. "That's it," he encouraged. "More, D. Take more of me. You're doing great."

He pushed in deeper and slammed her gag reflex. She coughed him out, which he didn't mind in the least, growing harder as he watched her lips grow sticky and slick. But Kress was listening to a different drummer. "Get him back in there," he commanded. "Or the wheel digs back into your ass, darlin'. I want to see his balls against your chin. You're being punished, not primped."

David helped by cupping her chin and gently guiding her back onto his head. Her mouth did the rest, getting his cock down until his balls did, in fact, slam her chin. The torture got worse as she let out a long groan around his flesh. He looked to discover the cause. Kress now switched up his efforts and simply went at her with his fingers. David stared in a heated trance as the guy applied lube to both his thumbs and then settled himself right behind the sweet, mottled swells of her ass. With a savoring grin, he pushed both fingers into the crevice David had penetrated himself a while ago.

Dasha quivered and whimpered, tickling his erection with more erotic ruthlessness.

"Holy...shit." He gave it from locked teeth. "You're really earning your Sir's favor again, D."

Kress let out a low chuckle. "Maybe she's earned herself a fuck at last."

"Hmmm." David stroked her cheek with the back of his hand. "I did tell her I was going to do as much, if she behaved. But technically, she's still being punished."

"Maybe a compromise? I think you'd satisfy all requirements if you got over here and took your girl in the ass."

Dasha groaned again, though he couldn't tell whether it was in protest or acceptance. He desperately hoped the latter, for the sound pulled him with irresistible force. He recalled how he'd promised they'd be fucking by the end of the night. Very soon after that, he'd had his finger deep in her backside. Now realization dawned. The two actions were meant to merge into this climax of reality.

Kress rose and stood back, extending a condom packet with a bad-ass grin. "Lucky fucker," he quipped, though David hardly heard. Lust was a hurricane in his head and a firestorm in his cock. Just sliding the latex on was a chore in self-control. He managed to keep it together a few seconds longer, drenching himself in lube and then spreading Dasha's asshole wide enough to get plenty of the slick liquid inside her too. With his fingers still wet, he reached around to the folds of her pussy. Locating her clit was the easiest feat of the night. Her most sensitive flesh was hard and erect and pleading for his touch.

"Mmmm," he murmured, rejoicing in her gasp as he worked his fingers against her. "You ready for the ride, sweetheart?"

"Yes," she pleaded. "Yes, Sir, please!"

He tried to take it slow. He was damn near certain Dasha had never been fucked like this, and forcing himself like a cretin into the tightest entrance of her body would likely ensure he didn't get asked back for another jam session. But fuck—*fuck*—the way her tunnel constricted around him, squeezing him with pressure he felt all the way back to *his* ass, was a torment too agonizing to ignore.

The second he was sure she'd gotten used to him, he began to grind. It was magic. It was torture. She started to gasp and then grunt in time to his pounding pace. Her little sounds, a mixture of ecstasy and suffering, were like a hit of crack to his balls.

"Tell me how it feels," he commanded from clenched teeth. He needed to hear it from her lips.

"Hurts. Tight. Hard. *Hurts.*"

"But you want more?"

She took a second to get to that one. "Yes...Sir."

"Yes," he hissed back. "Yes. You please your Sir. You—"

Words went the way of his thoughts—into nothing—as the explosion shot up his cock. He pulled her cheeks apart to get in even deeper, driving into her with animal abandon. Then the world was only his moan and her cries, her body accepting the invasion of his with hot, gripping submission.

He became aware of the new sound in the room as his brain circled back to earth. David looked up while gently pulling away from Dasha. The guy who'd gotten him here was still locked in torment, using the body cage he leaned against for stability as he unleashed his own cock. Moridian stroked the angry red length in a white-fisted grip, his face drawn in lines of total agony.

"Wait," he called. "Slow down there, cowboy."

Kress glowered. "Easy for you to say."

David smiled grimly. Slid all the way out, watching Dasha's ass quiver as if it missed him already. The rest of her body was still a slingshot of tension, her pussy still engorged with its need for fulfillment.

Carefully, he stepped aside and grabbed a bottle of water from the minifridge. He carried it around to where Dasha's head was still locked in place at the front of the stockade. Gently, he pulled off her blindfold. She blinked up at him, momentarily stunned even by the dim dungeon lights, her face awash in sweat, her mouth shimmery. He ran the pad of his thumb over her bottom lip, pressing it to open her farther.

"Thirsty, sweetheart?"

She gave him a slow nod, though her gaze went from adoring to stunned when she looked to Kress and what she'd done to him.

"Good." David knelt beside her, brushing the hair back from her face before cracking the bottle open and holding it to her lips. "Drink up."

She gratefully gulped the water. On purpose, David tilted the bottle a little higher so some of the liquid overflowed down her chin, neck, and breasts. "Beautiful." He pulled the bottle from her mouth and dribbled more water down her back, across her ass. Dasha moaned in pleasure as the cool liquid dripped down her sides. She undulated in her bonds, and the sinew of her muscles was sexy as sin against the dark wood of the stockade.

"Holy fuck." Kress groaned. "There's no slowing me down now, man."

"Perfect. Then get yourself over here. I think our girl still needs some extra hydration." He took her chin between two fingers and pinched gently. "Open for us again, D. The Sergeant's worked hard for you tonight. Drink him up while I get to work on your reward."

The words flipped her compliance button in a nanosecond. Not that Kress could wait any longer. The man was about the same size as him but didn't waste his time or patience on any half thrusts. He gripped Dasha's head and impaled her on his shaft, his breath leaving him in a passionate, appreciative grunt.

The guy wasn't going to last long, and David would bet his left testicle that their beautiful sub needed a climax just as bad. It was time to make good on his promise. Shifting to the back of the stockade again, he palmed her pussy and thumbed her clit. Indeed, she was hot and soaked. He gave her a hum of approval as she pressed into his touch and let out a pleading mewl around Kress's cock.

It was definitely time.

He'd noticed Kress had thought of everything when stocking up for the night, including a vibrator most normal people probably used as a back massager, the head was so large. But his incredible Dasha was as far from the norm as it got, thank Fate in all its awesome glory. If he flipped the thing on and then spread her cunt lips back just right and then slid the head over her distended nub...

Oh yeah.

Her orgasm tore through her with sudden, glorious violence. Another hit her practically right after that, dissolving her into screaming glory. The third explosion shook her just as Kress groaned, palmed her jaw, and then cut loose with his own climax. The sight was amazing, their good little sub taking his come as he thrust into her with mighty, hard stabs.

When Kress started pulling away, some of his juice spilled from the corners of her mouth.

"Shit," David said at the sight. "Sweet shit, D...my beautiful D."

She'd moved him like a locomotive tonight. A crazy slew of mental train stops that normally took him months, even years. He'd been blown past the gates of Lust. Careened across the plains of Astonished. Shotgunned down the tunnel of Wonder. And now, slammed in this abyss of raw, raging feeling. What was this? It twisted his chest like that locomotive had hit a wall.

He hated it.

He didn't know if he could ever live again without it.

And from the looks of things, a similar freight train had bashed into his little submissive too. Her tears had started again with the orgasms. She wobbled against her bonds. Only one word spilled from her lips. "Sir...Sir...Sir..." She babbled it in a rasping litany.

"Here."

Jesus. Had that croak come from him? He cleared his throat and stated, "Here, baby. We're gonna get you out. Hold still, okay?"

She sobbed into his chest as he pulled her from the stockade and folded her into his arms. David pulled her as close as he could, gratefully accepting a blanket offered by Kress. She felt smaller than ever as she huddled against him, clutching him. Or maybe she clung so tight because he gave her no choice. His own arms vibrated with the intensity of his grip.

At last, a new phrase came out of her. She spoke it into the crook of his neck with soft, simple, and very complete honesty.

"Thank you."

CHAPTER FOURTEEN

When had living become so complicated?

Dasha finally let the rumination sink in after an hour of locking herself away in the mansion's solarium. The bright circle of a room lived up to its name with ivory-and-green decor, currently dappled in midday sun. She'd retreated here in her favorite comfies with her guitar and a cup of jasmine tea, her go-to combo for times when stress threatened the roots of her sanity.

But so far, so not good. The clarity her music normally brought remained far-off and elusive, a dim light at the other end of a mental forest. A really big forest.

A forest filled with memories.

Memories she couldn't stop from coming.

Memories filled with every brutal, intense, incredible minute from last night.

The minutes that had made this whole life thing a lot more tangled than she'd thought possible.

She rolled her eyes at that drama but the next second fought tears. She could no more ignore the emotional impact of what she'd done than the fact she'd done it. And done it with consent. Greedy, grateful, hungry, passionate consent.

With two men who had fulfilled her more than all the other lovers in her life combined.

Her knuckles went white around the guitar. She'd tried to write off the Lifetime Channel line as a twisted justification for her behavior and probably would've succeeded had it not been for everything that happened after last night in the dungeon.

Oh yeah. It was the *after* that kept doing her in.

First came the gentle journey in David's arms to a bathroom that adjoined the dungeon, gleaming with black tile and gold fixtures, where Kress waited with warm towels that the guys swirled down every inch of her body. David disappeared then, while Kress laid her out on a velvet chaise and rubbed healing oils into her bruises, preparing each one with a tender kiss first. After that, he carried her into a palatial room dominated by a bed surely built for twelve people. She'd been glad to see only one occupant in the thing, however: David, his broad chest even more bronze and beautiful against the ivory satin linens, just before he pulled back the covers to let Kress slip her in next to him. The sheets were cool, but her two Doms were huge and warm; they held her and took turns murmuring praise to her. It didn't take long for their voices to become her lullaby as her mind plummeted into a sweet, peaceful sleep.

When she woke this morning, she'd been relieved to do so alone. Before instantly yearning for both of them again. Of course, that was before she saw their invitation to join them upstairs for breakfast—and in awkward fear, tore the note up.

"Crap," she blurted, setting aside her guitar and obeying her body's demand for nervous movement. Though her backside protested a little, she lurched to her feet. "Crap, crap, crap!"

And the Grammy for Most Fucked-Up-in-the-Head Artist goes to...

"Dasha?"

She spun at the quiet greeting issued from the doorway

and was stunned to see Mary standing there. Immediately, she wondered why. She knew David had flown Mary, Raife, and the show's whole creative team along with them to Atlanta. The hiatus provided a good excuse for some collaboration on adding new wow factor to the popular songs in the set. So her friend's presence wasn't the surprise...

Realization set in. She was bemused by Mary's bearing. Correction, lack of one. Her friend was so...calm. And that was so not normal. The little dancer was always a whirlwind. It even looked like Mary was on her way to rehearsal, dressed in a gray T-shirt and sweats, her blonde hair pulled into a tight twist.

"Hey." Dasha shook the weirdness free and gave in to genuine delight. She crossed and pulled her friend into a tight hug. "I don't care why you're here. I'm just glad you are!"

David would've been proud. It was the complete truth. When music couldn't calm her rampaging nerves, choice number two had to be a girlfriend visit or an ice cream binge. Mary arrived just in time to save her from the latter.

"Ditto," Mary replied. But when they pulled apart, her friend reverted to that strange concentration again, studying her from head to toe. "How are you? You look...really good."

"And you sound surprised by that."

"I think I am."

Her friend's voice was a knowing undertone. Dasha didn't recognize it but chose to ignore it. Her head wasn't bolted on properly right now.

Humor provided a safe distraction. "So did David give you the secret spy passcode to get in here or just send you with thugs who blindfolded you along the way?"

To her relief, Mary chuckled. "Actually, Raife brought me."

"Aha. So what's the deal? Is the torture master breaking out some dance steps I'm going to kill him for, all in the name of 'keeping the show fresh'?"

Mary's smile quickly dropped back to Mona Lisa territory. "Yeah, torture's probably on the menu." Her eyes went wistful. "If I know Raife."

Okay, it was official. Dasha wasn't imagining the woman's weirdness. Still, she tried half a laugh. "Well, thanks for taking the detour my way."

Before Mary responded, she scooped up Dasha's hands. Her sky-blue stare didn't blink. "David said you might need it."

So much for mystery. Her friend peeled off the veil of intentions with one clean sweep. "He said that, huh?" Dasha punched out a harsh breath, thinking—hoping—she still interpreted Mary wrong. "Well, well, well. What else did he tell you?"

Her friend's gaze softened—but again, her regard was way too steady for comfort. "Pretty much the *Reader's Digest* of what happened last night."

"Last night?"

"Downstairs."

"Downstairs?"

"In the dungeon."

Dasha knew now why the woman clasped her like a wrestler. "Let me go." She seethed with fury and embarrassment. How *dare* he share something like that, even if it was with one of her closest friends?

"No."

"Mary, don't—"

"No, *you* don't. Before you tear out of here to crucify him, hear me out."

"There'll be more than a crucifixion." Though a combination of hammer, nails, and David's balls sounded pretty good right now. Something to match how deeply he'd humiliated her.

"I know what you're probably feeling—"

"I don't think you do, okay?"

"Look at me."

Dasha froze. When the hell had Mary taken command lessons from a drill instructor? The impression doubled as she grabbed Dasha's chin, jerking it back up.

Fresh gasp. There was something new across her friend's face. Something beautiful. Everybody always called Mary "pretty," but this was something new and strong, turning her into a new creature. A confident, elegant person, wholly sure of her identity, especially after the next words she spoke.

"Dasha, Raife has been my Dom for three years."

For a long minute, she said nothing—too busy with the playback tape in her mind. She recalled all the moments where she'd marveled at the harmony between her two dance leads, all the subtle and thorough ways they seemed to know each other, as if reading each other's thoughts...

Because they *had*.

For three years. Even after these few short weeks with David, she understood that. Attentiveness, openness, and willingness... They were the very foundation of D/s relationships, weren't they? She thought about all the new things she'd learned about David since New York and then mentally multiplied it by three years.

She sank back to the couch. "Whoa."

Mary joined her. "I've wanted to tell you so many times. I always had the feeling you'd understand, but still..."

Dasha chuckled. "Not the kind of thing you can spill over a latte and a scone."

"To up your 'whoa' factor further, it's actually how we met David."

Dasha frowned. "He told me he saw you guys perform at a club."

"Not a lie."

"God forbid if David did that."

Her friend took a turn to laugh. "Right. Honesty is up there on Raife's list too. It was a lifestyle club. A place similar to your fantasyland downstairs, only open for lots of people to come and enjoy and learn new things."

Dasha let her amazement show. "They do that?"

"Oh yeah." Her friend's face lit up. "It makes for a *very* interesting night. And like I said, you learn new stuff too."

She watched the happiness light up Mary's features all over again, feeling a little like Dorothy tossed anew into Oz. She'd been living in a black-and-white Kansas, and suddenly the world was brilliant Technicolor, with roads to places she'd never imagined. And friends on them that she'd never really known...

Before now.

She had to force out her next question. "What...were you and Raife doing when David...uh..."

"Flying." Her friend finished it with a wink.

"What?"

"Raife is into suspension bondage." Her look took on a naughty twinkle. "Rope," Mary clarified. "Used in creative ways. *Very* creative."

Dasha stared at her friend for another long moment. Mary began to look half-sauced, her grin a loopy slide beneath glittering eyes. She remembered the same gleam in her own eyes, reflected back at her from the elevator doors at the Viceroy Miami. Right after David had given a very creative twist to the word piercing. A slow smile curved her lips.

"So...he tied you up and was doing what?"

Mary shrugged. "Little of this, little of that. Some twirls, some spanks, a few whips, a few kisses, and some...other things." Her eyes drifted shut; she sank against the cushions with a sigh. "Ahhh. Nobody does it better than my Master."

Dasha looked away, grinning wider. Funny. She'd just thought the same thing about David.

And...right after that...Kress too.

Thunderheads curled in her chest again. The darkness curled downward, twisting her stomach. She knotted her hands there, forced her next words out.

"Mary...have you and Raife... I mean, has he ever..."

"Shared me?" Shockingly, she jingled with a new laugh. "Okay, I sort of suspected you'd ask." She reached for Dasha again, resting a soft hand on her shoulder. "And yeah, it's part of why David asked me to come talk to you."

The words came out like such normal conversation, they didn't register for a long moment. Then they hit like a piano tossed off a skyscraper. "Oh God." Dasha gasped. "You mean—you and Raife—with—"

"Oh *God*!" Mary echoed. "With David? Oh my fucking stars, no!"

Dasha was actually grateful for the mirth they shared at that. It gave her a comfortable way to continue. "But...you have been with Raife and...someone else, then?"

There. She'd gotten it out. Even so, the statement was astounding. Just a week ago, she and Mary had gone shopping in Miami, chatting about fashion, nail polish colors, and the hot-but-gay valet boys. Her friend had even let her rant about Crystal the Pistol, as she'd taken to calling Dad's new wonder staffer. Now they sat here discussing spankings, whips, and being at the mercy of two amazing men at once. Well, amazing in her case. She glanced at Mary, suddenly realizing her friend's story might not be the same fairy tale. What if Mary's second "prince" had really been a terrible wolf? How would that change how she felt about Kress?

Well, damn it.

Her mind and heart came to the same realization in the same moment.

She *did* feel things for Kress.

A lot of things.

Her thoughts got interrupted by Mary's new statement.

"His name is Philip," her friend gushed. Yeah, *gushed.* Mary's eyes twinkled with brilliant blue joy—though her lips quivered in blatant sadness. "And I'm missing him something fierce right now."

Two feelings hit. Dasha was sympathetic for her friend's heartache but was hit by a rush of relief. "So he still..."

"Plays with us?" Mary filled in. "Hell, yes. Though it's been entirely too damn long since Master and I have seen him. The three of us met when we were touring with J.Lo. When David hired Raife and me for your gigs, Ms. Lopez promoted Philip to her lead slot. He couldn't say no."

"You don't say no to J.Lo," she quipped.

"Not if you're sane."

"Especially if you've got the name of an ancient English prince."

"Okay, biatch, watch what you're saying." They giggled

again, but Mary sobered fast. "So if it makes any difference...I think I know what you're feeling right now."

Dasha leaned her own head back. "I guess you do." She sighed. "Tell me it gets easier?"

Mary gave a contemplative hum. "Which part?"

She stopped to ponder that. Mary's answer wasn't what she'd expected. She'd hoped for another flippant laugh and a reassurance that the happy-ever-after button was going to get tripped any second...that all of this would start making sense and life would work itself out. Whatever *that* meant.

"The confusion," she finally said. "And the...guilt. The crazy sense that you're walking in a dream but the never wanting to wake up from it. The feeling that you're doing something so wrong..."

"That's never felt so right?"

Dasha swallowed back tears. "Crap. Yeah."

Mary copied her sigh. "I wish I could give you the answer you want, hon, but the path doesn't get simpler. Discovering your submissiveness is just the first step. Figuring out what that entails and what to do about it... That's where we're all different. And a lot of times, it's where all the shitty head-trip stuff comes in."

"Well, hell." Dasha appreciated Mary's little snicker. Sort of. "I just know...that nothing has ever made me feel so..."

"Complete?" Mary whispered into her silence.

"Yes," she rasped.

"Free?"

"Oh yes."

"Loved?"

"Damn it." She slammed a hand over her burning eyes. "Yes," she finally confessed. "Loved."

"Which means, if I know you, that you give the love back in return."

She didn't move for a long second.

But at last, nodded.

It was true. The confession clamped on her heart with searing, scorching surety. She was in love with David. And every time he bound her physically, more of her heart got tied to him.

"But it can't be real...right? How can you fall in love from doing this?"

Mary smiled softly. "Don't you mean how can you fall in love when it involves taking so much pain?"

Dasha winced. "Shit. Yes."

"Because it's the pain that frees you, D. It's what gets you to that pure place in your soul, beyond all the walls you've built around it, so the love gets set free."

She could only nod. It was true. Every word of it.

"But the journey to get to that freedom," Mary went on, "it's not an easy one. No *regular* person would willingly pick up a flogger and use it on you, even if you begged them for it. It takes extraordinary men to understand women like us... to see the spaces in our minds that crave this and then find the courage in themselves to take us there. But it also takes exceptional men to control themselves when it's time to stop or if they hit a trigger that brings a safe word. None of that is easy. It takes a lot of *cajones* to be that guy."

Dasha lowered her hand. "You're right." She didn't hide the amazement from her tone. How the hell any of that made logical sense, she had no idea. But it did. Crazy, wonderful sense.

Her friend shrugged. "Why shouldn't you be in love with

your Dom, hon?" An entrancing sparkle entered her gaze. "I'm totally in love with mine."

Like they were in a play and those words were a cue, Raife strode in. Dasha imagined the guy would look different to her now, but his ensemble drove the change home. The handsome guy wore a black formfitting shirt overlaid with a pewter vest, black cargo pants with carabiner hooks at the belt line, and boots made for commanding a battle ship. His black hair, normally a just-out-of-bed mess, was slicked back from his sharp Italian features.

"Well, look at this." He intoned it in the voice Dasha normally heard when the guy got ready to persecute the dancers with a tricky new step. "Two lovely pets in a row. Very nice."

Dasha felt her cheeks flame, but Mary's face was a sudden forest fire, alive with longing. "Master." She jumped up in an eager swoop. "Your timing couldn't be more perfect."

"Really?" Raife paced over, eyes dancing but black brows arching. "I'm not inclined to agree, love." He tugged at the front of her plain gray shirt. "Is this the state you intended to greet me in?"

Fresh heat lit up her friend's eyes. Without hesitation, Mary threw off the shirt—revealing a shiny latex corset in a rich, dark blue, with black laces cinched to push her breasts up into matched swells. Along the side of one breast, Dasha noticed a swirled tattoo: the letter R.

Before she could see if Raife's last initial got honored on the other side, Mary shucked her sweatpants as fast as she'd lost the top. Beneath them was a barely-there pair of black latex shorts layered over Caribbean-blue fishnet stockings. Both showed off the woman's toned dancer form to naughty perfection. Since the dancers often wore heels to rehearsals, the black Mary Janes on her friend's feet had clued nobody, including Dasha, to what the sweats really hid.

"Better?" Mary lifted a hopeful smile, but Raife stole it by jerking her head back with one hand and then smothering her lips with his own. Dasha fidgeted, knowing she should look away but instead gawking at her friends. They barely came up for air before sealing mouths again, clearly not caring if she watched, left the room, or started swinging from the ceiling fan.

When they finally pulled apart, Raife used his hold to push Mary to her knees. As she dropped, her shining eyes never left his face.

"Better," he finally crooned, stroking her hair. He broke the contact for just a second, letting a wicked grin fly free. "Hey, Dasha."

"Uh...hey."

In an instant, Raife only had eyes for his subbie once more. With desire flashing in his eyes and hardening his jaw, he leaned and plunged his tongue into her again. This time, he also scooped a hand inside her corset, pinching the treasure inside. Mary moaned, running a hand up his arm, but her action made him stiffen. He twisted, caught her wrist, and angled it sharply back.

"Forgetting manners already?" He added a harsh tongue click. "Oh, it has been too long, hasn't it?"

Mary visibly trembled at that. Dasha couldn't figure out if she'd gotten terrified, aroused, or a combination of both. "Yes, Master." Her rasp didn't clarify it either. "It certainly has."

"Maybe it's good that I called in some reinforcement."

New emotions lit up her friend's face. Anticipation. Lots

of it. "You did?"

"Hmm. Perhaps."

Mary let out a delirious squeal as a stranger strolled into the room. Dasha had to admit, the guy bumped the BPM on her pulse too. Though dressed in similar attire to Raife, his tanned face, gold hair, and leonine grace made him more suited for a gladiator thong. When his gaze found Mary, he gave her a smile of both lover and predator.

"Well, well, well." The man's voice sounded like velvet over sandpaper. "How's my favorite little play toy?"

"Naughty." Raife supplied it as Mary jostled at his feet, clearly yearning to jump up and attack the guy. "And ready, Sir Philip. Look at the way she can't control herself. Just had to pull her off me for getting handsy during a reward kiss."

The golden god issued some tsks of his own. The sounds carried the same sand-and-silk quality of his voice. Dasha began to regret using his name and anything ancient in the same sentence—especially when he threw an openly sadistic stare at Mary.

"Is that so?" Philip crossed the room until he towered over her. "Does someone need a refresher about pawing their Master correctly?"

Dasha watched Mary's reaction. Mesmerizing. The little blonde stopped squirming, though her breaths came fast and furious, shoving her breasts against their constraint. Her lips fell into an obedient line; her stare dropped to the tips of Philip's boots. "Yes, Sir Philip," she answered. "Your toy would appreciate the instruction...very much."

"Perhaps the toy shouldn't be neglecting her manners again."

Mary frowned. "Sir?"

"Is there a ghost in the room, or do you have a friend here?"

Dasha skittered back as the Dom nodded toward her. She'd been absorbed with the interaction of the three before her, joyful their dynamic unfolded in such a natural way. Observing Mary's adoration for her men had eased a lot of Dasha's self-inflicted labels—words like *deviant, degenerate, weirdo,* and *wrong*—making her feel nearly normal again. In this new world view, she was simply a woman with a lot of love in her soul to give and a couple of men who knew how to free it from her.

She exhaled softly as a few of lines came to mind, recognizing the tickle of what would soon be a new song.

What a different world this would be...
If everyone could just be...
Singing the songs they're meant to sing...

She put the tune on mental simmer, redirected by the new smile on Mary's face, directed her way.

"Permission to rise, Sir?" she asked Philip.

"Well done," he praised. "Granted."

Mary approached and took her hand. "May I introduce my dear friend, Dasha?" To Philip, she added, "She's called 'D' by her Sir."

Dasha had the strange urge to curtsy or bow or something, taken in by the romantic formality between the two. Thankfully, Philip took charge, lifting her hand to his lips with courtly style. "A pleasure, my dear. You do your Sir proud."

"Thank you," she mumbled. "Um...you know David, then?"

"No. Just met him today. But he's a good man. He's upstairs with Agent Moridian." He gave her a deliberate nod. "Who's also a good man."

Her to-the-hair-roots blush didn't deter him.

"They're both concerned about you, little one. Doms need a little TLC too, you know. And the assurance you haven't gone catatonic."

As Dasha managed a nod, Raife came forward. "Okay, the therapy couch is closed. If you don't get some knots on your toy's wrists and some lashes on her ass, we'll both have hell to pay."

"He's right," chirped Mary, bouncing on her toes. "I'm waiting, damn it! I'm waaaaiting!"

Philip transformed back into a provoked lion. Without skipping a beat, he dropped to one knee and then flung Mary over it, punishing her backside with a few smacks loud as gunfire. "Why don't you try that request again, little one?" he finally growled.

Mary, droopy-eyed and limp-limbed, muttered, "May I ask for more of that, Sir?"

Philip's elegant lips curled. "Perhaps. Once we're in the dungeon."

"I'm ready, Sir."

"No shit, sweetness." He pressed a hand into the small of her back. "So why don't you follow your Master downstairs? I want to see correct posture and distance as well, or I'll stop and go get the posture collar. I'll be right behind you to make sure you don't fuck up."

Dasha took that as her cue to leave too. Philip's statement had sunk in. It was time to get the inevitable over with. Hiding out with her guitar wasn't helping matters at all. The music to be faced here was with David and Kress—even if it was in the key of awkward, with a resounding backbeat of uncomfortable.

CHAPTER FIFTEEN

Kress clicked the Pause button on the security camera footage filling his computer screen. His team in Miami had done a great job of pinpointing a half-dozen pertinent clips from the Viceroy Miami, but his eyes felt like dust balls from watching them a hundred times. He rubbed his lids and grunted in exhaustion.

"Not riveting shit, I take it." The support came from Pennington, who sat on a couch nearby. The guy was buried in piles of surveillance photos from Miami International, background dossiers on the Buenos Aires outfit to which they'd tracked the cell phone, and a complete workup on Ambrose Smith, who remained a "person of interest" in case they'd missed any connections to their crackpot from Miami.

"No," he stated. "But you're not getting to read the top of the *Times* bestseller list there either." He gave a gruff nod. "I appreciate the help, man."

David pinched the bridge of his nose. "Anything to catch this bastard faster."

"It's still above and beyond. Especially after your dancers invited you to go watch their playdate in the basement."

Pennington dropped his hand and reopened his eyes. They were dark as thunder. "Right. And you think that'd be fun for me at this point?"

"Got it," he returned. And he did. Clearer than he wanted to admit. He understood every note of frustration in the guy's voice, betraying exactly what—more correctly, who—lay front and center in their minds right now. "Sorry."

"Forget it. I just wanna know if she's...you know..."

"Going to speak to either of us again? Going to speak to *anyone* again? Not freaking out by probably the most intense sexual experience she's ever been through?"

"Thanks for the reminder." His friend jolted to his feet, looking ready to punch the wall. "Goddamn it. I watch after my subs, you know? Aftercare is fucking key for me."

"Same page, man. You know that."

"Yeah, I do." He pressed his fist into the side of a bookcase and let out a dark laugh. "I've had subs send *me* flowers for my aftercare excellence. But *waiting* for the chance to do it..."

"Sucks serious ass?"

"It's just new. *Really* fucking new."

Kress folded his arms. "Maybe...in this case..."

"In this case, what?"

"Maybe the waiting *is* the aftercare." He leaned back in his chair. "Dasha's not exactly in a usual profession to begin with. On top of this, her world has been upended in less than a week. I've seen fewer plot twists on most cop shows. Maybe she just needs space to process. She's not a stupid woman."

"I know that." Pennington's tone went grittier. "But she bottles up, damn it. To hide out. To avoid dealing with herself behind the facade of stressing about everyone else."

Kress took that statement and connected the dots in his own head. "Everyone else," he echoed. "Like what I witnessed during the call from dear Daddy last night."

David arched both brows. "The lightbulb starts to come on."

"But this case, the 'everyone else' is—"

"Us."

"Shit."

"Yeah. Shit."

Kress shook his head. "She's a forest with a few shadows, isn't she?"

Before Pennington could respond, a soft rustle came from the doorway. "She's also a forest who's way late for breakfast," came a soft soprano voice that robbed him of a few heartbeats. "And...she's sorry."

How the woman could get any more gorgeous than she'd been last night, Kress couldn't understand, but here she was, irresistible even in her tied-up hair, *twenty-one pilots* T-shirt, black capris, and nothing on her feet except lavender polish. He remembered the color all too well—from every moment she'd tried to squirm away from his flogging.

Concentrate on something else.

He cleared his throat and forced an affable smile. "Hey, stranger."

Fuck. *Hey, stranger? What, now you're Woody Allen with the dork-dick lines?* But what *was* he supposed to call her? Were they back to Miss Moore and Agent Moridian? He sure didn't expect her to keep up the Sergeant act, though his cock twitched just at the thought. And taking that one step further, imagining the joy of calling her his good girl once more...

Best to cut that one off at the head right now, figuratively speaking.

Hell.

David had been right. This was new territory. Mental domain filled with landmines.

Okay, so he'd gotten to share some beautiful submissives before—just never any he had to get back to work with the next morning. Even worse, the definition of that work: tracking down the lunatic who wanted to kill them. On top of that, he had to pretend last night hadn't blown the doors off every other D/s experience he'd ever had—meaning a vanilla relationship comparison was pointless too. Especially when he had to give a few thousand brain cells on acting as if Dasha, with her trusting eyes and sweet spirit and open eagerness to please, hadn't likely ruined him for any woman who knelt for him again.

More importantly, he had to quash the hope of Pennington ever letting her do it again.

"Hey, stranger," she said in return, though her gaze already raced to her man. "David." It almost sounded like a question, until David opened his arms for her. Kress clenched his jaw behind his smile, dealing with the mental dagger of watching her race into the man's embrace.

"Hi, sweetheart." David murmured it into her hair as she burrowed against him. "How are you?"

"Good. Really good...now."

David tugged the little tie off of her ponytail. "You don't sound so sure about that."

Kress grabbed a chair, surely refinishing it with his grip as D's sunshine-colored curls spilled into the guy's fingers. But he caught a glimpse of her scrunched brow too—though the next moment, she insisted, "I'm fine. Just getting my shit together, you know?"

"Understood." Pennington pressed a kiss to her temple. "But we still missed you at breakfast this morning. Yeah, Kress?"

He went for the easy out of sarcasm. "Yeah. He's a bitch before his caffeine."

David grunted with humor, but Dasha looked to both

of them, features still troubled as a fallen angel. "I'm sorry. I shouldn't have ignored your request."

"It wasn't a request," David stated. "And you're right, you shouldn't have ignored it. We needed to know you were okay. That's our right and responsibility after what we asked of you last night."

The angel huffed. "Sheez. You know my status quo on how I deal with stuff. I thought you'd just figure it out."

David's hand tightened in her hair. "We're not dealing with status quo right now. Not on a lot of levels. I thought you'd figured that out."

"Okay." She sighed. "You're right; you're right."

"Hmm. Thanks. Now say it like you mean it."

"I *do* mean it." She added, with a soft jab at his ribs, "Sir."

Kress caught Pennington's fast glance. "I don't think she means it, Kress. What's your scope reading?"

He doubled a stare back at his buddy. Sure enough, the subtext in David's words gained reinforcement in his intent stare.

Whoa.

Was he really thinking of more discipline for D...now?

And including him in the mix too?

Yet the man knew her, maybe better than anyone else on earth. Dasha's gaze, conveying a brown-sugar mix of fear and lust, confirmed she was considering the idea too.

Considering it...and excited by it.

The *holy shit* had just had begun its victory dance in his brain, when a video call rang from his computer.

CHAPTER SIXTEEN

Dasha was both relieved and peeved by the sudden ring from Kress's computer.

She hadn't realized how thick the air had gotten in the room...and how she'd hoped Kress would answer David's question with one of his blatant, down-on-the-floor-now stares at her. It'd been easy to imagine it and even easier to envision her compliance. That was what the man got for jump-starting her libido with his stubbled jaw, unruly hair, and tight black T-shirt...

But real life was determined to have the last laugh.

The computer rang out again, sounding even more strident than before.

"Who the fuck?" Kress muttered.

She giggled before breaking into a singsong. "Hello, Agent Moridian? It's the president on the line..."

The humor didn't help. Kress's glower deepened as he peered at the laptop. "Damn. It might just be."

Her laughter halted. "*Huh?*"

"It's from Washington." Kress sat down with a hard grunt. "And it's a secured number. But it's likely my director or one of your daddy's security team."

She lifted her head from David's shoulder in astonishment. "Daddy's team?"

"Oh yeah. The bunch of them have been all over my ass since this thing started."

A mixture of emotion hit. Surprise and shock, though infused with an odd sliver of comfort. While she felt lousy Kress had to deal with more Washington asses, it eased the ache from Dad's abrupt good-bye yesterday. In his roundabout way, maybe her father really *was* looking out for her.

Her chest continued aching, though it seemed a fraction of the torment plaguing Kress. As he shifted in his chair, a grimace commanded his face—while a discernible bulge took over the front of his jeans. The observation made her smile. She wasn't the only one aching for a reprise of last night. The knowledge warmed her, though Kress's face hardened to granite.

"Oh, this is gonna be a joy," he grumbled. "You two might as well go watch another movie. They'll want a full debrief on the mall throwdown."

He finally clicked the Answer button. The screen came to life. A face appeared at the other end of the call, making Kress blink with surprise—and hauling Dasha off David's lap. She took a couple of stiff steps and then stopped in disbelief.

Crystal Corso looked like Snow White in Prada, with those big blue eyes, the bouffant with tube curls at the bottom, and even a pristine business shirt starched into perfect collar points. The woman's voice shattered that parallel, though. Her no-nonsense tone came over the speakers with clipped, queenly efficiency.

"Agent Moridian, I presume?"

"Yes, ma'am," Kress replied, his posture still composed, his face all business. "And may I ask who..."

"Crystal Corso. I'm Senator Moore's Chief of Staff."

Dasha gasped. Kress spun around as she plunked back down to the couch, back into David's hold. The agent looked like he thought a crazed psycho had gotten in. Maybe one had, Dasha concluded, and that nutcase was her.

"Chief of Staff!" She snapped it in a harsh whisper. "She was hired as a senior *aide*. Only a month ago!"

"Moridian?" Corso demanded from the computer. "What's going on? Is everything—"

"We're fine here, Ms. Corso. Naturally, we're taking all kinds of precautions for Miss Moore's safety, even inside the compound. I overreacted to...uh...something."

His features, now in profile to Dasha, dropped fast back into respect—though she saw him scrutinizing Crystal in a new light. His immediate credit to her opinion was a huger gift than he probably knew.

"How can I be of service?" he prompted Crystal then.

"Simply checking in on your progress," she replied. "As you know, the senator has asked for regular updates on his daughter's case, and in light of the protracted pace of the investigation, I assured him I'd make it a top action item on my own list."

The woman's dig, even given in her friendly press-conference tone, clearly chafed Kress. "A manhunt like this doesn't get solved like a TV show, Ms. Corso," he said through tight lips. "If you let a lunatic know you're on to him, he's likely to hide deeper or run farther."

"The senator is aware of your sensitive position," came the whittling knife of a reply. "So you believe it's a man?"

"Point of speech," Kress clarified. "But, yes, the Bureau's psychologist has indicated we're likely looking for a male."

"Good. That's good, Agent Moridian."

"Really?" The brow Dasha could see clicked higher. "And why is that, Ms. Corso?"

"I just mean good progress." Crystal gave him another canned smile. "Senator Moore is extremely concerned about his daughter's well-being, and—"

"Then why doesn't Senator Moore come and tell her himself?"

As she cut Crystal off, Dasha surged up again. She couldn't stand by any longer and watch the woman try her smooth-operator routine on Kress. He wasn't falling for it anyway. She let her glare say exactly that as she leaned in at the computer monitor.

"Dasha." If she took the woman by surprise, it got covered well. "What a lovely surprise. You look well, darling. How are you?"

"I'm not your darling." She was cordial about it. Mostly. "We've only met once, Ms. Corso."

"Of course." The fairy-tale smile tightened. "It felt like a natural thing to say. How fortuitous that you're there, however. The second purpose of my call was to speak with you."

She felt the guys' tension levels ramping in tandem.

"This'll be entertaining," David muttered—tempting Dasha toward a bizarre giggle. She bit it back at the last minute. She didn't trust Crystal as far as she could toss a bushel of poisoned apples at the woman, and it felt good to hear David sharing her instinct.

"Speak with me about what?"

For a long second, Crystal didn't reply. The woman scanned as much of the library as she could see through the laptop's camera, as if expecting their dove killer to magically pop out from the volumes and turn himself in. She was so busy conducting her little Scooby-snoop-swoop, she didn't notice Kress scrutinizing her in return.

"Crystal?" she prompted again.

"Yes. Forgive me, dar—erm, Dasha." Corso popped back into character, tilting her head with practiced ease. "Well. I have some exciting news. Your father will be flying to Atlanta at the end of this week."

A handful of words. That was all it took to flip her mind from Angry Girl to Stunned Daughter. "He—really?"

"Oh yes. Really."

She caught Kress's skeptical stare, as well as David's unchanged brood. She ignored both, focusing instead on her own face in the corner of the Skype window. She connected with her joyous gaze and excited grin. "So what time—"

"We'll be there midday on Friday, give or take a bit," Crystal interjected. "Your father has a couple of early appointments; then we'll head for Dulles. I've booked a private charter."

"That's awesome." Her elation gained momentum. "He'll probably be in time for lunch. The chef at this mansion is amazing. Dad will love these peach things she makes for—" That's when her face fell. "Wait," she blurted. "*We'll* be there?"

Corso's expression remained as lacquered as her hair. "Of course."

"Dad and...you?"

"Dad and everyone. This is a huge trip, Dasha." The woman curled an evocative smile. "I've saved the best part of this for last. Your father has been identified as a potential front-runner for the candidacy in two years, and CNN wants to tape a special interview with him. Only him!"

The woman's eyes gleamed as if world peace had just been achieved. But on this side of the conversation, Dasha felt like she'd just tossed smoking grenades. "What're—you—" she stammered. "What candidacy?"

"Why, *the* candidacy. For the presidency."

She blinked hard. A lot of times. "P-President? But—"

"Isn't it thrilling?" Corso gushed. "The numbers we've gotten back so far look phenomenal!"

"He never told me he wanted to be president." Something upended her heart again. Shock wasn't the right word. Broadsided seemed more fitting. She shook all over. Kress gripped her arm gently and guided her to sit in his chair.

Crystal had no trouble chugging right on. "Dasha, this could be the start of a snowball effect. Your dad is starting to comprise a team for the campaign—"

"I wonder who thought of that," Dasha muttered.

"—and of course, we're planning follow-up trips to Iowa, New Hampshire, and Florida after this. We may stage Florida first, though. Even the blue hairs there know your dad now, thanks to his daughter's little incident at the Viceroy last week."

David came forward. "Ms. Corso, the details of what happened in Miami are not for public consumption." He added, for the ears of the three of them alone, "For many different reasons."

"Of course not," the woman returned. "Which is why everyone's wild to see Dasha herself."

Dasha jerked her head up again. "See me where?"

"At your father's side, silly! Where else?" Corso's precision-plucked brows jumped higher. "They're going to do an extended personal piece, covering your father's childhood and your mother's passing, of course...ending with a thirty-minute, commercial-free interview featuring the two of you!"

Broadside, part two.

Dasha worked her lips together, unsure how to react. Or even how to feel.

"It's wonderful, isn't it?" Corso continued. "The special

will air next Monday, and the timing couldn't be more perfect. You've canceled all those concert stops, so you have the time to spare. We understand you're set up in a lovely mansion there in Atlanta, so we can shoot there."

"Stop." David leaned in again. "Ms. Corso, this is a lot of presumption."

Finally, Snow White looked like one of her apples was shoved up the correct end of her body. "Excuse me?"

"You heard me." David grunted. "Just because Miss Moore is on a temporary break from her tour doesn't attach your puppet strings to her schedule."

At first, the woman absorbed that with a wild flare of nostrils. Within seconds, she was schooled back to graceful calm. "I think Miss Moore should have something to say about that."

"She does," Dasha injected. "And she says Mr. Pennington is right." The tension from the other end had become nearly a physical force, but she went on. "I support my father always, Ms. Corso, no matter how much he's been coached to think something else. I'm here for him."

She lifted her chin—and felt damn good about it. The action wasn't compelled by strings or motivation from the outside but by a strength that came from a deep place in her soul. She looked to Crystal with a clarity she'd never known before—because she knew it was right. The men flanking her had given her the courage to embrace that and claim it as her truth.

"I'd be happy to be available for the interview," she stated, "with one condition."

Corso's nostrils flared with dainty impatience. "Condition?"

"Dad must do the asking. Himself."

"Dasha." The flare never happened. The I'm-talking-to-a-toddler tone did. "I'm sure you understand that he would if he could, but—"

"*He* calls, Crystal. *He* asks. Or the Moore Family Special is a no-go."

CHAPTER SEVENTEEN

Two very fast days had passed since that ultimatum. Now David took a chance to slow down, stand back, and contemplate the remarkable woman who'd issued it.

He'd lived nearly every day of the last five years with Dasha Melodia Moore. Five years full of countless moments to be crazy proud of her. All her award-acceptance speeches. The time she'd first gone platinum. The morning she'd sold out the Garden. The half marathon she'd run for cancer research. Those were just the highlights. The list was endless.

The number-one slot just got a new contender.

It was a perfect afternoon. A little breeze played at the trees, making the sunlight dance across the golden halo of Dasha's hair as she and the senator chatted with an attentive Anderson Cooper. The journalist sat opposite them on one of the mansion's shady patios, in a setting of ideal Southern charm. Lemonade was poured in cut crystal glasses on the table. The senator looked relaxed in a crisp shirt and casual Geoffrey Beenes. Dasha wore another of those sundresses that screamed for David to rip it right off her pretty shoulders again...

But definitely not right now.

Right now, he watched her hold those shoulders with a newborn strength, a fresh dignity.

Right now, she wasn't the insecure daughter, afraid of being a liability to her father.

Right now, her gaze sparkled with flecks of pride, confidence, and fulfillment. They all glowed across her face too, drawing one's eye completely off the man all this shit was supposed to be about.

The change had started forty-eight hours ago. The senator had abided by his daughter's request, calling her fifteen minutes after the ultimatum. He'd been a gentleman about it too, treating her with respect, warmth, and not-so-subtle fatherly pride. He'd sealed the deal by ignoring Corso and her gaggle of advisors, lingering on the line to talk in private with his daughter for a few minutes. When the conversation ended, the look Dasha beamed was a dazzling reward for every third-degree he'd given her about it over the years—and every disciplinary spank he'd delivered most recently.

His satisfaction grew when the senator arrived today. Granted, Crystal Corso was right at his side—correction, clinging to his side—but the senator scraped her free for an hour to tour the mansion alone with Dasha. When they'd strolled onto the patio for the interview, David had noticed the continuing transformation in his girl. Kress's small nod said he did too.

It had been a moment of genuine *kumbaya* victory— leading to the guilty dilemma that dogged David to this moment.

What excuse would he use *now* to redden her sweet little ass?

The buzzkill to his fantasy involved just one look to the opposite side of the set. There, Corso kept her own vigil, a vision of flawless Washington chic. A doting preppy-boy assistant practically sprinkled holy water at her platform-heeled feet, adding to her creepy vibe.

He flushed the feeling by refocusing on Dasha. She laughed at a crack from Cooper, transforming her face again, captivating him anew and consuming him with fresh pride. She had *it*: the built-in strength and honesty that made her more than a passing trend of a star. He'd known it for years; it was just damn satisfying to watch her claim it for herself. And to know he'd helped her get there...

Fuck satisfying.

It was magical.

Incredible.

He let the force of it drench him, flooding him with all the feelings he'd kept so carefully chained back. He struggled to lock the chains again, but the consummation of this moment made him the Hulk along with the Incredible, exploding out of those chains, succumbing to a force beyond his control.

The force of real love.

Holy. Shit. He'd fallen in love with Dasha Moore.

The realization impacted him like a physical shove. He regained his balance only by anchoring his attention back to Dasha. The song in his heart. The submissive of his dreams. His beautiful love.

His love.

Crap.

What the fuck did he do now?

"So...what now?" The question got echoed with too level a tone to be his head talking. Cooper phrased the query so artfully, nobody doubted where he led the senator with it. This was the moment. CNN wanted its ratings magnet.

"What now?" The senator flashed a one-sided dimple. Dasha followed with nearly the same look. "Could you get a little more specific, Anderson?"

The silver-haired star winked. "I suppose you can afford to be coy, right? When you're about to announce you're going to run for the presidency?"

Another moment stretched. Even the bugs and birds seemed to stop. David realized he held his breath, along with everyone else in the garden. It was disconcerting. He'd always followed politics with a distanced curiosity, never understanding their drama, but this sure as hell changed his mind.

Moore took his time smiling at his interviewer. "Anderson, I'll be honest. I woke up this morning prepared to give you a 'yes' on that." He turned that warm look onto Dasha. "But something extraordinary happened on the way to that particular podium."

"Oh?" Cooper's return lifted with surprise.

"I got to spend an hour with my extraordinary daughter."

Dasha shot her father a stunned stare. The senator chuckled. To Cooper, he drawled, "Do you realize all the stuff this kid has done with her life?"

"Uh...yeah." Cooper flashed his signature grin. "We're all aware of Dasha's successes, Senator."

"Well, I wasn't." Moore's smile faded. "Not all of it. That's because I wasn't there for most of it. I fooled myself into thinking she was okay about it too—that she'd chosen good people to surround her and she understood I was serving the people of our great state." The man's tension spread through his posture. "I even told myself that when a madman breached her team's security last week in Miami. Then again when another opened fire on her and a thousand people here in Atlanta."

As her father let out a ragged sigh, Dasha reached for his

hand. "Daddy. It's all right."

David curled one hand into a fist. *No, it's not.*

"No," said the senator. "It's not." He looked Dasha in the eyes. Cooper's camera team moved in for close-ups. "You only have one parent, and you needed him there. And I wasn't. Instead, I drowned my own grief in my work, and...I'm sorry. Oh, my beautiful girl. I'm sorry."

David didn't unlock his fist. He was happy for it now. Used its tension to fight the heat behind his eyes as Dasha and her father shared a tearful embrace. He glanced up and over to Moridian, strangely satisfied to notice the guy waging the same battle. The camera guys had given up and backhanded their eyes.

The only person who continued to resemble one of the garden statues was Crystal Corso. David sneered. Why wasn't that a surprise?

The stunner came with his next thought. His ruminations wheeled toward....Josh. And, incredibly, attempting another bridge with his brother. If he'd helped Dasha get to this place with her dad, maybe there was hope for him and his hard-ass brother. Okay, so he'd inherited plenty of that stubborn streak himself. But maybe that was their problem. Further, if the attack at the mall had shown him anything, besides his terror of losing Dasha, it was that life was too goddamn short, especially to spend seven years of it at war with your only sibling.

He drew in a long breath, again observing Dasha's radiant happiness. The woman had wrought a miracle in his life. She'd unraveled the pain of Sophie. She made him want to believe in things again...in people. And she'd inspired him to believe in *them,* in the reality of maybe, just maybe doing this life thing together and building a life outside the mayhem and the spotlights...

Goddamn, how he wanted to finish her day in a romantic corner of the mansion, with a single rose and a corny-ass declaration of his feelings. But even the fantasy felt selfish. In the last three weeks, he'd taken her as his submissive, altered her body in a couple of kinky ways, and shared her with another Dom in a night that redefined the word intense. And there were likely a few *other* things on her mind, like two weeks of postponed tour dates to make up, along with a stalker who still roamed free.

Gee, D, I know you've got a full plate, but let me heap this mush in the middle of it. Doesn't your head want to explode a little more?

Not the right time. Not the right place.

But he could honor her by digging deep for his own courage and making his own life-turning phone call.

Well, shit.

He hadn't seen this coming when he'd gotten up this morning.

CHAPTER EIGHTEEN

It wasn't the day Dasha expected when she got up this morning. But it had turned out to be one of the best of her life. She still smiled when thinking of the last hug Dad had given her, along with the promise he'd be there for the first concert after the tour started again. This time, she believed him. This time...was different.

Life was different.

She was different.

She looked at her mystified smile, reflected from the vanity mirror in her and David's bedroom. All her features were there, exactly where they always were, only...not. There was a new person there, alight from the inside out, not only confident in her truth but holding her head high from having stated it, no matter how hard, to someone she loved in a spirit of love. And in return had healed a lot between them. And helped Dad make a pretty huge decision. She really was important to him. He really did need her. Wow.

She had so much to thank David for.

Her stomach responded to that thought like it always did, jumping in a delicious mix of anxiety and anticipation. The feelings she'd had for him just weeks ago...they were crumbs compared to this incredible feast. As his business partner, she'd been happy. As his friend, she'd been delighted. As his lover, she'd been ecstatic.

As his submissive, she was free.

It was the thought consuming her mind while giving her hair and makeup one last check. After that, she wrapped herself in a robe and turned out of the bedroom.

She needed to find him. The day wasn't complete until she did.

She was surprised—okay, stunned—by the distance David had kept since the CNN crew left. Right after, they'd all enjoyed a big Southern-style dinner that even Dad and his posse stayed for. When David disappeared after that, she'd assumed he went off to return phone calls and emails, but that was two hours ago. He was officially MIA. More specifically, he hadn't come back to her, now clad in the special outfit she'd gotten online with Mary's help, a gorgeous black leather body harness inlaid with ornate silver stitching, guiding the eye perfectly to the places it didn't cover—namely her breasts, ass, and the freshly shaved folds at the crux of her thighs.

All places aching for her Sir's touch again.

It had been five days. Too damn long.

A quick stop at the library still turned up nothing. Not even Kress was pulling duty in their makeshift command center—not a news flash. At dinner, he'd traded a dozen hot glances with one of Dad's staffers, a cute brunette in a pencil skirt and red-trimmed eyeglasses. The girl had been hanging all over Zack, Crystal's pretty-boy assistant, who hadn't stood a chance as soon as Kress appeared. By now, Kress had likely shadowed the woman back to the hotel—and her room.

Dasha set aside the weird twinge of jealousy she felt about that. She had no right to the feeling. The agent didn't belong to her any more than she belonged to him. Tonight was for tracking down the man to whom she did belong. Her body zinged with sexual tension. Even her nipples pulsed against the piercings he'd put there.

Where the hell had he gone?

After padding down the back stairs, she looked in the kitchen and workout room. David was a sucker for leftovers and then sweating them off on the weight machines—but the kitchen staff declared they hadn't seen him since dinner. The weight room was dark and didn't smell like sweat had hit it lately.

She frowned. Retightened her robe. Finally conceded she might have to go back upstairs, fetch her cell, and turn into the needy girlfriend she'd forbidden herself to become. But damn it, she needed David's hands on her. Inside her. Taking her. Possessing her. Tonight.

Maybe a bit bossy, little sub.

She could hear him saying it already, every syllable turned to arousal by his suggestive growl.

I need you, Sir.

She passed the back study, now enclosed in darkness, on her return trip to the back stairway.

Movement.

There it was, deep in the shadows, drawing her back to the room.

She peered deeper into the thick layers of light. Well, lack of it. The dark furniture thickened the dimness, intensifying her conflict. What had she seen? Heard? No. Neither of those. She'd *felt* it. Felt him...

A floor lamp flickered to life.

In its sudden glow, she found him.

His presence was oddly still. He sat in the center of the couch, nursing a glass of Scotch.

"Hi." No growl. Just a soft murmur. He still wore his white

dress shirt and dark blue Zegna suit pants but at least had yanked off his tie and jacket.

He looked up with a fathomless gaze and an equally unreadable smile. Radiating an energy she could only describe as weird.

"Uh...hi. What're you doing here in the dark?"

"Thinking."

The weirdness radar went off again. She twisted one of her robe strings around a finger. "About what?"

"Not important."

"Hell it isn't." The retort flared as easily as the instinct that spurred it. "Maybe a rewind will help? Viceroy Miami, about four thirty in the morning? 'I'm not a hide-in-the-dark Dom, Dasha.' Shadows aren't usually your style, remember?"

David lifted both brows. "Maybe they are. Look what came to me as a result."

The ongoing enigma of his voice, sounding panther and prey at once, melted her. She went to him and, without thinking, sank to the floor at his feet. "You didn't have to wait in the dark for that."

To emphasize that, she raised a hand to his knee. David stretched his touch to the top of her head, steady and strong but too damn gentle. She deepened her hold, shifting it to the inside of his leg. They passed a long minute like that, in silence that felt like a thickening blanket, a shroud she would've gladly wrapped herself in if not for the self-built cage she still felt from David. This was different from his work tension and even separate from the strain he gave off when he wanted to get her naked.

Weird graduated to eerie. She tried to stay calm. Tried not to conclude that now she'd reconnected to Dad, it meant David was hitting the release cable on their relationship.

"I called Josh an hour ago."

Dasha snapped up her stare. The eerie vibe earned a PhD in what-the-hell. It almost eclipsed her relief at knowing this had nothing to do with her. "You're not kidding," she said, looking deep into his eyes. The gray had turned a beautiful light blue.

"Nope."

"You two are Anakin and Obi-Wan. You never speak unless it's time to try to kill each other."

"And I've never told you why, did I?"

"You told me to never ask."

"I did, didn't I? It was...messy. And stupid. And—" His hold stiffened. "It was because of a woman."

His gaze intensified. Dasha held his stare, tried to look into him through it, to comprehend him as he always did her. He slid his fingers to the side of her face. "But because of another woman, I realized it was time to put the lightsabers away."

She swallowed. Or thought she did. The emotion flowing off him thickened, so intense she almost couldn't bear it, yet she wanted more. So much like his domination. She wondered if being with him would always mean this push-pull of feeling. And if she would ever want it any other way.

"What was this woman's name?" she asked softly.

"Sophie. She was young and hungry for a D/s dynamic. I was her first Dom. We clicked—at first. She liked it. A lot."

Despite the irony of his frown, Dasha smiled. "I relate to that."

"No," he retorted. "You don't. You're nothing like her." He shook his head, took in a deep breath, stroked her cheek again as if apologizing. "Sophie... There was a lot in her life she was running from. She started using our dynamic more and more as an escape valve. She went sub frenzy faster than anyone I've seen."

Dasha crunched her brows. "Sub what?"

"Sub frenzy. It's...an addiction of sorts. Some submissives, once they get a taste of the endorphin rush that D/s can bring, hunger for it like a six-year-old in a candy store. And some of them start acting like that six-year-old too."

"You're serious?"

"Wish I wasn't. At least not in Sophie's case. She got lost, really lost." He squeezed his eyes shut. "Needy is just the tip of the iceberg to describe what happened to her. She couldn't stand being apart from me and got more and more demanding of everything. She insisted on floggings and fuckings on a daily basis, even when she wasn't healed from the previous day, physically or emotionally. When we met, she was a brilliant PA at Fox. She quit that job and started hanging around the house to be my slave whenever I wanted her there."

Dasha sat up straighter. "Whoa. You're still serious."

His jaw scissored. "Oh yeah."

"Well, most men would call that a dream come true."

His gaze became a knife. "Dream? I don't want a goddamn slave, Dasha. I want a woman who knows her mind, heart, and her body and gives them to me freely. Who makes me earn her submission. Who makes me want to earn it."

She couldn't control the little smile that rebloomed. "Okay, Tarzan."

"You're fucking right, Tarzan." He pushed up, launching into pace mode. "Any overbearing ass on this planet can have a slave."

An awful lightbulb snapped on in her brain. "Oh God. And Josh became that ass for Sophie."

"No. Josh thought I needed to be that ass."

"Now I'm really lost."

"I know." He released a hard breath. "Time to back up." He slowed the pacing a little. "I began to try to force Sophie back to reality. I couldn't exactly release her, but I started to make it damn hard for her to be little domestic slave girl."

Dasha frowned in confusion. "Release her?"

"The Dominant's version of a breakup," he clarified. "But like I said, I couldn't go there. Not then, not in the state she was in, not when I was the one who'd put her there to begin with. But I could make it difficult for her to be stuck there. I had the locks changed on the house, ordered her to come over only at times I designated, set a crapload of limits on our time together. I also stopped helping out with her bills. It killed me, all of it, but I figured a week or two of real-world challenge would be the bucket of psychological ice she needed."

"And somehow that's where Josh came in."

He'd turned away, and his shoulder muscles bunched. "Yeah. That's where Josh came in."

"He supported her side?"

"Supported it? Hell, he gave her the idea in the first place."

"*What?*"

He pivoted back with a dark smirk on his lips. "Yeah, baby, the Dom gene runs high in the Pennington DNA." The smirk dropped. "Only Josh got a thousand more strands of it than me."

She sat back, trying to take in all that information, imagining what insanity his life must have been. Loving that girl...feeling bound not to mess up her life, even though she'd turned his upside down...and then finding out his own brother facilitated it... God, no wonder he didn't just ask for honesty but commanded it.

Suddenly, perplexity latched on to her brain. "Wait. Hate to repeat the obvious, but why didn't Josh just—" The words felt awkward, but she finally got them out. "Well...take her as his own...um...slave?"

"Full plate," David replied. "He already had one, and they were training another together. Besides, messing with mine was like another conquest to him. What better way to justify your alternative tastes than by converting your own brother?"

She tamped down a bizarre urge to laugh. *Alternative tastes.* Three weeks ago, she couldn't imagine anything more alternative than sexually dominating a woman in a Madison Square Garden dressing room. To think of David being called a prude about anything... Unreal.

That's when the mirth got replaced by irritation. Protective claws of it. "Tastes?" she snapped. "Wait. It's not like freaking ice cream."

Of course, *that* was when David jumped on the humor bandwagon. "No." He chuckled. "It's not, sweetheart."

His grin, huge and dazzling, grew as he crossed to her again. His hold, urgent and commanding, yanked her head back. With his free hand, he shoved the hair from her face—before dipping his head to slam a long, adoring kiss onto her.

She sighed beneath his assault. If this was D/s prudeville, so be it. She'd die a perverted prude.

"What were we just talking about?" she stammered when he finally let her go.

He laughed again. "My splendid brother and the fact that he wrote checks to my submissive for two months before I found out."

Dasha returned her hold to his knee. "Wow."

"Yeah. Wow."

Sadness weighted her chest. "So *that's* when the lightsabers came out."

"And a lot more."

The words spoke a dozen volumes of meaning, but Dasha had seen his mouth make that line before. A line she knew not to cross.

For now, she just wanted to help with the healing he'd begun with his phone call—the courage to which she related with crystal clarity. She'd had recent experience with finding it in herself, but the chasm between her and Dad...like the erosion of time, it hadn't been intentional. What had gone down between David and Josh was wrought by intent, deliberation, ego, and stubbornness. On both sides.

"That phone call took guts." She stroked his hand. "I'm proud of you."

David threaded fingers through her hair. "No more than I am of you."

Dasha huffed. "Two different scenarios, Mr. Pennington. Dad didn't intentionally hurt me. What Josh did to you, going behind your back *and* enabling someone with scrambled eggs for brains, took more heart to look past. It took—"

He cut her off by palming the back of her head, dragging her up to his lap, and ramming his lips to hers again. "Hush," he said. "We're done with it for now."

Dasha licked at the sting he'd left behind. She wanted more of it. Equally bad, she yearned for the voice she'd gotten with it too. *That* voice. The one with no more mystery but plenty of darkness. The one that sluiced arousal through her in brand-new ways...and injected her with a rush of boldness.

She jerked her chin a little at him. Then arched her own brows in open challenge. "Who says we are?"

A strange scowl took over his face. His eyes narrowed at the outer corners. His mouth, grinning at her just moments ago, pursed with intensity.

He looked...

Dangerous.

For a long moment, she was certain he debated on whether to roll her onto the couch or drop her to the floor before he stomped out of here. She braced herself for it.

Instead, David coiled his hand tighter into her scalp. Pulled, fast and forceful, baring her face completely to him.

"Games don't become you, D. Say what you mean."

After all his introspection and calm, the move came as a surprise. And an irritation. She flung back with quiet decision, "I'm not the one who was playing hide-and-seek in the shadows."

Just like that, he whipped his other hand around, bracing it at the corners of her jaw. "You've got a little bug in your panties tonight, don't you?" He traced his touch down to the V where her robe closed. "What is it?" He flattened his index and middle fingers to her skin. "What do you want, Dasha?"

Against her efforts otherwise, she shivered. His touch shot heat to the apex of her thighs, and she quaked trying to hide that from him. Thirty seconds ago, she'd been terrified he'd leave. His nearness wreaked three times that havoc.

She loved it.

Every second.

"Say it," he commanded in a rough rasp. "I have nothing to punish you for. This time, you have to take the steps. What do you want, D?"

Did that ragged inhalation belong to her? Her tight lungs said yes. "I just want to please you." She ran her tongue over her lips again. "Sir."

"Thank you."

So now he was back to being Gentleman Jim?

Dasha considered what kind of a glower she'd fling for the mixed signals. It was a costly moment of distraction. She never saw his next move coming, flipping everything back into raw animal territory. He turned his two fingers into hooks, securing them into her robe. Ripped it from her shoulder in a single slash. Not wasting a second, he tore off the other side.

Once again, all was silent.

If nobody counted the adrenaline pumping in her ears.

"Well. This is a good start."

His tone descended to deeper shadows, taking her mind and body with it. Dasha rejoiced in the journey, breath quickening and pussy throbbing. Judging from the way David's hands ran up her rib cage, following the patterns of silver thread to the base of her breasts, he did too.

Seeking him out had been the right choice. This was where they both needed to be, physically and mentally, especially tonight. Leader and follower. Panther and gazelle.

Dominant and submissive.

She let out a long breath, letting her brain dip into that wonderful mental space of surrender, as he rolled his hands up to her breasts. "Thank you, Sir." She mewled as he coaxed her nipples into hard beads, pushing them against her piercings.

"Shhh." His voice grated on the reproach as he suckled the curve of her jaw. He squeezed her areolas harder, making her gasp and writhe. "No more words," he commanded. "Lock your hands behind your head, please. You may nod if you understand."

Dasha bobbed her head, hyper-aware of her new position. Her sparkling nipples were lifted higher for his view, inciting David's hum of appreciation. He dipped his head to one swell, biting it gently just beneath the glittering letter embedded there.

She yelped, trying to jump back. He caught her around the waist, anchoring her against his body, continuing his assault on the flesh below his initial.

"David!"

"Hmm?"

"Shit!"

"Mmm." His voice was smooth, filled with sadistic beauty. "I'll forgive you for the words—only because you're so pretty when you're in pain."

As if to prove the point, he let go of her left swell, only to flick his finger against the diamond P there. If she was pretty in pain, then she must've been gorgeous now.

"Damn it!" she cried, trying to escape again. "Bastard!"

To her shock, he let her get free. But she'd no more whirled and stumbled a couple of steps than he caught her around the waist, letting her momentum propel her forward and down. He wrested the robe all the way off and then tossed it across the room. Cool air blasted her upturned ass. Her heartbeat tripled in a second. She knew what was coming next, dreading it and wanting it in the same heady rush.

Sure enough, without warning or pause, he pummeled her backside with a series of brisk spanks. Dasha dug teeth into her bottom lip, taking the discipline in silence. She'd invited the punishment with her outburst, but her breasts still throbbed from his torment. Gravity wasn't helping things.

What was that she'd just been thinking, about making the right choice to come get him?

The swats continued, increasing in strength until she squirmed, though the effort was futile. His grip dug into her flesh, gripping her tighter—exposing her purely for his pleasure.

Crazily, the admission made the spanking a little easier.

A *little*.

Her gasps turned into whimpers, but just when she felt more choice words bubbling to the surface, David stopped. She got in half a breath of relief before he flipped her back to her feet. Dasha thought she'd crumble to the floor again, but he hauled her back against him, hard and tight, one arm cinching her in. With his free hand, he caught her jaw again. Locked around it with steady fingers, cinching her head into the crook of his neck. Her pulse thundered in her neck. Her blood roared in her senses. The tumult grew as he took the skin beneath her ear, licking and kissing and biting until her eyes drifted shut.

Brain, meet goo. Body, meet surrender.

Yes. Oh, yes.

This was why she'd sought him out tonight.

He gnawed his way to her ear, where his growl filled it. "Bastard, hmm?"

She pushed out a sigh through her dizzy haze. Oh, yeah. She'd said that, hadn't she. It felt like days ago. No. A lifetime.

"Shoe might fit, Mr. P."

He laughed softly. "Well then, tell me, sweetheart...what bastard owns you tonight?"

"You."

No-brainer there. A gasp followed as his other hand slipped to the folds between her legs. With expert precision, he homed in on her clit, pulling the sensitive nub between two fingers. *Goo* really had been the perfect description. Her pussy dissolved, melting into glorious heat around his touch.

"What bastard is going to take you to the dungeon and do whatever he wants with this?"

"You!" Her heartbeat thundered. Her body accelerated. "You. Please..."

"Excellent. Say it again. Beg me for it, D."

"*Please.*" She grew aware of his clothing, rough and demanding, against her nude skin. Every contact sparked her higher, consumed her deeper, beckoned her into the abyss of submission. "Sir...please take me to the dungeon."

He rewarded her by angling her face toward him and snaking his down. He kissed her deeply once more, mating her tongue with his. Before long, Dasha didn't know where she ended and David began. He continued to tease her clit as they kissed, kneading the slit of skin until her breaths came faster and harder. Until her body climbed to a precipice of bittersweet sensation.

Oh dear God...yes.

David yanked his mouth away. "Don't you dare," he ordered. "Don't even think of coming yet. Control it. Rein it in."

She searched for the retort to that. Couldn't find it. The abyss had her now. His will was her will, even if it meant the hell of dominating *herself* for a long minute. She took deep, harsh breaths, forcing her heartbeat to slow. "Y-Yes, Sir."

She sounded like a child who'd just had a lollipop ripped from her mouth. David clearly got that too. As he turned her to fully face him again, the shithead unfurled a grin of cocky satisfaction. Dasha couldn't help but glare back, still gasping for control.

He cupped a hand to her cheek. She bared her teeth,

letting him know what she longed to do to those teasing fingers. His eyes twinkled. "You're gorgeous."

And I'm not going to show you how that dissolved my bones. "Thank you, Sir." She purposely clipped it.

"So...you want a trip to the dungeon."

She let him hear the hitch in her breath. "Oh yes, Sir."

"Then present yourself properly for that." He answered the question in her gaze by jerking his head toward the dungeon door. "On your knees in front of it, please. I think you know what position to take as well."

"I do, Sir."

"Perfect. Remain that way until I come get you. I won't be long."

He pointed to a spot on the floor near the entrance to the dungeon. Dasha felt her anger fading back as the mental abyss again beckoned. They'd come so far together since David had first instructed her to do this...yet every time still felt like that first time too. Her womb came alive from the recognition, using her feelings like gasoline on a fire. Her labia quivered from the rush of cool air over her wet skin. Fresh juices dampened the bare folds at her center.

It was ecstasy. It was agony. She already yearned to climax again.

Instead, she dug fingers into the carpet and watched David slide back the door to the dungeon. That was when she frowned a little. The second door, the one that was actually part of the building, was already pushed open. Did she hear music drifting up the stone stairway? It was a melodic but gothic sound...thoroughly hypnotizing. But how had he turned it on? He wasn't even at the first step yet. Remote control?

Her question got answered when she heard a female

shriek from below. The sound penetrated the velvet curtain, shooting straight up the stairs.

"Outstanding." Every syllable shot off David's lips with equal fervor. He flashed a breathtaking smile. "Seems we have some company, sweetheart. Back in a second."

"A second" was a tad inaccurate. Lying there on the carpet, waiting for her Sir to return, she almost gave in to the urge to curl into a don't-look-at-me ball. Short of being completely naked, she was as exposed as it got. Her nipples jutted toward the ceiling, still puckered and red. Her mound was open and wet, her arms spread to her sides. If anyone walked past the study, it'd be as if the harness didn't exist. They'd know exactly what she was waiting for. What if that anyone was one of the mansion staff? What if that anyone was Kress? What if he had the little brunette from Dad's staff with him? Oh shit, what if the girl told *Dad* what she saw?

She got so agitated imagining that scene, David startled her a little when he reappeared. He offered both hands to help her stand, yet that shit-eating smile still adorned his wicked lips. "Come on," he bade. "We don't want to miss the show."

The show?

She ached to actually say it as he took her hand, guiding her down the stairs. As the music got louder, now backed by a Gregorian chorus who sounded like they'd hit purgatory, so did the real-life outcries.

What the hell?

When Dasha entered the dungeon, all was explained. The screamer was...

Mary.

Holy. Crap.

Her little friend's naked body was crisscrossed by an

elaborate web of red and black ropes, all secured on one of the suspension rings in the middle of the room. Mary lay sideways in the bonds, her wrists and forearms encased in a black rope gauntlet over her head. She was suspended a good four feet off the floor. Whoever had tied her left her backside free of ropes, and it was easy to understand why. Raife stood near her head, using one hand to swing her back toward Philip, who waited with a single-tail whip. With every pass, he used the thing to lash her ass, flicking with precision. When Mary came back toward Raife, he stroked her breasts with a long red feather on a glittering stick.

Dasha only had to give her friend one look to know the conflicting sensations drove her crazy—in all the right ways. Mary's face contorted with forced pain one moment, divine pleasure the next. Her body strained against the ropes with her fast breathing, but her eyes were hooded and glossy with the double sensory assault.

She was incredible. She'd seen her friend in a lot of stage finery and makeup, but in this moment, with her face adorned only in surrender, Mary was at her most beautiful.

Dasha breathed harder. She couldn't look away. Part of her wanted to be Mary but was terrified of ever being that exposed and helpless—and swinging midair over a concrete floor. She couldn't even think about being at the mercy of that whip. Every crack filled the dungeon like a lightning strike.

Raife pushed Mary back toward Philip again. Dasha watched her friend's body tense for the lash, but instead Philip caught her, having shoved the whip into his back pocket. Mary whimpered as he traced a finger along several of the bright-red welts he'd put into her flesh.

"Lovely, precious toy," he murmured. "I love what my

leather does to your skin." He sidled next to her, wrapping one arm around her waist as he bent and slowly licked one of the lines. Mary let out a deep moan.

Dasha gulped hard to avoid doing the same.

"Hurt a little, sweet Mary?" he said with lips still pressed to her skin.

"Y-Yes, Sir."

"Are you ready to be fucked, then?"

"Yes, Sir!" She gasped it. A cry followed it as Philip pressed a finger into her core. He lifted his head, frowning at Raife.

"Wet," he pronounced. "But not wet enough. I think five more lashes should have her ready."

Dasha's gut knotted, but her own sex got wetter as Mary gazed at Raife with eyes full of dread and joy combined. After Philip swung her back over, Raife greeted Mary with a passionate, deep, openmouthed kiss.

Dasha watched the embrace with awe, almost wanting to trade places with her friend in that moment, lashes and tears and all. And David standing in Raife's place, of course. And the stand-in for Philip?

She knew the answer to that too. She wanted it to be Kress there, waiting for her at the other end. She could almost see him there already. Powerful. Rugged. A grin curving his lips, conveying one thing. *I can't wait to get my hands on you.*

She closed her eyes. Forced the image from her mind.

Until she turned and realized the four of them weren't alone.

There was somebody else in the room.

That person shifted in the shadows.

Dasha glanced in time to see David give the person a familiar, guy-to-guy kind of nod. She peered the same direction.

Oh, God.

It was Kress. Very alone. And looking very uncomfortable—and just as turned on—as David.

Her body responded immediately, churning fast toward the realm of pure need.

Which gave brand-new meaning to the term "dazed and confused."

CHAPTER NINETEEN

Kress looked at the turmoil washing over Dasha's face and called himself five kinds of a shithead.

He could've downplayed how he'd gotten down here. How he'd done the class act by the cute Natalie, despite the brunette's either-you're-dead-or-you're-gay-not-to-notice moves on him all the way to the hotel. How he'd pleaded a stressful day and a migraine to her rather than the real ache assaulting him: the need for sweet gold hair, an equally delicious mouth, and a certain soprano voice crying from his touch.

How he'd returned to the mansion beating himself up for that line of thought, intending to go straight to bed—*alone*—but drifted toward the back stairs and the study instead.

How he'd hoped to find the door to the dungeon open. And had.

How he'd found Raife and Philip setting up for a scene, with Dasha's dancer friend waiting with bright, eager eyes.

How he'd accepted their invitation to stay and watch. And how he'd hoped the night would turn into *this* moment. How he'd hoped David and Dasha would join the party too.

Shithead.

Why had he wanted this? Now he longed to take back any karma he'd put into the universe with his selfishness and erase the desperate look consuming Dasha's sweet face. Especially because, as his stare drifted lower, he knew it wouldn't soon be returning to her face.

"Fuck." He grated it beneath his breath. That black-and-silver half-corset thing was good for one sole purpose. It all but ordered a man to rip it off her. The way it cupped her breasts, which looked like Pennington had taken some fun plucks at already, but then fast drew the eyes down to where it framed the V of her pussy and edged around into a sculpted Valentine arc across the top of her ass...

"Fuuuuck." The second time around was a doomsday prophecy for his self-control—as well as the erection ramming at his pants.

He had to get out of here. Had to escape before David started pulling her to the equipment. Then got her naked. Then restrained her. And then...

He ground his jaw. Commanded his legs to move. Made his arm shove the velvet curtain back. *You've train-wrecked this one real good, Moridian. Greedy bastard, you should've been grateful David shared her for even one night. She isn't yours. Forget her. Go upstairs, grab Natalie's number, and get yourself somebody who's not practically wearing her Master's collar already.*

"Moridian."

He ordered himself to complete the exit. He could just pretend he hadn't heard the call. But something in Pennington's voice hooked him like a carp. He felt like one of the ugly fish too, as he gave the guy a who-me look. The entire time, he fought not to stare at Dasha again. He failed, of course.

"Are you being a fucking party pooper?" Pennington's tone made it seem they were all at a frat party instead of a bondage dungeon with the world's most perfect submissive standing nearly nude between them.

What the hell. He could play the act too. He gave his

friend a shrug. "I crashed the soiree to begin with. Raife told me they'd be roping up their girl, and I was interested watching his knots, so—"

"Bullshit."

Dasha's shoulders went a little stiff. Her lips parted, and she flicked her gorgeous pink tongue over them. Like she had no damn idea what that did to his very bone marrow.

"Excuse me?"

"Don't throw that FBI tone at me, pineapple boy. You know what I'm talking about."

"Pineapple—I should turn heel on you for that alone, asshole."

Though David laughed back at that, the guy snaked a hand to Dasha's ass and gave her a solid whack. Her eyes went wide, but she said nothing. Against his will, Kress watched her. She fascinated him as a woman and a person but even more as a newly initiated submissive. In some moments, she completely forgot her place and turned into a spank-worthy brat. But the very next, she'd commit to the dynamic so deeply, he figured they'd already lost her to subspace.

In others, like now, she was at her most adorable. When she oscillated between the extremes, bratty and skittish nearly at once, she was three times cuter than the others. And thirty times sexier.

"Sweetheart." David spoke the directive to her but looked at Kress. "Be a good girl. Take Kress's hand and lead him to the bedroom. I'll be there in a minute."

Dasha kept her eyes toward the floor as she obeyed her Sir. In that instant, Kress wished she'd opted for willful-disobedience mode. He needed to know if she had a clue about David's grand plan here, because he sure as hell didn't.

By the time they got to the big bedroom with the matching four-poster, he was certain Dasha had no more of an idea about this than he. She kept her gaze riveted to the floor, where she gave the ivory carpet a nervous massage with her toes. Her fingers shook as she twisted them in his, trying to disengage their grasp.

He didn't let her go so easily. "Dasha." He locked her hand in his. "Look at me." She didn't comply. He wasn't surprised. So he let his voice go to iron. "Okay, I direct you to look at me."

She actually stamped her foot. It almost made him laugh. "And who says your directions bear any weight here?"

"Only you."

Just two words. But Dasha's sigh told him she recognized their power. And was supremely uncomfortable with it.

The next moment, when she raised her head, Kress understood why.

Her conflicted gaze in the dungeon was the paltry start of what she seared into him. The copper depths of her eyes looked like three-alarm fires. She wanted him but hated herself for it. Ached for him but damned herself for that too.

And felt for him.

He wasn't sure what, but...

Christ. Whatever it was, it scared the shit out of her.

"Happy now?" she whispered, blinking back the sheen of tears.

"Fuck." He couldn't say anything more because David strode back into the room. A key on a velvet rope hung from his fingers. He slid the thing into a double-doored wall panel Kress hadn't noticed before, even during their little sleepover in here.

Ohhh man, did he notice it now.

The twin doors swung out to become the outer walls of a domination toy store. He gaped at the shelves full of devices they hadn't even found in the outer dungeon's armoire. Strict discipline collars in red and black leather. An assortment of gags, bits, wire spreaders, and speculums. A rack of gels and lubricants. Some handheld fucking devices, and even a set of twenty glass fire cups.

He only had to imagine using half those things on Dasha, and his erection soared back to the category of torture.

David slanted a grin. "Now you know why they call this the bonus room."

Dasha didn't say a word—but *did* visibly tremble. Kress tried not to notice how her nipples went three times more erect too.

"Look, man..." He spread his arms. "I appreciate the gesture, but after playing voyeur to Raife and Phil for an hour, I don't think I can repeat the favor—"

"Who says you're watching?"

Hell. That made everything trickier. As in forgetting-to-breathe tricky.

Dasha went still—well, *more* still—too. "Sir? Excuse me?"

"Ditto," Kress added. "What the hell are you saying, Pennington?"

David eyed them both again. Straightened and folded his arms. "What the three of us haven't been saying." He let a long silence stretch. Stepped to Dasha and lifted her chin with one finger. "You know what I'm talking about, don't you?"

Kress heard her shaky intake of breath. "Y-Yes. But—"

"Hush." David kissed her fiercely. "The only 'butt' we're addressing tonight is the lovely one at the top of your thighs."

"David." Her whisper was thick with wonderment. "Sir.

How did you—"

"You've given me so much, D." He tightened his grip, boring his stare into her. "And I want to give you everything in return. Everything you could ever want or desire." His attention swung to Kress. "Right now, that includes you, Sonny Crockett."

Kress's breath returned in a rush. The generous reality behind David's sarcasm...it was too good to grasp. But more than that—was Dasha was all right with this? Wanting his domination was one thing; getting it was another. Their golden beauty was a passionate woman, but she was also a new submissive. Fresh arrivals to the lifestyle sometimes let their kink-hungry eyes agree to stuff they couldn't eat. Additionally, she'd already had a day of explosive emotions. Could she handle a whole fireworks display of more?

Kress pressed against her on the other side. "Are you sure?" When her answering gaze went molten, it turned his cock into hot lava too. Still, he said, "This time isn't a punishment, D—but my dynamic won't be any easier to take. You know what I demand of my submissives. Tonight, you're openly agreeing to that. You understand?"

Like a defiant princess, she lifted her chin higher. "Yes, Sergeant. I understand."

Sergeant.

Well, hell.

That sure as fuck unraveled any last protest he could conjure. It also uncoiled the last tethers on his lust. God, she was incredible, a gift of generous passion and insatiable fire, mixed with an actual heart and a beautiful brain. He couldn't wait to claim her again, to work with David on giving her even better ecstasy than they had before.

He acted fast on that resolution. Moving yet tighter on her, he deepened his hold, splaying one hand along her neck and lowering the other into a commanding cup on her ass. "Why don't we let her prove it?"

Dasha tensed as if expecting a swat. Kress grinned, enjoying the psych-out. He squeezed her cheek harder as David circled behind her. The guy joined D in looking directly at Kress, moving his lips close to her ear. "Now it's your turn to answer to me, D. Do you understand that we're inviting Kress to join me in using you tonight, to dominate your body in whatever manner pleases him?"

Her little gulp was one of the sexiest things Kress had ever seen. "Yes, Sir." The little catch in her throat, a betrayal of her mounting anticipation, was even sexier. Holy Christ, if she changed her mind at this point...visions of diving off a cliff into a river of glass came to his mind.

"And will you submit to him with all the respect and willingness you'd give to me, with the exception of any hard limits we may encounter?"

"Yes." It was a bare rasp. "Yes, Sir."

"Do you remember your safe word?"

"Yes, Sir. Sound check."

"Perfect. Now answer this: do you remember how to suck cock?"

She licked her lips again. It mesmerized Kress. Though he longed to look at what the challenge did to the rest of her body, he couldn't rip his stare from her face. The burnished desire in her gaze. The racing pulse in her throat. That shimmering sheen on her lips. *So fucking beautiful.*

She finally murmured, "Yes, Sir."

"Then get on your knees—and show Kress your gratitude

for his domination tonight." David guided her down himself. "Suck him well, sweetheart. I'm going to watch every minute."

Heaven.

He really, truly, had to be in heaven.

Not a point he wanted to debate, though—especially as the golden goddess dropped before him. He gulped hard, battling the tremors of his fingers as he fumbled for his belt.

"No." David's command sliced into his mental haze. "Let her do it, Moridian. Don't lift a finger. *She's* servicing *you*."

"I enjoy full service." Never had he said words more true. As she set him free, tenderly working his erection with those same sweet fingers, he groaned. He dug appreciative hands into her hair, combing through its long, soft waves.

Yes. Heaven.

Maybe just a damn good dream.

He'd think about the crapville of waking up from it later.

Much later.

CHAPTER TWENTY

David's words echoed in Dasha's head like a dream. *Show Kress your gratitude.* But gratitude flowed in her heart for both these men. For David, who'd been her strength. For Kress, who'd been her safety. And the two of them together, for becoming her freedom...for tearing down the walls of her heart and setting its love free again.

Yes, she loved them. God help her, *both* of them. And yes, she wanted to prove it to them both too...right now, with every fiber of her body.

The body that quivered in awakening now as she stroked Kress's cock in appreciation.

A hiss escaped him as she ran her fingers up his velvet length, tracing the pulsing veins beneath the skin. "God, yes, Dasha." She loved the moan that followed, coinciding with the milky drops that leaked from the slit at his tip.

"Lick it off."

Not Kress this time. David's whisper stunned her for a moment. He really was watching, pressed up against her, his now-shirtless torso pressed to her back.

"Use only your tongue," he instructed further. She obeyed with joy, lapping up the pre-come, reveling in another hiss from above. "Now lick the rest of him like that." David reached forward and cupped her breasts as he ordered it. "Long strokes, baby. Good. Anchor your hands on his thighs. Get his balls wet too."

She closed her eyes, inhaling Kress's musky scent as she dipped her head, angling her mouth toward the sizable sac at his root. He tightened against her tongue, tasting like raw man and pure arousal. David shifted with her, watching every motion, dragging her senses into a whirlpool of sensual awareness. Knowing David looked at every action of her mouth...was assessing her...made her yearn to satisfy him as much as she pleasured Kress.

"Very nice." Her Sir's praise made her heart sing. "Now take all of him."

"Fuck, yes," Kress seconded. "Fuck...*yes.*"

Dasha opened her throat, lowering herself completely on his shaft.

Kress's grip crushed into her hair. The man had never lied about how he liked things; he was passionate with a hearty dose of military-level control. A passive blowjob didn't register in his vocabulary. Dasha rejoiced in his strength but struggled to accommodate his rhythm as he pumped into her mouth.

"Stop fighting him, D," David commanded. "He's fucking you now. Relax and be a good little mouth."

She let her eyes drift shut. His words worked dark magic in her head. *A good little mouth. Yes.* She wanted to be good for them. She wanted to be better than good. She longed to forget who she was for these magical moments. To truly let go. To be their good girl...

But why did Kress suddenly stop?

He didn't take long to clarify. "I'm going to fuck her on the bed," he said. "And throw a blindfold on her. I want her complete surrender."

"Great idea." As David guided her to the bed, Kress began peeling off his clothes. She stopped for a second, watching him. Years of chasing down bad guys had been extremely good to him. His thighs were as thick and powerful. His torso was muscled perfection, with a high, meaty chest. His arms really could be described as "guns." He looked...dangerous. And David, while slightly leaner, was more chiseled and defined. And *beautiful*. His body was the product of focused conditioning, with defined striation everywhere.

Danger and beauty. Both hers—for the whole night. And now, with a leather blindfold lowered around her eyes, both plunged into sensual blackness.

With her sight taken away, every other sense was sharpened, intensified. As David laid her down on the big mattress, her skin turned into a thousand splinters of ice and fire. She breathed in and smelled fresh sheets, hot skin, and the unmistakable tang of her own arousal.

Suddenly, all that awareness got eclipsed by vertigo. The men turned and pulled her, and the world cartwheeled.

Kress's baritone came from overhead. "No. This way."

David chuckled somewhere near her feet. "Hmm. Another good idea."

Her equilibrium went off-kilter again. A hand gripped her nape. Big and rough. Kress. He tugged her head backward, over the side of the bed. She gasped in confusion as blood rushed the direction of the floor, her chin jutting toward the ceiling. Instinct kicked in. She flailed, trying to right herself, but more hands caught and restrained her—this time, David. He locked her wrists into soft-lined cuffs, securing her arms like wings at her side.

"Relax, sweetheart. Trust us."

A pair of thumbs started stroking her cheeks. "Goddamn it," came Kress's tight murmur. "Look at you, darlin'. You're gorgeous."

"Couldn't agree more." Slight clinks sounded at her sides. She assumed David was checking the chains he'd secured to her wrists and then the bedposts. After that, he ran both hands up her arms, along her collarbones, down to her breasts again. He kneaded the swells gently. Warmth flooded her sensitive peaks, and she moaned.

"Nice." Kress's murmur came with husky emphasis. "You're ready for me again, aren't you?"

He didn't give her a chance to answer. One of his hands braced the back of her head. The other stroked along her jaw, prodding it open. She had no choice but to obey. Her world spun more, her mind shut off as sensual awareness took over. It heightened the delicious, salty taste of his flesh as he pressed his cock to her mouth again. She instinctively opened, letting him roll his hard knob along her tongue, teasing her with it. Her brain careened. She prepared her throat because she knew what he was about to do with that burning rod.

"Good girl," he ordered in a low grate. "Open up and take me deep."

In one slow slide, he filled her. Every inch of her throat became his. With that first stroke, Kress's grip went from demanding to savage. He angled her head to receive the stabs of his body. His equally primitive groans made every moment worth it. She loved making him sound that way. Rejoiced in feeling his wrist tremble with need. Exulted in serving him with the gift of her body and the submission in her heart.

As her jaw began to ache, David got busy in the distraction department. She felt his hands descending, making short work of the zipper to her harness. "Ready to be naked?" he drawled, ripping the garment. His hand raked back in, zeroing in on the apex of her body. Dasha shivered and moaned, especially because he restrained his touch on her pussy to the barest pressure. When she protested by shoving her hips up at him, he retaliated with a swat on her mound.

"Greedy again, sweetheart? Does this pussy need a little discipline?"

Discipline. The threat—no, the promise—hammered in her brain harder than Kress pumped in her mouth. She'd seen the wicked devices on the shelves in the closet—and now wondered if he eyed any of them. Her heart thundered, nerves and anticipation mixing as the weight on the bed changed. He'd reached for something in that cabinet of sin; she just *knew* it.

Her trepidation went nuclear as he pressed his long, strong fingers at the inside of her thighs. "Wider." David pushed her thighs out. "Yes. So lovely." He ran a finger down her most sensitive flesh, causing her hips to jerk again. "Be still now. If you fight me, D, this'll only hurt worse."

His statement didn't match what she braced for next. *It'll only hurt worse.* That implied she was going to hurt *somehow.* But the next sensation she felt was a rush of cold liquid spilling over his fingers as he spread it. A tangy strawberry scent gave away the liquid as lubricant. David seemed to know just how she liked to be caressed with it. She moaned, the sound strangled because of Kress's cock, but the way David worked her nerves, sliding the lube deep into her vagina, made her never want to stop. *Don't stop. Don't stop. Please—*

Stop.

He'd warned her. But the sharp bites came as a shock anyway. It was like he'd let miniature alligators loose on her pussy lips. *Hungry* alligators. The little monsters latched on to her flesh and didn't let up, even as she writhed. And David, the bastard, merely hummed in appreciation. He explored her with equal languor, pressing fingers deeper into the entrance he'd widened.

That wasn't the end. With his other hand, he delivered another surprise. The clamps seemed to have wire extensions, which he pushed out to brace against her inner thighs. He locked them into place. He'd spread her even wider, rendering her completely helpless, so he could taunt her flesh however he wished.

This moment, that meant the relentless flicks of his fingers, pulling every layer of her pussy open—except the one place she longed to be touched the most. He came close, so damn close, so many times...*dear God...*

Her lungs heaved. Her hips trembled.

David turned his hand into a paddle instead.

"Breathe it down, D." He only spanked her once, but it was enough. Her pussy throbbed and ached in a dizzying combination of agony and ecstasy.

She seethed but worked at calming herself.

Kress came to her rescue in that department, pulling his cock out of her mouth and replacing it with a kiss. "Thank you, beautiful. That was magnificent."

"You're finished?" Disbelief clouded David's tone.

"Not by a long shot. But I don't want her getting an aneurism. Besides, you've got her bucking like a colt on crack. What the hell are you doing?"

"Just enjoying our girl." David pulled her so at least her head now rested on pillows, and the tension in her arms made it seem like she went from forming a T to a V. Though the blood in her head returned to normal, David wasn't so merciless on her bottom half. With the pussy clamps and thigh spreader still in place, he now scooted a foam wedge beneath her lower back, lifting her pelvis high for both men's scrutiny.

"Isn't that pretty." Kress. And, judging from the direction of his voice, it was his hand that wrapped around one of her ankles to steady her. "No," he added, sliding fingertips down the inside of her leg, "not pretty. Fucking gorgeous."

Dasha moaned again, long and low, telling them both how deeply she ached...how much she needed them. *Both* of them.

"Now *that's* pretty." There was a smile in David's voice. "Keep up the soundtrack, sweetheart. Maybe this will help you out."

The *this* to which he referred happened so fast, Dasha bypassed moans and went straight to screams. First, one of the guys released the spreaders. Her thighs turned to pools of relief—which was short-lived. The next second, the clamps got pulled off. Blood rushed her pussy. Before she could process the pain, somebody's mouth delved into her core, ruthlessly ravaging her clit. Every nerve ending there, which had been desperate for the contact, gave in at once to the assault of raw passion. Her buttocks clenched. Her arms wrenched at the chains. Even her toes tensed as she spiraled into a frenzy of fiery need.

"Shit," she cried. "Ohhhh, shit! Oh, please!"

"Please what?" David betrayed himself as her pussy's tormenter. "Say it." He bit her thigh with savage intensity. "Tell me, D. Tell me now."

Rational thought, she surmised, probably got left behind on the floor where her brain had been between Kress's legs.

Kress...*oh Kress*...

Now that she could identify the lover at her other side, she turned her face toward him, seeking him. She needed his brutally honest strength. He grunted, acknowledging her, wrapping his hold around her calf. She felt his erection against her inner knee, his desire at full attention.

Please. I need you.

But he didn't budge. Just devoted himself to watching over her, adoring her—and with that, lending her the strength to answer David.

"I need you," she blurted. "I need your cock inside me. Please."

David's teeth scraped her skin again. "Whose cock?"

The words burst from her without compunction. "Both of you. I—I want you both."

Asking it was like freedom. She knew damn well what she'd asked for. David would take her however he fucking pleased. Kress would do the same. Neither would show her body mercy. She was really glad she didn't have anything strenuous on the schedule for tomorrow, like performing. Or walking.

"Better than Beethoven to my ears." Kress's voice was a low, sensual drawl. His grip descended to her center, stroking her where David had just sucked and then dipping even lower. She shuddered in fresh arousal when his fingers got to her anus—but tensed when he stayed there, prodding the rim of her back hole with steady intent.

"Right." David snorted. "Because *you* listen to Beethoven."

"The hell I don't," Kress retorted. "And this"— he pushed his finger deeper up her backside—"is more beautiful than 'Moonlight Sonata'." He worked a second finger into her tight opening, persisting even as she jerked from his invasion. "Easy, darlin'. Relax and let me warm you up properly."

"Use this," offered David. The sweet scent of the lube tinged the air again. As Kress grunted his thanks, squeezing some onto the third finger he worked inside her, a strange uneasiness set in. His exhortation was a specter. *Relax. Let me warm you up proper.*

Warm her up...for what?

She didn't have time to ruminate. Seemed David had helped himself to the lube first. He slicked a generous amount up her vagina, working sensual magic with his long, knowing fingers. "You're so hot, babe," he murmured. "Your beautiful cunt wants me, doesn't it?"

"Yes." She was captivated by the lust in his voice and the torment of his fingers. *No,* she wanted to scream when he pulled out. She let out a distraught sigh until Kress compensated for the emptiness by getting one more digit into her ass.

Her breath launched to a tight cry. The pain was consuming, intrusive—but Kress kept pushing, widening her asshole with careful intent.

"Easy," he admonished again. "We're gonna do this nice and easy."

"G-Going to do—what?" She had to force it out, largely from being terrified of the answer. Kress poured more lubricant into her ass. His fingers started thrusting. Plunging deeper. Spreading her back hole wider. The slick shucks of it resounded in the air.

"Damn," David said. "That's such a nice sound. I think we need to sample it. We could lay it in as the backbeat of D's next single. The thing would go triple platinum."

He added some sound effects of his own. The rubbery slide of a condom. His deep groan of pleasure.

She flashed a sarcastic grimace his way. "Ha fucking ha."

Payback for that was the proverbial bitch. Two sharp strikes, one on each of her inner thighs, were accompanied by shocking stings. "That's two times you've spoken out of turn." David's tone carried the timbre that both thrilled and maddened. "So that's two turns with the crop. The disciplines get doubled from here, so if you want to take a little pain break..."

"No!" she exclaimed. "I mean—no, Sir. Please. I'll be—oh!" Her voice caught as Kress resumed his torment to her ass. "I'll t-try to be good."

"That's beautiful." David's voice slipped back to a husky rasp. "Beautiful, sweetheart."

Without another word to prepare her, he parted her labia, seated his cock, and drove inside her. Though Dasha gasped from the size and suddenness of him, she breathed and took his first strokes in obedient silence. Somehow, she knew this was also David's way of disciplining her. And testing her. For now, as Kress continued to slicken her back entrance, a clearer comprehension got pried open. It started in her mind and then slithered lower. Burned down to her stomach. Turned into a ball of apprehension.

"I'm in." David said it past locked teeth. One of his hands still gripped her thigh; the other dug into her waist as he shifted his angle, letting Kress get better access to her anus. "Damn, I'm in. Sweet God, D, you're gripping me like a vacuum."

"Yeah." Kress's tone was equally tight—with frustration. "And my fingers too. And that's gonna be a problem, darlin', unless you let a few muscles go."

Dasha bit her lip. Discipline or not, she had to speak. "I'm...scared."

Kress caressed her waist. "No shit. When you agreed to us both...you didn't know you agreed to us *both*, did you?"

"Crap." David slowed his pace in the wake of her affirming silence. But the other man didn't relent. Kress left his hands right where they were and continued in a voice she'd only heard out of him once before. It was the way he'd issued the mandate that he was coming to Atlanta with her and David.

"Okay, we're gonna be clear about it now. Let's start at the obvious. Do you *like* getting taken in the ass, D?"

Her mind did a rewind, remembering when she'd been in the other room with them both last week. She'd been locked in the stockade, spinning through the wonderland of subspace, and David had taken her in that illicit way. The pain had wrenched her back to reality—hard. But once he'd hit his rhythm, it'd taken naughty to a whole new level for her. And knowing she'd satisfied his body with that service... It'd been glorious. And ohhh yes, the way he'd pleasured her afterward... It'd been better than glorious.

Finally, she replied to Kress, "It's not bad."

"And do you like pleasing me too?"

That didn't take a mental trip at all. "Oh yes. Very much."

He changed his pressure at her back hole. No...shifted it. The intrusion wasn't from his fingers anymore. *Oh God.* It was...

"It's going to please me to be in your ass tonight, D."

It was the tip of his cock.

"But...what about...David?"

"Right here, sweetheart."

"He's going to stay right where he is. You feel him there, don't you?"

"Yes..." And she loved the position David took too. He straddled her left leg, curling one of his own across her abdomen, holding her thigh high so he could penetrate her with deep, long strokes. He was so close, so hot, so strong and solid against her.

"Good." Kress's voice came from a few feet above. She got the impression he was on his knees. He lifted her right leg a little higher, angling her back hole even better. "Now your body's just inviting me to the party too. And like I said, we're gonna take this nice and easy."

As if to prove that, he eased her blindfold off. She beheld Kress's beautiful face, gazing down at her with a satyr's smile gleaming against his stubbled jaw. She turned to David. His features were defined by unfiltered lust. He penetrated her with an intent stare. His mouth was slightly open as he dragged in air.

Only then did she dare a glance down. David's cock, still buried inside her, gleamed with her juices. Right next to it was Kress's erection, covered in a condom and thick layers of lube, the velvet head kissing her back entrance.

Shit shit shit.

She didn't know if she could be this naughty.

She curled her fingers, desperately grabbing the chains still holding her wrists. And gulped.

"You're so fucking amazing," David said. "What a good girl. Let him in, D."

She drowned the last of that with her shriek, as Kress finally breached her back opening. The size of him, in addition to David's occupation of her already, felt like she was being ripped down the middle. Torn. Filled.

A lot.

She hissed hard as he pulled out and then plunged back in. He went deeper this time. Lube sloshed inside her ass. Her thighs quivered from the pain.

"Christ," David declared. "Christ, this is good. He's almost there, sweetheart. Shit, you're amazing. The hard part's nearly over. Then this is going to feel incredible for you, I promise."

"Fuck. Off."

The bastards should've been glad they'd secured her arms. Both of their laughing faces would have brand-new black eyes otherwise. Making their arrogance tougher to take was the realization, over the next couple of minutes, that David's words proved more than empty platitudes. Dasha didn't want to prove him right. She wanted to hang on to her fury and tension, though admitted the stuff was a shield to hide what really happened in her heart as she gazed at her two dark lovers. Outrage was easier, *way* easier, than letting in the adoration that flooded her heart. The stuff wound deeper in as she watched their faces, both awash in passion, and their bodies, sleek portraits of the pleasure she gave them.

The pleasure she didn't want to share.

Oh...God...that she *couldn't* share.

Could she?

"Oh." She sighed as the first nibble of fire teased at her core.

"Oh," she repeated as the flames spread deeper.

The hot tendrils ignited her from the waist down. The feeling was, even to her thesaurus brain, indescribable.

"That's it." Kress's voice was one part encouragement and ten parts authority. "That's it, D. Take me deep."

Her eyelids started to flutter. Her breath came faster as her whole womb shook. Deep, indeed. It was like their cocks were sticks, rubbing against each other to kindle a secret forest inside her, faster and harder, setting flames free to consume her vagina, her pelvis, her pussy, her clit.

"Holy...ohhhh..." Her own voice sounded lost in a great wood, wandering through the inflamed mess but never wanting a way out. "Wh-What's happening?"

"Enjoy, sweetheart." David had never more been her lifeline to reality while at the same time never more her commanding lord in this surreal sexual journey. "He's helping me get you at the G-spot. Just let the fire take you."

How did he know? She didn't care. Hell, she could barely think. Her whole being became pure feeling, complete surrender, total immersion in how their bodies filled her. She shook everywhere as the inferno raged, blinding and resplendent.

"Oh...my..."

Words fled as the first inner orgasm rocked her. Her head jacked back, her arms strained, and the world exploded in shades of red and orange and white. It was heaven, hell, and everything in between. She'd never come like this, her pleasure going on and on, without an end in sight. She couldn't get enough, and yet, it felt like too much, too much, too—

"Damn." From somewhere in the fire came Kress's dark eruption. His fingers twisted tighter to her thigh. His cock drove deeper, harder into her ass. "Damn...*yes,* D."

With an equally conquering bellow, David came too. He kept pumping even after Kress slid out, repositioning himself for maximum contact with her clit. Again, it was exactly what she needed. Her next orgasm wasn't just fire but flood. David confirmed that, uttering past gritted teeth, "That's it, baby. Soak me. Give it all to me. Don't hold anything back."

Right. Like that was an option.

But not just her pussy wept. She was shattered. Exposed. Drained of any defenses, physical or emotional. As the sobs racked her, dual hands worked to free her arms. Then the guys cradled her together, dark bodies encasing her, as she shuddered and sobbed...

And wondered how she'd ever gone through life without knowing what this was like. No, not this. *Them.* These two brave, giving, passionate, beyond incredible men. They held on, stroking and silent, as she dissolved from the inside out. Her body trembled from the joy they'd given it. Her heart burst with gratitude and love.

She choked as the comprehension rocked her.

Ohhhh, shit.

She loved them.

Not so shocking where David was concerned. He'd had her heart long before he'd commanded her body. But Kress...

Kress, with his dorky metaphors. With his macho-man strut. With his crazy-ass protective streak.

Oh, God.

In just ten days, he'd roped her down and made her fall hard. *Hard.*

"Hey," said the object of her thoughts, cupping her shoulder with a big hand. "You're still shivering."

"Noticed the same thing," David said. Since she faced him, he kissed her on the lips. "You okay, sweetheart?"

"Yeah." She probably muttered it too fast—but getting the words out was miracle enough. "Yeah, I'm—" She dipped her head and burrowed deeper between them. More words begged for release. Her head wrestled them back. *Screw it,* her heart flung back. "I just...love you guys."

She kept her head down, hoping it sounded like something a subbie spilled in the afterglow of a typical bondage-ménage-orgasms-to-end-all-orgasms hour. Just the usual, flippant statement as you rested between the two hard, sweaty bodies of one's adoring Doms.

"Now *that's* something to sample into the next hit single."

Kress pressed closer along her back as he grabbed a soft towel from a supply in the nightstand and then gently cleansed her off.

"Agreed," David said, shifting his lips to her forehead. "And for the record, I love you too."

Though the words lightened her heart, she didn't reply. Extended conversation felt like focusing on a star after discovering the universe. She was glad David and Kress seemed to agree. She lay there, yearning for this moment to really become a universe and stretch into forever, until her brain went to fuzz and she fell into the bliss of sleep.

★ ★ ★

She woke up many hours later from the overriding need to pee—not a fabulous condition for slipping out from under the guys. The task was tantamount to peeling an orange from the inside out, almost inciting her to giggle aloud when done.

Kress really *was* rubbing off on her—and she had to get over it. He was going to be out of the picture soon. As soon as they found the weirdo behind the texts, he'd be on the next plane to Miami. They'd all return to life as normal. Whatever "normal" meant anymore.

She lingered in the bathroom after doing her business, lost to that rumination and all the conflicted feelings around it. It wasn't that David wasn't enough. Her Dom was more than she'd ever dreamed of in a lover, a friend, a leader. He'd opened the door to a world that was Oz, Middle Earth, and Wonka's Chocolate Factory combined, only better. All the magic, none of the calories. Trouble was, he'd pushed the door wide enough for Kress to fit too. There'd be a horrid emptiness for a while without Mr. Moridian around. She knew David would be the first to back her on that too. She knew it because she began to think of all the time they'd been together. So many times, these ten days had felt more like ten months, even years. The three of them just...meshed. And the magic was about way more than the sex...

Images filled her mind. The scenes ranged from serious to sublime to outright silly. She loved watching the two men laugh—and fight—with each other. They'd nearly come to blows the other night about whether to watch *Ghost Hunters* or *Deadliest Warrior*. But they agreed about many more things, stupid shit like German beer and Nike over Reebok...and not-so-stupid stuff like their mutual obsession for finding out who threatened her life.

They were both aggravating, stubborn, and dominating about it—and smart and funny and passionate...and dominating about all that too.

And she really wasn't getting back to sleep now.

She rounded the corner back into the bedroom and indulged in another long gaze at her men. The pair formed a strange hit single of their own, with their dueling snore rhythms. She smiled while throwing on the robe she'd found in the bathroom and then turned and headed upstairs. In the bedroom, she stole a glance at the clock while she changed into some sweats, a plain white T-shirt, and flip-flops.

4:12 a.m.

Another wicked grin came on as she remembered the last time she'd been sleepless around this time and what she'd done about it...and what David had done about *that*.

Fat chance he'd catch her sneaking in an orgasm this time. Number one, she'd learned that lesson. Number two, everything between her thighs and buttocks still throbbed in memory of what it had recently been through. But it was a beautiful pain, accompanied by the best memories of her life. To paraphrase Mary, a bondage that had set her free. A valley that had climbed to the most breathtaking cliff...a song that beat at her soul now, begging for release.

Without hesitation, she scooped up her guitar. She needed to be outside. For some reason, that was where she composed her best power ballads. And there was a full moon tonight, which meant the back garden was going to be beautiful.

By a small miracle, she found a can of green tea in the "magic beer fairy" refrigerator and popped it open. It was easy enough to pull a chaise to the middle of the garden lawn. The moonlight made everything magical, shining through the branches of the old magnolia tree, splaying a lattice of light on the grass. A little fountain was nestled at the base of the tree. Its streams pattered against marble cherubs, comprising the only sound around right now. Even the cicadas slumbered as the night held on to its last minutes.

She picked out a tentative tune. The music flowed naturally right now. The words played harder to get.

She tried a tentative verse. "Loving you both..." That ended on a fast grimace. "Ew. Disgusting, party of one!"

She started strumming again. The fountain cherub was an impervious audience.

The footsteps on the patio weren't so subtle. They came steady, sure and even—like the man to whom they belonged.

Her heartbeat did a fast forward, until she realized that was exactly what David wanted her to do. "You still slinking around in the shadows, Pennington?" she cracked. "Fine; you scared me for a second. You got m—"

She tried to suck in air for a scream. But that just helped the cause of the figure now consuming her vision, a stranger clothed completely in black, including his hands, feet, and ski-masked head. Her sharp intake pulled in more of the stuff on the cloth he rammed into her face. It smelled sweet. Really sweet. But artificial, like plastic. It overpowered her in nausea. But the bile wouldn't come up. Terror rammed it back.

Not David. Not David.

Oh God, *not David.*

Or Kress.

The fountain stopped gurgling. Then the clouds and the moon faded, just like the energy in her arms, her legs, her whole body. They went dark, numb, powerless.

Just like her vision.

Then her consciousness.

CHAPTER TWENTY-ONE

David yearned to succumb to exhaustion again. Since New York, his brain had been jacked on nonstop stress of one kind or another. It'd been heaven to pass out next to Dasha, knowing Kress literally had her back. With that assurance, he'd let his senses fall into obliteration. And damn, this bed was comfortable.

Only one thing could've coaxed him to move at all. Mmmm. Dasha was close and warm. He smiled, running a hand over her flesh, loving how she shifted a little beneath his touch and then scooted nearer. Maybe, he mused, they could rouse Moridian and think of some creative ways to greet the day together—

"Whoa! Gaahh!"

"Ahh!" he echoed. Moridian *was* roused, of that he'd almost gotten firsthand experience. He gaped across the tangled bedding now separating them. "Dude. Man. Sorry. I thought you were—"

"Got it." Kress tried to tame the rat's nest of his hair while throwing his brilliant stare around the room. "Speaking of which..."

"Yeah. Hear you." He wrapped the sheet around himself and called out, "D? Hey, D, where are you?"

He got up. Swept the bathroom and then peeked around the corner into the dungeon. The dark shadows gave up only the smell of disinfectant. Raife and Philip had left things spotless.

By the time he got back to the bedroom, Kress had yanked on his briefs. "I don't hear my favorite soprano yet."

"I think she's gone Dasha-style AWOL again."

"Okay." It came out nearly as a question. "So you're gonna call the ball on this one. Do we let her play hermit again, or do I really pay attention to the tickle in my gut this time?"

He tugged on his pants. "*You* get tickles?"

"Not often." The agent stepped into his jeans. "And not the good kind."

David did a double take at the guy's developing scowl. Kress wasn't kidding. Not even a little.

He forgot about locating his shirt and ordered his brain straight to logic. The simplest explanation was usually the truth. "She probably went upstairs to shower and change. Didn't want to wake us." He couched the last two words in air quotes.

"Yeah," Kress muttered. "You're probably right."

He peered harder at his friend. "Okay, the last time you wore that look, we were in Gap Kids before the shit went down at the mall."

"That's the last time I had the tickle."

He didn't waste another second to turn and bound up the stairs to ground level. Once he saw the normal world all appeared—well, normal—he forced a calming breath. He was going to find Dasha, give her a good-morning kiss to curl her toes, and then hit the intercom for the dungeon bedroom and give Moridian shit for being such a drama queen. After that, maybe the two of them could convince D to join them in making it a *really* good morning.

As he went up the back staircase, he took care to skip the third and sixth steps, knowing by now that they squeaked.

A little grin slid out as he stopped at the top. This place was actually starting to feel like home. Despite the insanity that'd forced them here, he and Dasha had started building something in this hideaway, a something that'd turned them both into better, more courageous people. And when Kress got added to the picture...Christ; small cities had been lighted on less electricity.

No wonder he smiled at those squeaky steps.

No wonder his pulse clamored at him to find Dasha.

He found their bedroom empty. The robe from the dungeon's bathroom lay sprawled on the bed. The bathroom was dark and silent too.

His heart rate spiked again.

"Get a goddamn grip on yourself."

Her guitar was missing too. That explained a lot. So Miss Music recluse *had* sneaked off somewhere. He'd just find her, assure that she was all right, and then leave her be for a while. His johnson could wait a few hours. His brain, and its need to confirm her safety, couldn't.

A peek into the solarium yielded only lazy motes in the early day sun. Pool deck turned up nothing too. That left the back garden.

David mentally kicked himself for not starting there. Would've been her first choice; it was where the senator had gone public about rededicating himself to their relationship. The space was sufficiently froufrou for her poetic songwriter's side, with the fountain and the flowers and...

She wasn't there either.

He turned to start back inside.

Just before his body kicked a new sensation at him.

A tickle, deep in his gut. An instinct making him want to puke.

"Shit."

He stalked across the patio, into the grass where one of the chaises had been dragged.

"Calm down. Calm the fuck down." *It's not like someone can waltz past the security system, get past the billion cameras between the perimeter and the house, and then just wait for Dasha to stroll by and—*

A weird smell teased. It was the faintest thing, but he knew it didn't belong here. Sweet but not floral.

What the hell?

His toe hit an overturned can of green tea. He picked it up and sniffed the opening. Not the smell.

He continued, following the tracks in the lawn leading to the chaise, swallowing hard with every step. They looked fresh. So did the nick in the lounger's armrest, which he stooped to get a closer look at. The finish was cleanly broken, as if something had rammed it. And the chaise's cushion...shouldn't have been askew like that. The bottom part hung over the side of the chaise, like whoever had been here had slid off the thing.

Or been dragged off.

Calm. Down.

So said his brain...

Before his stare caught on something else. A curious, crazy something else...in the ferns surrounding the fountain. Yeah, the fountain right next to the stone bench he'd envisioned in his little I'm-in-love-with-you-D fantasy.

No.

It couldn't be.

You're seeing things.

His legs, now disembodied from the corkscrew in his chest, somehow carried him across the grass.

He didn't want to look.

He had to look.

Just get it the hell over with, you stupid shit. You do know it's not what you think, right? Just because her guitar is in the flower bed...

Her broken *guitar...her prized Taylor acoustic...in the fucking flower bed...*

"Shit!"

He barely fought back the need to rip up the bushes. Instead, scraping a hand across his skull, he wheeled back toward the house—and began praying like hell that his horrific conclusion was seriously wrong.

★ ★ ★

He was disgustingly, hideously right.

He stood next to Kress in the mansion's security room, watching the man's rage balloon, as they watched the security video footage from the mansion's perimeter cameras.

The scene had been ripped from his nightmares. Dasha, limp as a rag doll, was carried past the pool, through the orchard, and out the front gate. Seconds later, an Escalade pulled up, black as the ninja outfit of the bastard who dumped her into the back seat. As he hopped into the front, the car took off.

"Son of a *bitch*." Moridian let out a guttural snarl before breaking into a full bellow. "Stratham! Parker! Why aren't you on the line to Atlanta PD yet? I also want all traffic-light footage within a five-mile radius taken between oh-four-hundred and now. I want it five minutes ago!"

David wished for his own excuse to tear off the roof like

that. Hell, in any form. Witnessing that bastard's hands on Dasha, grabbing her ass to secure her better on his shoulder, handling her like a fucking *commodity*...

Maybe he still *would* tear the goddamn monitor off the wall.

Then hurl it out the window.

Where the hell had a mistake been made? More importantly, who'd made it?

"He knew the code," he stated, peering at the footage again. "Am I right about that? If the guy forced the gate—"

"This place would've lit up like the Fourth of July," Kress supplied.

"So he found a way to get the code."

"Yeah."

"The code we changed yesterday morning?"

The agent's whole stature seethed a silent *yes*. "The only people who had it except us were key players from the CNN crew and the senator's entourage."

"So he found a way to get onto one of those teams." Frustration chewed his gut. "But we checked every goddamn credential. *Everyone* on those lists was cleared. No psychological blips. Not a single therapy session on their records."

"None that was traceable."

He closed his eyes. Pinched the bridge of his nose. Fought back another surge of bile. "*Shit.*"

"*Wait.*" Kress bit it out at the same second.

"What?" David leaned over, not missing how Kress had gone suddenly still.

The agent scrubbed his unshaven jaw before punching the computer's Back key. "This behavior." He tapped a pointing finger. "It doesn't add up."

David forced himself to peer at the same image. It was the shot of their ninja friend about to slip out the mansion's service gate with Dasha. "What do you mean?"

"He's carrying her like a tackle dummy."

"Thanks for the four-one-one."

"No, no. Don't you see? It doesn't fit. If this was our demented fanboy, he'd be pulling a Romeo Montague. He'd be cradling her like a lover."

David barely silenced a growl. "The fruitcake left a dead bird in her luggage, Moridian."

"Aware of that detail, man."

"Then you're aware he's not sane. He wants to *kill* her."

"Because he thinks he's worshipping her by doing so. 'Dasha dies and saves us all.' That's a statement you give to a martyr...or a lover. *This* bastard...he's delivering a product, not stealing a woman he's obsessed with."

"Which means...what? The real lunatic is still out there, and this guy is another crazy cocksucker?"

If it was possible, Kress's face contorted harder. "It means we might have been looking in the wrong direction the entire time."

He released a low snarl. "You mean...maybe there never really was a lunatic. That the note and the dove in Miami—"

"And maybe even our friend Mr. Smith in Atlanta," Moridian finished. "All part of something else. Something designed to make us look at the loony-tunes fans and the fringe society elements, instead of—" He interrupted himself with his own confused frown. "Instead of *what*? Damn it, that's the piece we're missing."

David let a heavy pause go by—just to see if the dread in his gut dissipated.

It didn't.

"Fuck."

Kress snapped his head up. "What?"

He forced his jaw to unclench. "The senator."

"What about him?"

"He's been heading up this development task force in Iraq. It was designed to open up commerce possibilities. *They* apparently love us for it, but—"

"Not everyone else in the region would," Kress filled in. "Or anyone over here who shares those world views."

"And if one of them got onto the senator's team and had access to all his *daughter's* information—"

"Stratham!" Moridian cut him off with another shout. "Let Parker continue the light checks. I want you to check the location of every member from Senator Moore's team who was here yesterday. Where are they right now, what are they doing, when they last took a shit. Everything!"

"Agent Moridian." Another agent stepped up, apparently out of the wall itself, though David recognized him at once. It was Phelps, the asshole who'd first grilled Dasha back in Miami. Same scuffed loafers. Same by-the-book gaze—which, in this case, was the guy's redeeming virtue. "I've already started the job. As soon as you and Mr. Pennington linked the breach back to yesterday's visitors, I began cell traces on all the senator's staffers."

Kress expelled an audible breath. "Good thinking, man."

Phelps shook his head. "Only by half. The numbers we're able to trace all show up at the Four Seasons, where the senator is staying. But there's at least a half-dozen numbers we *can't* trace. They're secured lines, invisible to us."

Before Phelps finished the sentence, Kress started bolting

out the door. "Not anymore they're not."

The library, appearing more a command center by the day, was down the hall. In less than a minute, Kress reached it, hitting the threshold like a man possessed. Less than a minute later, he'd opened a secure video line on his laptop. "I'm damn glad I told Corso I needed to have at least one way of accessing her," he clarified.

They watched, both barely containing their tension, as the call started ringing through. When Corso didn't pick up the summons after four rings, David backed toward the door. "That's it. I'm gonna go find D's phone. The senator's private line has to be on—"

On the sixth ring, the call was picked up—but Corso's features didn't fill the screen. A sleep-tousled brunette in a barely-there tank top squinted into the camera. "Hello?" The next second, she lost the mumble. Her eyes opened wider. "Oh! Kress! Hey." She scraped chunks of hair into her face. "Crap. I look like a toad right now. I didn't think it would be you. Shit."

For a second, David wondered about the woman's familiar tone. Then he recognized her from dinner last night. Petite. Glasses. Eyes behind those glasses, containing very naughty plans for Moridian.

"Natalie." Kress's response was cordial but complete business. "Where's Corso?"

"Uh—who?" The woman's fuzzy stammer confirmed her flirtations with Kress last night had been lent liquid courage.

"Crystal Corso." Moridian stressed every syllable to the breaking point. "Your boss, remember? Isn't this her secure video line?"

"Uh...yeah. Um, not here. She told me she'd be getting up early to handle some business with her company in Buenos

Aires. She took her right-hand guy, Zack, to help. I'm on video duty." A sultry smile crept across her lips. "You into a little voyeur action, sweetie? Or do you just wanna come over and—"

"Buenos Aires?"

David fired it in unison with Moridian. They exchanged knowing glowers.

"What company in Buenos Aires?" Kress demanded. Thankfully, the woman was too bleary to notice their uptick of urgency or that she'd just spilled the biggest heap of incriminating shit of the morning. Hell, of the entire investigation.

"Her dad left it to her when he died a couple years ago, but she's a silent partner, because it's not great for her political rep to have an off-shore business. It's all boring stuff like shipments and commodities and exports and imports. She calls them a couple of times a month and—"

"Natalie!"

The woman actually jumped as Kress shouted it. "Jeez! What?"

"Listen to me. I need Corso's cell phone number. Now."

It looked like his order penetrated her hangover haze— until she stuttered, "Kress. I—"

"*Now,* damn it! Dasha Moore's been abducted. Does that part register? The only way we can find her is through that number."

The woman's face crumpled. "Oh, Kress. God, I'm sorry. I don't have it. She changed it yesterday."

"*What?*"

"She said it was for security reasons and she'd give me the new number when she got back today."

David kicked a dent into the wall while Kress shoved

a stack of files to the floor. He disconnected the call without saying anything else to Natalie. The guy lurched to his feet, clawing back his hair, as haggard as the woman he'd just switched off. His gray T-shirt looked like a trash bag. The fly of his jeans was barely zipped.

But when he spoke again, the agent was completely confident of every syllable. "All right. We're gonna have to do this the hard way—which means we do it right, every second of it, the first time."

"I'm in," David stated.

"Damn straight you are." The agent grimaced. "Now go find D's phone. It's time to tell the senator the truth about his adorable little Crystal."

CHAPTER TWENTY-TWO

Sweet little Dasha. Sweet little Dasha.

She moaned, fighting her way back to the dream. Mom was singing to her, making the tune a little half whisper so she'd fall asleep, but she giggled, trying to stay awake.

Sweet little Dasha.

The dream grew fainter. She couldn't see Mom anymore. And her head felt like a gigantic, pain-filled boulder. "Don't go," Dasha begged the dream, only to wonder why her tongue wouldn't cooperate. Cotton lined the inside of her mouth. Dirty cotton. She just wanted to go back to sleep...

"You're awake."

Definitely not Mom. It was more like a school nurse with a thermometer caught up her butt, crossed with Crystal "I'm-Too-Perfect-For-My-Pants" Corso.

"Well. I was hoping you'd stay a good little pseudocorpse, but so be it. Soon enough for the real thing."

Dasha forced an invisible crowbar beneath her eyelids. It took a couple of seconds more for her eyes to fully focus.

When she did, she wished she hadn't.

It *was* Crystal. The woman wore a silky ivory turtleneck and matching cashmere pants, which seemed a ridiculous outfit, given the surroundings. The place looked like a man-cave designed by Davy Crockett, with dark-wood walls crossed by heavy timber support beams, a stacked-stone fireplace, and accents of iron and steel everywhere. A real bearskin rug lay underfoot; the animal's head had been mounted on the wall just before the entrance to the black granite kitchen. Sure, because *that* was appetizing.

All of those observations faded when Dasha's gaze fell to the pine dining table in front of her. Red candles, yet to be lit, rimmed three sides of it. They surrounded a surface upon which thousands of pictures and photos had been dumped.

Thousands of images...of her.

"What...the...?" Even her whisper sledgehammered her brain. Surely she'd imagined the sight. Time to rub away the sleep completely.

Not happening. She couldn't raise her hand. Or any part of her arm. She looked down to discover all four of her limbs bound to the dining chair by tight rope gauntlets. Her torso was also secured, the ropes wrapped just below her breasts. They dug in so tight, breathing felt like pushing on a wall.

She repeated, with deepening outrage, "What...the...?"

"Relax," Crystal crooned. She added with a slick smirk, "*Darling.*"

The utterance put an icy edge on Dasha's fury. The woman's voice was a verbal scalpel, slicing with deep deliberation—and complete confidence in her control.

Of everything.

Sure enough, as Dasha's mind shifted beyond first impressions, she noticed discerning—and disturbing— elements about this place. Beyond the cabin, she heard only the wind in trees, some small creatures scampering, and the distant tap of a woodpecker. She smelled only pine and sap.

A forest. And not a pretty, pseudo-wilderness-at-the-edge-of-town deal.

They weren't in Atlanta anymore, Toto.

"Shit." It sounded lonely and defeated, instead of the terror beating her blood. "Crystal, why..." She shook her head, unable to voice the hideous truth at the edge of her conscious. But she fought to force it out. "Is this—are you—"

"Have something you want to spit out? Or do you just want to shut up and keep still, as I've always preferred you?"

Though Crystal's tone still dripped honey, Dasha was certain the woman meant to suffocate her remaining courage with it. And perhaps, a couple of weeks ago, Crystal would've succeeded. The Dasha of that time would've succumbed to the role of petrified kidnap victim and then bargained with Corso for her life. But not now. She'd confronted so much about herself in these last weeks, stripped clean of her excuses for honesty, just as her body had been stripped by the most generous men she'd ever known. For the surrender of her body, she'd been given emotional freedom, physical ecstasy, and sexual highs beyond words.

For the honesty of her spirit, she'd gotten even more.

She gotten back her father.

She wasn't about to let that go now. No way in hell would she let David and Kress down.

Or Dad.

Which meant she had to handle the lunatic bitch in front of her, here and now, on her own.

"It was you, wasn't it?" She drilled an unblinking stare across the room. "You sent the text to everyone, back in Miami. You'd have the security clearance to get all the addresses, so you did. And then you—"

"Don't be ridiculous." Crystal strode to the stove, lifted a lid on a pot, and stirred the savory-smelling stuff inside. "As if I have time to blast texts to all those idiots." She flashed another demure smile. "I had Zack do it, of course. That's what he's there for."

Forget the chill in her blood. It turned to sheer ice. She thought about those terrifying hours, after the texts had hit everyone's phones. The confusion in everyone's eyes. The fear and the uncertainty. So many wondering if one of their own was even responsible—until she'd found the mutilated dove atop her suitcase and the realization striking that only an outsider could be that sick.

"I don't understand."

"Oh, come on." Crystal rolled her eyes. "You do remember Zack, my personal assistant? Cute little hipster type, would do anything for your father and me?"

"I know Zack," Dasha snapped.

"Then what's the problem?"

"I don't understand...*why*." She stared at the witch who stood there so serenely, brewing her damn stew...undoubtedly laced with arsenic. "I've never done a thing to you. So why did you go through all that? Send the texts...and the dove..." She swallowed, throat clutching. "And what about the shooter at the mall? Did you sic Zack on him too?"

"I'm not a complete monster, Dasha." She set the pot's lid back with a hard *clang*. "Mr. Smith and his rifle were a fluke we didn't expect. Granted, a fortuitous fluke, but—"

"A fluke?" She shook her head, struggling with the wild ride of her senses. Horrified ice, then an inferno of outrage, and then back again. "A *fortuitous* fluke? People could've been killed. Do you understand that, you half-baked psycho-bitch?"

Crystal wheeled. Pounded the counter with her stew ladle. "I. Am. Not. A monster!" She grimaced at the culinary spatter art she'd inflicted on her perfect pants. "Everything I did—*everything!*—was for your father. Damn you! Don't you understand? I did it for the great politician he can become!"

"Really?" Dasha found her quiet sneer easy to achieve. "Enlighten me on that."

"You stupid girl. As far as your star has risen, it amazes me you don't get this." Crystal crossed her arms and leaned against the wall. She stood right under the bear head.

Sometimes, irony did have a sense of humor.

"Fine." The woman rolled her eyes and huffed. "Here's your enlightenment, dear. The party came to your father about the possibility of the presidential bid. He was, as he always is, modest to a fault about the idea—but we needed to show he could sway influence in Florida. We needed some publicity there..."

"And I happened to be there too—with the tour."

The woman's flawless Revlon brows arched. "For once, you were in the right place at the right time."

Dasha ignored the slam. "So you staged the texts and the stalker-style stuff, knowing it would land my name in the local press?" She snorted. "Okay, that's a big stretch. The FBI told us they didn't talk to anyone about the case. And I believe them."

"And *we* wouldn't have it any other way," the woman assured, going velvet cool once more. "Controlling the information leaks is key on a project like this, *n'est-ce pas, cherie?*"

Dasha didn't give her the satisfaction of rising to the bait. Besides, the more Crystal relaxed, the more she turned back to the stove, which meant the opportunity for Dasha to visually sweep the room for a means of escape. Not that a lot of possibilities sprang up.

Inspiration hit. Loosen the ropes by tipping herself over?

Hop the chair backward to the large oak chest behind her and hope one of those drawers contained cutlery? She'd already noticed the hefty chopping knife on the counter. Its blade was littered with diced vegetables. Dasha swore that if Crystal tried another "darling" or "cherie," she'd get to that thing somehow and add the woman's guts to the mess.

Crystal stirred her pot and continued. "The fact that Ambrose Smith took it upon himself to expand the case so publicly...well, that was an unexpected twist." She chuckled and shook her head in wonderment. "Talk about accelerating the process!"

Dasha narrowed her gaze. "Nice to know nearly killing my bodyguard could help you out."

"Dasha," Crystal returned, "grow *up*. Do you know how many downloads your new song got after the incident at Lenox Square? Sentiment for you grew exponentially. And we had to bump the campaign announcement up by three weeks!"

The raw delight in the woman's voice was worthy of an open squirm. Dasha shoved against her bonds, knowing what claustrophobics felt like for the time in her life. It wasn't just the ropes around her body. It was the place Crystal's explanation led her to, the question she had to ask...

The answer she did *not* want to hear.

"Okay, so all of this"—she rolled her head, indicating their surroundings and her ropes—"is another episode for the saga, right? Another gripping drama to somehow re-spark the campaign?"

Crystal went still. Too still. "Darling, thanks to you, there *isn't* a campaign right now." She tilted her head, looking troubled, as if delivering a hard life lesson to a small child. "And you see...that's not acceptable. Not one single bit. I won't let it be. I've worked entirely too hard to get this far." She turned, smooth as the cashmere encasing her body, to check her stew again. "So that really leaves me with no choice about our next actions, does it?"

Another breath.

Another breath.

The words were easier to obey if she mentally layered David's and Kress's voices over the words. She didn't question why. She only knew it worked.

Breathe.

The strength of their voices fused with her lungs.

Breathe.

The force, even their echoes, fortified her will.

"Okay," she found the strength to say. "I'm going to ask again: What the *hell* do you mean?"

No answer from Crystal—because she was too busy cocking her head, sharp and birdlike.

Because she'd just heard something.

A car had arrived. Was rolling to a gravelly stop in front of the cabin.

A long stillness followed.

"Ah!" Crystal's happy chime rang in the air like a gunshot. "Perfect. Just in time."

"F-For wh-what?" It was shrill and scared, and she couldn't help it. Crystal's manic joy conveyed the horrid truth. This really wasn't just an episode of *The Perils of Dasha*. This was a well-orchestrated plan, formed in the mind of a woman not used to getting "no" handed to her in the middle of a live CNN interview. A woman not used to *no*, period.

The front door swung open. A rush of late summer sun brought along blinding sunlight as its buddy. Another pair of pals filled the portal. First in was Zack, Crystal's assistant, whom she recognized from the events of yesterday. The guy's plaid mountain-man shirt and jeans were a far cry from the Brooks Brothers suit in which she'd first met him, though his haughty frown hadn't changed an inch. Zack dragged in a second man, also wearing jeans, though this guy's outfit was topped with a T-shirt from Dasha's first concert tour. At the moment, however, the prisoner's biggest fashion pieces were shaking shoulders and unsteady steps, worsened by the black cloth bag covering his head.

As soon as Zack shut the door, he yanked the bag off.

"What the fuck?" The oath was a contrast to the guy's boyish features. "What're we doing *here*? This is just my family's stupid cabin, man."

Zack backhanded him. Dasha winced. The poor kid couldn't be more than nineteen or twenty.

"Watch your language," Zack ordered. "There are ladies present."

"What's this all about, asshole? You show up at my dorm, tell me I've won a contest to meet Dasha Moore, but then you make me wear this goddamn hoodlum thing, and now—"

The kid's jaw fell open as his gaze fell on her. Dasha tried to give him a reassuring smile because she had a feeling what he'd go through next. Sure enough, Zack jerked the boy's hands forward, cranked his wrists into a pair of handcuffs, and then kneed him in the back. With a stunned groan, he crumpled to the floor between her and Crystal. The kid cried out, still half-furious, though terror rapidly took over and doused his voice to a whimper. She didn't blame him one bit.

"Darling, I'm pleased to introduce Mr. Austin Taylor," said Crystal. "He's the one who's already left a confession note in his dorm room about sending all those nasty texts to your show crew. And he's about to send another round of texts too... this time with pictures, showing them how he's succeeded in killing you."

CHAPTER TWENTY-THREE

"This has got to be a mistake."

It was the twenty-fifth time the senator muttered it. And the twentieth time Kress followed it by exchanging a glare with David.

His friend's face conveyed exactly what it had the previous nineteen times. *You wanna deck him, or can I?*

Kress longed to be tapped for that honor, but the circumstances were the worst setting for it. They were surrounded by the finest ops guys on Kress's team, twenty square miles of forest, and a shitload of anxiety-amped atmosphere.

The only one who didn't share their collective mindset of *holy crap* was the senator—AKA King Head-in-the-Sand. Dude still believed a string of theories reading more like a bad soap opera. Dasha was grabbed by a mansion employee gone rogue...or an exceptionally resourceful, wing-nut fan... or a lunatic they'd somehow missed. Because any or all of them could've pulled this off after a sweeping, two-week investigation. At five in the fucking morning. In a mansion with such tight security, air molecules needed a password.

He was just waiting for Moore to throw an alien abduction into the mix.

In the next damn thought, granted the guy a mile of leeway.

Given the same circumstances, would *he* be reacting any

differently? Avoiding the truth any more than the senator was? Denying to see how the woman he most deeply trusted was also the puppeteer behind his daughter's stalker nightmare—and now her disappearance?

There wasn't time for philosophical debate.

They had to stop Corso from making Dasha vanish forever.

He prayed, for the countless time today, they weren't too late.

"Senator." David locked Moore's stare directly in his own. "You're all for keeping an open mind, right?"

Moore gave Pennington a head-to-toe assessment. "Of course."

David didn't surrender his stance. "Good. That's all Agent Moridian and I ask of you now."

Kress had no idea if this was the first or the five hundredth time his friend had undergone the Papa-Bear-Protective thing from Moore, but David climbed a few more rungs of esteem in his book for the way he handled it now.

"Let's just get the hell on with this," Moore finally muttered. "But if you're wrong, so help me God, I'll—"

A harsh *zziippp* raked the air, sounding like a hummingbird on steroids. Kress stepped between the two men, slashing his hand in front of his throat in the universal command for silence. He recognized the *zip* as their greeting from Whitehurst, his number-one recon agent, a warning that they approached the location of Zack's traced cell signal. Since they were at a blind spot about Crystal's phone, they'd taken a stab and guessed their ninja from the mansion's security tapes was in fact Zack, invited in on a cut of Crystal's glory once Dasha was out of the way.

With a tap to the comm-pod at his ear, he opened the radio line. "Hey there, Tighty-Whitey," he murmured to his friend.

"Glad you all could join us, Kress-Man," said the recon agent. "We still have the ride-alongs?" He referred to David and the senator.

"Affirmative," Kress replied.

"No prob. Just advise how we alter the plan, then?"

"Not by a damn thing." Kress cast a cautious glance around. "You just make sure we got the bogey first. But after that, you have my authorization to move in."

They moved another fifty feet, and that was when a sizable vacation cabin appeared through the trees. The place looked like a magazine ad: wind chimes jingling in the breeze, the sunlight skittering across the roof, designer porch furniture, a gleaming black Escalade parked in front.

"License plate on the car checks out," came Whitehurst's voice over the line. "It's the rental signed off to Zack Crean, two days ago."

"Got it," Kress confirmed. "Let's all move in quietly. Get a visual first if you can."

"You're really dragging the senator with you?"

"I have no choice about that, Whitey. Some hardheads need a burning bush to believe."

Any comeback Moore might have had for that got eliminated by a scream, full of pain and fear, bursting from the cabin. Though the outcry carried a distinct male timbre, their "slow and careful" plan got instantly scuttled.

Kress whipped out his Glock and darted to a deep shadow beneath one of the cabin's side windows. He motioned for David and Moore to follow. After a few seconds to assure they hadn't been heard, he prepared to dare a look inside, but Corso rendered that risk unnecessary.

"Damn it, be *careful,* Zachary!"

"How else do you expect me to make him cooperate?"

"I don't *care* how you make it happen; just don't get him all bruised up. It needs to look like this was all *his* idea, right?"

"All his—what?" The interjection came from someone young, male, and terrified. Likely the source of the scream, Kress deduced. "You people are fucked up! What the hell?"

There was a sigh, also male. "Can't I just get him a little high, maybe? I've been dealing with his disgusting mouth since we left the city, Crys."

Kress snuck in a sideways look at the senator. Instinct told him Zack's use of the nickname wouldn't sit well with Moore. He was right, judging from the tension at the man's mouth and temples.

"No," came Corso's retort. "You're not going to jeopardize this, damn it. We only have this last piece to slide into place. Then the wheels will start to turn again." She took a pair of demanding steps. "Nothing is going to stop me from getting to the White House. *Nothing.*"

"You?"

This time, it was Dasha. Relief flooded Kress so completely, he indulged a peek through the window. David joined him, though the guy swore beneath his breath once they beheld the state she was in. Corso had her bound at multiple points to a sturdy wooden chair. The table next to her looked like something out of a "World's Creepiest Murders" documentary. Dozens of candles. Thousands of photos.

One gun.

As if the weapon wasn't lying there in front of her, Dasha spat, "The last time I checked, it wasn't you they wanted for the job, Crystal."

"Who says I want it?" The woman laughed. "First Lady will be just fine for now, darling. And when I'm the one to help your daddy pick up the pieces of himself after you're found as the first half of this murder-suicide, that wedding ring will be locked on my finger."

Kress and David got to the senator in time to clamp him down by his shoulders. If they hadn't, Kress was sure Moore would've dived through the window. Kress tried to flash an assuring glance. It sucked that Moore had to learn Corso's true colors like this—but sometimes it took a burning bush to create a believer.

"God." Dasha's rasp seemed deafening against the onerous pause inside. "Austin's right. You *are* fucked up, Crystal. And if you think you're going to pull this off without anyone investigating, then you're fucked up *and* stupid."

Kress's chest swelled with fierce warmth. *That's my girl.*

Corso answered D with lethal calm. "Shut up."

"No. If you think David Pennington and Agent Moridian will accept all of this at face value—"

"Shut *up.*"

"If you think they won't tear the facts apart, if they won't tear *this* place apart—"

"I said *shut up!*"

The woman's voice busted into a shriek—a blessing in disguise. Kress used the cover to scuttle undetected to the cabin's corner. "Southeast corner secured," he gritted into his headset. "Whitey, let me know the *second* you've got the perimeter locked in." Another blessing: concentrating on ops made it easier to ignore the loud *smack* from inside. From Dasha's pained grunt, it sounded like Corso had decided to get physical—and not in a fun way.

"God," the woman gritted. "You really are a little idiot."

Kress lifted his head, able to spot Corso directly now. Her head was dipped low, her stare slicing down at the woman who'd forever altered his heart.

"Sweet, cute little Dasha," she sneered. "You know, you wouldn't be in this position if you'd only stayed in your place. The gap between your father and you was such a perfect fit for me, darling. Why, *why* did you have to go and close it up? Now all you've created is a mess. Happy with yourself?"

He should've expected Dasha's reaction, but even now, even knowing her and caring for her as he did, the woman could stun him.

"If this is between you and me, then let's make it between you and me." She nodded at the young man on his knees next to them, who grimaced in numb terror. "But don't drag Austin into this. He has nothing to do with this. Don't let his blood be on your hands too."

Goddamn it, Dasha. You pick the strangest times to put everyone else ahead of yourself.

That was when the realization hit him.

Forget caring about her.

He loved the woman.

Undeniably. Uncontrollably.

Fuck. And he derided *her* for crappy timing?

Focus. There'd be time to think about that mess when Crystal Corso wasn't laughing like a giddy sitcom track. "Blood?" she echoed. "Oh no, darling. The only thing on my hands will be this stew I whipped up for your dad. He loves my stew, you know. He's always grateful when I find a way to make him some, even when we're on the road together. As soon as it's done, we can get on with having our friend Austin put a bullet in your brain."

"Fuck you, lady!" Austin shrieked.

Kress liked that kid. *Keep it up, Austin. Your Wolverine act may come in handy.*

In direct contrast, Zack's voice was a low, rich-boy sulk. "I still think we should wait until nightfall. Less chance of being ID'd as we leave the woods."

"By who?" Corso snapped. "A handful of squirrels and that ancient excuse for a man who runs the store at the bend? He reeked of Jim Beam anyway. Any testimony he'd give will be tossed like last week's polls." She sighed. "Besides, much as I hate admitting it, darling Dasha is right. Moridian is a bulldog. He won't turn over rocks to try to find her; he'll blast through the damn things."

"You're right about that, bitch," Kress muttered.

"Fine." Zack's comeback took them all by surprise. The guy went from cool-hand to hothead inside ten seconds. "You want to do this, then let's do it, damn it."

Kress didn't like the sound of that. Not one fucking bit. "Whitey." The growl clawed up his throat, rough and urgent. "What's the sitch on the perimeter, man?"

"Nice and pretty," Whitey came back. "We're good, K. Repeat: we're good."

Inside, Corso cackled again. "What on earth got all over you?"

"Lately?" Zack snapped. "It hasn't been *you*. And I'm done with the games. So you wanna do this? Let's just do it."

Kress popped to the balls of his feet at the same time bodies scuffled inside the cabin.

"No!" Austin shouted. "Fuck you! No!"

"Crystal!" The scream was Dasha's. "Please! You don't have to do this! Please!"

If her outcry wasn't enough to rip his guts out, what Kress saw next took care of that job with horrifying force.

He dived forward without another thought.

CHAPTER TWENTY-FOUR

Your whole life in front of your eyes.

Dasha knew the words, of course. She even imagined she'd know what such a thing felt like, if she ever knew her own death was coming. She'd envisioned what images would come to mind. A journey through her childhood? High school music shows? Maybe a visit from Mom, taking her hand and serenely welcoming her to the other side.

She didn't see a thing.

Everything was only...

Sound.

The strains of the first song she'd ever composed, at the age of eight. The music at Mom's funeral.

Then just the voices.

Dad whooping in joy when she'd won her first Grammy. The shouts of her fans at the mall in Atlanta. And then David...

Oh, David...

His sarcastic drawl. His biting one-liners. The first time she'd ever heard his adoring murmur. *You're beyond beautiful.* And the lower cadence that took her heart and soul to amazing places. *Kneel. Good girl. You please me so much.*

And Kress. Yes, he was there too. His gruff bark of a laugh. The growl that consumed him when she aroused him. And the words *he* used too. *Look at you... You're gorgeous...*

She used their voices to get the strength. Clung to them as she stared into the barrel of the gun Zack forced into Austin's hand—and then pointed at her face. Felt the heat of them in the tears scalding her cheeks as she braced for the coming explosion.

Soon enough, her Doms' voices would be hauntings in her soul instead of memories in her mind.

No.

No.

She hated that thought. Struggled to find their voices again, but all was black and dark and scary. Forget about going Zen or seeing radiant light. There was nothing radiant about this. There was nothing peaceful, complete, or celestial. *I don't want to do this. I'm not ready to do this.*

Where were the voices? Where were David and Kress to keep her sane through this?

"Move in! Now! Everybody move!"

"You heard the man! Let's do it!"

There they were. But she barely had a moment for gratitude. The detonation came. The world was a blast of motion, sound, noise, chaos. Windows crashing. Voices bellowing. Feet pounding. The timber floors shaking.

And then, the noise she dreaded the most.

The gun went off.

The pain hit hard.

Only not in her head. It flared from her shoulder. She blinked, disoriented. It took a strange second to realize she'd been...pushed over. She was on the floor, still bound to the chair, now staring at an army of booted feet and black-clad legs. *Black*—what Zack had been wearing when he took her from the mansion—which confused her deeper. Were these more of the bad guys or—

"Don't move, Corso. Not a single fucking muscle."

A sob escaped. Kress's command at Crystal was the best music she'd heard in a long time.

The good guys had arrived. Definitely the good guys.

"Hard-ass." She couldn't help cracking it, even with her cheek mushed on the floor.

"Don't you forget it." His voice was a miracle of warmth. She pulled that ribbon into her heart and wrapped herself in its beautiful strength.

The world spun again. She'd been jerked upright, and the asshole FBI agent from Miami wasn't looking such a jerk-off anymore as he went to work on her ropes with lethal-looking scissors. She forgot all about him the next second anyhow. More joy turned the ribbons in her heart into a delirious Maypole dance as David appeared next to her. He fell to his knees, not taking his gaze off her. Tears careened down her cheeks as she stared back. A full smile lifted his noble lips, though exhaustion tormented his temples.

He was the most perfect sight she'd ever seen.

"Holy fuck, Dasha." It grated out of him.

Thank God her arms were freed first. Every inch of them stung from being in the ropes so long, but she wrapped herself around him with all the might they'd give. When the ropes fell from her legs, she dropped into his lap, shaking and crying harder.

His lips pressed to her forehead, warm and incessant. "Are you okay?"

She managed a nod. Burrowed against his shoulder. From that vantage point, she took in a scene she hadn't dared hope for. Kress slammed a pair of handcuffs on Crystal, rattling off her Miranda rights with glee. While he did, a couple more agents carefully took steel-cutters to the cuffs on Austin, who didn't let even that distract him from his grip on the gun Zack had forced on him—likely because he now aimed the weapon at Zack himself. Like the guy was going anywhere fast with that bullet planted in his shoulder. Zack moaned, trying to push upright with his good arm.

"Stay prone, ass-face," Austin ordered. "I purposely aimed for your shoulder instead of your eyes, thinking these gentlemen might want to fry your ass in court. I'm not opposed to rethinking that if you give me cause."

Kress chuffed. "Whitey, get this kid signed up for agent training as soon as he clears college." His stance tightened, though, as Crystal wheeled on him.

"You have *no* idea what kind of mistake you've made, Agent." She seethed every word.

Kress actually lobbed back a shit-eating grin. "Is that so?"

"What kind of evidence do you have here? It's circumstantial at best, and when Senator Moore gets words that you've treated me like this—"

"He'll wonder why Agent Moridian didn't cuff *and* gag you."

Dasha's grin disappeared in the wake of her gape. She struggled to stand, but her knees crumbled, still half-numb. David swept in from behind, supporting her with little effort so she could launch herself at the newest arrival in the cabin. "Dad!"

He returned her embrace with a crushing hug. "Dasha. Oh darling, I'm so sorry."

"It's okay," she whispered. "I'm just glad you're here."

She pulled back to see Dad trading a long stare with David. Her father's smile glowed with respect as he angled her toward him, kind of a bizarre twist on wedding day symbolism.

"Take care of her, Pennington."

David tucked her hand into the crook of his elbow with heart-melting surety. "I will, sir."

"Damn straight you will." Dad said it with a smirk, but his face took on a resigned slant. "If you'll excuse me, I need to take care of something urgent."

"Of course."

Dad pivoted with the precision of his Marine Corps background and then paced right to Crystal. Dasha swallowed, now very interested in his "something urgent."

"Mark." Her lips trembled with poor-me perfection. "Oh, thank God!"

"Crystal." Dad's tone didn't betray a thing. As a matter of fact, the last time Dasha heard him sound so flat it was to tell her about Mom's cancer prognosis. Just like then, her heart responded in raw fear.

"Mark—"

"Shut up. Just shut up, Crystal."

Everyone in the cabin went still. Her father turned, scrubbing a hand across his jaw. "I need to say just two things to you."

Crystal raised her chin with queenly dignity. Dasha admitted it: ballsy move. And delusional. Definitely delusional.

Dad leaned toward her. Dasha watched his shoulders bunch up. "First—if you even sneeze in my daughter's direction ever again, I'll hunt you down, wherever you are, and end your sorry life myself. And second—"

He grabbed a dish towel, using it to lift the big pot off the stove top and dump its contents down the front of Crystal's pants.

"I hate your goddamn stew."

★ ★ ★

The setting sun painted the pines in deep gold and amber. A twilight breeze brushed the air, crisp and sharp. Dasha took in a deep lungful, trying to ingest the peace it promised. But like the other ten times she tried, the effort was futile.

She was alive. It was a miracle. A gift from fate she couldn't ignore.

Which meant she had to honor the other gift she'd been given in these crazy, amazing weeks. She'd learned the lesson of speaking her truth...especially when that truth involved the two most important men to her.

She just had to stop thinking about what would happen afterward.

Telling them both would mean losing them both. David and Kress had played nice so far, but that was with the understanding that everything was temporary. On a day-to-day basis, they both woke up and poured possessiveness into their coffee along with the cream—and she didn't envision either of them going cold turkey on the shit.

But your alternative sucks. Big-time.

The alternative *wasn't* an alternative. She'd almost died with this confession still locked in her heart—her personal glimpse of hell.

They both had to know. And then she had to deal with the consequences, whatever they'd be.

What *did* a double broken heart look like?

She was saved from the brood about that by a rustic creak behind her. Somebody stepped from the cabin and then started approaching. Her heart, still thrumming in her throat, sped up again. The forceful footsteps in the pine needles gave him away.

David.

As soon as he stepped into view, her throat closed completely. It was so unfair, how total fatigue made him look this good. The dark stubble across his jaw, the roguish spikes of his hair, and the overcaffeinated sparks in his eyes all flipped pancakes in her stomach. In this moment, the effect was even worse—or better, depending on the outlook—because another element defined his features too.

Total adoration. Funneled on her.

"It's getting cold." He took off his jacket and swept it around her shoulders. "What are you still doing out here? I opened the car. The heater's on."

"I know." She pulled one of his hands to her lips. "And thank you. But..."

"But what?" He coaxed her face up with the pad of a thumb. "You okay?"

"I need to say something."

Well that *was graceful.*

No points for grace, D. Stick to the mission.

As she expected, his gaze turned dark pewter. "All right." His voice hardened to the same texture.

"It...involves..." She escaped his scrutiny for a second by glancing toward the cabin. "Where's Kress?"

The subject of her question lumbered out just as she said it. Kress looked modern-Highlander hot in his head-to-toe black and wild hair. His own face went heavy metal when he saw her. He jerked a brow at David. "I thought you put her in the car ten minutes ago."

"I thought the same thing. But sometimes, as we know, this one doesn't listen the first time."

The corner of David's mouth hitched. "Creates endless

possibilities for discipline, at least."

David grinned. "Well said, my friend."

"If only half my guys weren't still crawling all over this place."

"Hmm, yeah. If this place wasn't Grand Central Station right now..." The grin became a sinful smirk. "Talk about a subbie who wouldn't be safe."

Dasha folded her arms. "While we're on that subject, let's stop talking about the subbie like she isn't here, okay?"

Both Kress's brows jumped this time. "Oh-ho-ho." He cocked his own grin right at her. "Yes, ma'am. Or should I say Yes, *Mistress*?"

David sobered then. "She's told me she needs to say something."

Kress caught the don't-mess-around vibe. "Oh?"

"And I'm thinking it involves us both."

Dasha stunned herself by taking her own turn to smile. "You're right. It does."

"Oh?"

Kress echoed the word with an overlay of tension. Dasha wheeled her smile to him with a dose of *down, boy* in it. She took in one more breath of the forest air, really needing its crisp power.

"I almost died today." Again, no grace points. But an excellent place to start. "And when it was happening...when I was looking down the barrel of that gun...my head filled with a lot of things. The things in my life that really mattered. And what kept me together, what kept me from completely giving in to fear...was listening to you guys. Both of you."

Almost as if they shared one brain, the two men frowned. "Listening to us?" David charged.

"Yeah." She nodded and looked up into their beautiful, rugged faces. "I heard your voices. I heard them, and I hung on to them, and it made things better. I felt so strong." *Deep breath. Deep breath.* "But...I also felt terrible."

"Great," Kress quipped. "Thanks."

"I felt terrible because I was about to die without telling you both how much I loved you."

There. She'd done it.

She wanted to squeeze her eyes shut and throw up. But it was like she watched a car wreck; she stared at both of them, taking in the total vanishing act of their frowns. She tried to read their subsequent unblinking stares. She watched as both their mouths gyrated, struggling with words but not meeting success.

"I—I know you both thought I was babbling when I said it last night, after we finished at the mansion..." *Idiot, idiot.* She wasn't making this better by elaborating in a stutter. "But...I wasn't. And I should've been clearer. I know that now, but I freaked out. How is it possible that I've fallen in love with two men? What kind of a woman does that make me? I still have no clue. But...God...just an hour ago, all I could think was that my brains were about to be blown out, and I'd never had the guts to make sure that both of you knew how amazing you are...and how lucky I've been to have *two* men in my life to feel this way about..."

She finally stopped. Yanked in a sharp little breath, nervously bouncing on the balls of her feet.

"So there it is. If *you're* freaked, that's okay. I won't blame either of you. But you both needed to know it. I love you, David Pennington. And I love *you,* Kress Moridian. And if that makes me wrong, then—"

David was the one to steal the rest of it from her—with a solid, thorough kiss.

He deepened it by grabbing her nape and angling her face high and back for him. She couldn't help but open up, joyously letting his tongue rake wherever he wanted, surrendering to the hot flood he shot through her body with it.

He only broke away because Kress took over, whirling her against him, picking up the sensual assault where David left off. By the time Kress let her go, her senses swam in dizziness and delirium. David grabbed her back, his arms a wonderful vise, holding her flat against him. Her world careened...in all the best and most perfect ways.

"I've loved you," he finally murmured, "from the second you first knelt at my feet, D. Probably before that, though I was too terrified to admit it."

"Oh...David!" She gripped him in return, gulping hard to keep from bursting into sobs.

"So that takes care of the shit about thinking yourself wrong," Kress declared. Authoritative as the words were, he kicked at the ground in his own version of the uncomfortable-as-hell shuffle. "And for the record, I love the crap out of you too, Dasha Moore."

That took David's pancake-flip on her senses and turned it all into a giant waffle. Hot, yummy...yet filled with a bunch of hidden nooks, pooled with pure anxiety again. She looked up to David, wondering how that little bomb sat with him.

Shock popped up her eyebrows. Her Sir grinned at them both like a very satisfied panther. "Well, hell. You two are making this way too easy for me."

"Making *what* easy?" She and Kress blurted it together.

He let out a deliberate sigh as settled her back to her

own feet. Dasha was glad for the distance. She peered at his expression and recognized it. David got it when he really wanted to roll his eyes but had to refrain. He usually saved the expression for people like asshole record-company execs and reporters who asked her stupid questions.

"All of this bullshit has shown me something pretty fucking clear." He waited, almost like he expected one of them to fill in his "well, duh" blank. "*Security*," he finally stated. "Think about it. Do you think we've seen the last threat to your safety, Dasha?"

Think about it? Like she'd done anything except that lately. "No," she muttered, not filtering the tremble in her voice.

"Yeah," David replied. "You hear that? You understand now? We need a dedicated team, not the rent-a-cops we've been relying on in each city. Those people don't know you, don't give a crap about you." He swept his gaze to Kress. "They wouldn't throw themselves in front of a bullet for you."

Realization started to hit, especially as Dasha followed the trajectory of his gaze. A crapload of emotions played across Kress's bold features. Confusion warred with comprehension. Denial stabbed at hope.

She admitted to the same roller coaster of feeling. *Holy shit*. Was she interpreting David's message right?

"What are you getting at, dude?" Kress finally charged.

"I'm getting at offering you a job, *dude*." David spidered his fingers into Dasha's. "We need someone who has a deep, personal interest in protecting this superstar, body and soul. You think you could be that someone?"

"Does the Mississippi flow south?"

"So what's the confusion? Unless you *want* to stay in Miami with the feds? Maybe traveling the world in five-star hotels, helping me protect and pleasure this woman every day, isn't your thing? The whole pop-star package just feels too intense?"

Kress surged forward. His gaze went a little silver, making him look part wolf. "Who you calling a candy-ass about intense?"

"Why are you worried about any ass except this one?" David delivered a fast swat to her backside. Dasha squealed in surprise but beamed a new smile. She'd gladly bend over his knee here and now.

Instead of letting that delicious fantasy take root, she gave her bottom lip a sultry bite. Peered up at them both from beneath her lashes. "Maybe now's a good time to think about getting in the car."

"Good girl."

As her Doms gave the praise together, a fresh song bubbled in Dasha's soul. This time, she had a feeling the lyrics would come very easily.

EPILOGUE

"Hurry up, baby!"

The subbie hurriedly buckled her boots and mumbled an apology to her Sir. He laughed, not really that pissed with her, but the opportunity to land a swat on her backside was too good to pass up. She giggled, letting him grab her hand and lead the way up the gray stone driveway.

It was an early summer night in Southern California, the kind featured in classic rock songs and unretouched postcards. The air smelled like star jasmine and bougainvillea, with a tiny tang of ocean blended in. July hovered around the corner, teasing at the wind.

The Dom and sub rushing their way inside The Mansion Club definitely didn't stop to notice.

They were both dressed in their fetish best—leather, lace, latex, metal—for their first visit to the Southland's newest, and arguably finest, BDSM club. They'd heard the same story as everyone else: the grand Victorian residence, tucked at the end of an acre-long driveway and equally huge gardens, had a set of "ghost" owners who'd redesigned the place based on an authentic antebellum estate they'd played in last year.

To look at the place, one could only imagine what erotic goodness had gone down during those playdates. Crystal lighting. Scented candles. Velvet couches. Carpets that begged for bare feet and knees. Flocked walls that boasted alcoves instead of paintings. In these alcoves, nude performance artists beckoned to club guests with feathers or fans or the simple command of their smiles.

But tonight, nobody noticed those performers either.

The crowd made their way toward the largest playroom of the club, murmuring like excited guests at a celebrity wedding. The festive mood of their murmurs was contradicted by the music that beckoned them from hidden speakers. The ethereal Celtic tune featured a backbeat of moans and lashing sounds in place of bass and drums.

As everyone filtered into the wide living room, they formed into a crescent around the massive mantel, as well as the two wingback chairs in front of it.

The energy in the room escalated as the music changed. A new song came on, mysterious as the first but now possessing a strong drum track, cadenced into double-time sequences, like a heartbeat getting stronger. There were voices in this song too, blending in a sensual harmony of male and female tones.

People angled for better views on the center of the room.

It wasn't often one got to witness a double collaring ceremony.

The music swelled as the two Dominants entered the room. It was appropriate that they did so at the stroke of midnight, for they looked like nuances of the night itself. The first was sleek, powerful, and effortless in his strength. His friend was decisive, dangerous, and sweeping with his steps. They both wore nothing except black leathers on their legs, prompting a number of women in the crowd to shift again. One could have even been heard whispering, "Lucky bitch."

The subject of that comment emerged then. All the men in the room began lustful fidgets.

Like her Doms, the submissive was barefoot. Her toes,

painted shell pink, peeked from beneath a long, beaded skirt that might as well not have been there for all it covered. As she moved, every inch of her lush golden backside, thighs, and pussy got their own five seconds of fame. Atop the skirt, she wore an ivory corset, laced with iridescent silver and pink. On top of that, a shimmering head cover was formed of beads that matched her skirt, smaller in this garment so that it covered her head. The same beads adorned a mask that shielded the top half of her face.

But nothing covered the perfection of her joy-filled smile.

Indeed, the woman looked happier than a vanilla-world bride as she knelt to present herself, turning to kiss the palm of her first Dom's right hand, repeating the action with the other. The second Dom, belying his He-Man exterior, stopped the ceremony to tilt her face up. He smiled while swiping tears from beneath her eyes—before stroking the same fingers to her lips, clearly commanding her to lick them clean for him. Once again, every woman in the room got a little wetter.

The sub, still on her knees, turned back to face her first Dom. He grinned at his friend and then back to her while reaching for a box on a nearby table. Nestled on the velvet inside was a collar inciting everyone's gasp: a diamond-crusted circle turning to a blaze of decadence in the light. Breaking up the circle of bling were three larger stones, all rubies, inlaid next to each other along the collar's front side.

The Dom's grin mellowed into a smile of adoration. Tenderly, he curled the jewelry around his woman's throat. He leaned down as the other man closed the latch at her nape. When he was done, the Dom kissed her full on the lips, pressing her jaw so she opened more for him.

After several minutes of their open passion, he helped her to her feet. Gently circled her back to her other man.

The Dom behind leather door number two wasn't nearly so polite about sealing the deal. He grabbed her shoulders, jerked her close, and plunged in with passionate possession. His growl was audible even with the music pulsing.

At the same time, his friend bracketed the sub from behind, deftly twisting the hooks free down her corset.

The crowd gasped aloud from the sight of her bare breasts, sparkling with even more bling.

Her right nipple was adorned with a diamond initial *D*. A sparkling *K* was pierced into the other.

The submissive knew exactly who she belonged to now—and clearly didn't want it any other way. By the looks on the faces of her two Doms, neither did they.

The crowd burst into applause.

"Happy Ever After" came in a song of three harmonies tonight.

Continue the Suited for Sin Series with Book Two

Sigh

Keep reading for an excerpt!

EXCERPT FROM *SIGH*

BOOK TWO IN THE SUITED FOR SIN SERIES

She'd disappeared out the door before Mark trusted himself to push past his fury and speak. Even then the words left him with savage force, cutting through the laughter they'd given Rose as a send-off.

"I think we're done for the day, children. I suggest you use your free time to do something constructive. Like growing the fuck up."

They went silent. It was paltry relief for the protective fire roaring through his body. He let the heat take over and ignite his muscles, propelling him up the stairs two at a time.

Out in the hall, he beheld an empty corridor, a glass wall, and the patio beyond that. Bright hibiscus and lush palms swung lazily in the island breeze, mocking him with their peaceful perfection.

He bit back an oath. She'd bolted fast but couldn't have gone that far. He closed his eyes, drawing on instincts honed on the frontlines in desert shitholes, shutting down his reliance on a visual. He listened instead. And breathed. And hoped she'd give herself away with the patter of fleeing footsteps, maybe the lingering wisp of her fragrance on the air. In the last forty-eight hours, he'd tried like hell not to notice how she smelled. Now he was glad he'd failed. A hint of magnolia, a kiss of vanilla, and a lot of clean, creamy skin...

There it was. Off to the right. Her footfall, frantic and hard, confirmed his conclusion.

Without a second thought, he followed.

The corridor hooked to the left before becoming a flagstone pathway leading through gardens, grottos, and water features. Mark followed it past a koi pond and a gazebo, finally finding her stopped against a river rock wall, in an alcove that was nearly a cave, thanks to its other wall being formed by a waterfall. She glared at the thundering water as if she longed to drown herself in it. Her high, classic cheeks were already wet. But he knew, certain as he breathed, the drops weren't from the waterfall.

That look. Her tears. They almost caused him to turn and leave her be. They cracked him open. Decimated his logic. Shattered his professional composure. If he stayed for a second longer, he knew what he'd be tempted to do. To say.

She looked up and saw him.

He took a tentative step.

She jerked as if he'd thrown an electric charge across the grotto. Her lips, moist with her tears and berry bright from her bites, parted on a gasp. She drew breath for words. Mark cut her off.

"He's an ass."

He closed on her by two more steps. She stumbled back and slammed into the wall. "Oh, God!" Mortification stabbed the words. She palmed her cheeks.

As her hands came down, Mark grabbed them. And wondered what the hell he was doing. He didn't care about the answer. He only knew he longed to wipe out that pain in her eyes. No, it was more than pain. It was loneliness. He recognized it too damn well. Easy enough, when it was the same desperate glint he confronted in the mirror every morning.

"He's an *ass*." He let her see his locked teeth now. "Don't you see that?"

"Of course I see it! He pulls crap like this all the time at home. Earth-shattering surprise, huh?"

He let her look everywhere but at him. He softened his grip, elated when she didn't pull away. "But that's the first time he's ever pulled that particular wad of crap."

Her grimace confirmed that. He nodded, barely battling the urge to find Johnson, tell him to forget the maturity lesson, and just go the fuck home. Baghdad wasn't a place for sixteen-year-olds, even if they walked around in bodies twice that age.

While he got distracted with that fantasy, Rose finally took notice of how they stood. He nearly had her locked against the wall. Their hands, still joined, were the only thing blocking their chests from touching. "Shit!" she cried. "Look... Senator...I apologize—"

"What the hell for?"

She shook her head. "It's clear I can't handle this. Apparently I can't handle much of anything. I'm a mess. I'll save the company some money and go home now."

"The fuck you will."

She actually glared at him for three seconds. She seemed stunned he'd use that word, that tone, or both—making her response, calm as morning mist, even more a shock.

"The fuck I won't."

She dropped her head and tried to pull free from him. She had a snowball's chance of succeeding. "Rose," he reprimanded. "*Rosalind.* Listen to me. Nobody deserves to be on this project more than you. Nobody's got their head in a better space than you. Do you hear me on this? Rose?"

The top of her head, while a captivating crown of shiny russet, was unreadable.

The trembles of her shoulders, turning to the shudders brought on by sobbing, were crystal clear.

"Rose." He let out a weighted sigh. Then pulled her against him. "Oh, little pet, what is it?"

It was all he could not to give in to a tremor himself. Holy Christ, what was he doing? This protectiveness, this aching need to grip her and hold her... He hadn't felt like this for a living person since he and Heather had whispered their final goodbyes. After that day, he thought he'd never feel this way again. No, goddamn it; he'd vowed it. Best to just swear off the pain forever than risk ever going through that hell again. But here, it felt so perfect. So right. The only choice that made sense, even if it did make all this feel like jumping from a plane at thirty thousand feet without an oxygen mask.

With a deep inhalation, he spread his arms. Since their hands were still locked, Rose's followed along beneath. The action succeeded at making her his prisoner against the wall. She gasped. The sound hit him like a rocket, compelling him to lower his cheek. He scraped up Rose's tears with his beard while shifting his mouth, so all he had to do was whisper for her to hear.

"Let it go, pet. You've been holding it in for so long, haven't you?"

She trembled, still resisting. He understood. He waited. The significance of what he asked... It delved far beyond just the words he'd just spoken. He wanted her trust. To help shoulder a burden she'd carried so long, it likely felt like part of her. He practically felt her torment too. Surrender her burden to him and face the emptiness it left behind, or turn and run again...back to the safety of her life?

The safety.

And the loneliness.

Damn it, he wasn't going to make her choice easy. Or, if he

was being honest, his. He'd been safe for so long now, opting for the easiest way to think and the most comfortable thing to do, which was usually too damn much. His relationship with Dasha had nearly been the sacrifice for it. He'd only redeemed himself with her by tossing "safe" overboard.

Maybe that would work here too. Maybe that was why fate had brought him here to begin with. Maybe he was here to show Rose the truth about running. It wasn't always the answer—and safety wasn't always the key.

And maybe in showing her, he'd push away the loneliness for himself too. Christ, if only for a few minutes...

He shifted his hold, positioning his hands to circle her wrists. Squeezed in a fraction tighter. "Let it go." He lowered his mouth to her nape, unable to resist the elegant curve of skin. "I'm here, honey. Let it go."

Rose whimpered. Her wrists twisted in his hold. But when he eased his grip, concerned he'd hurt her from the rush of fresh Dom in his system, she still made the sound. Her lips were taut and her gaze shimmered, telling him one thing as clear as the sunshine of which she smelled. He hadn't pushed her physically at all. He'd rammed home a thousand emotional buttons—and now they all went off at once, overwhelming her.

Triumph surged. Yes. This was what she needed. Mental gears locked into place as he sensed it, knew it, savored it. He'd only just met her, but he *knew* her. He also knew he was meant to be here, to give her what she craved but wouldn't give to herself. Her worth to the world. Her beauty, within and without. Her desirability, an organic thing from her mind and her spirit, just as much as her incredible curves and her porcelain skin.

"That's it." He spread his legs, bracketing her body with his, rejoicing as she softened beneath him. "Don't fight it anymore. You don't have to. I'll be here to catch you, I promise."

"I...I can't..." It dissolved into a sobbing hiccup. "This...this isn't—"

"Anything or anyone but you and me." He murmured his next words against the furrows in her forehead. "I'll stop any time you want. Just say the word. But I don't think you want to stop, Rose."

This story continues in Sigh Suited for Sin Book Two!

ALSO BY ANGEL PAYNE

Suited for Sin:
Sing
Sigh
Submit

The Bolt Saga:
Bolt
Ignite
Pulse
Fuse
Surge
Light

Honor Bound:
Saved
Cuffed
Seduced
Wild
Wet
Hot
Masked
Mastered
Conquered
Ruled

Secrets of Stone Series:
No Prince Charming
No More Masquerade
No Perfect Princess
No Magic Moment
No Lucky Number
No Simple Sacrifice
No Broken Bond
No White Knight
No Longer Lost
No Curtian Call

Temptation Court:
Naughty Little Gift
Pretty Perfect Toy
Bold Beautiful Love

Cimarron Series:
Into His Dark
Into His Command
Into Her Fantasies
Into His Sin

**For a full list of Angel's other titles,
visit her at AngelPayne.com**

ACKNOWLEDGMENTS

Special thanks to Shayla Black, for believing this could happen from the start. And to Jenna Jacob, for scraping me off the ledge more times than I can remember. I love you two so much.

Sierra Cartwright, thank you for your amazing memory!

Gratitude for the AMAZING goddesses who have been there through every step of on this amazing journey and believed in these books from the very start: Victoria Blue, Cherise Sinclair, Tracy Roelle, Eden Bradley, Red Phoenix, Trish Bowers, and Jennifer Zeffer. I love you, ladies! More than you may ever know!

To all the readers who have so steadily supported, screamed, yelled, loved, and held me up: I have no words to say how much you mean to me.

Thank you!

ABOUT ANGEL PAYNE

USA Today bestselling romance author Angel Payne loves to focus on high-heat romance starring memorable alpha men and the women who love them. She has numerous book series to her credit, including the action-packed Bolt Saga and Honor Bound series, Secrets of Stone series (with Victoria Blue), the intertwined Cimarron and Temptation Court series, the Suited for Sin series, and the Lords of Sin historicals, as well as several standalone titles.

Angel is a native Southern Californian, leading to her love of being in the outdoors, where she often reads and writes. She still lives in Southern California with her soul-mate husband and beautiful daughter, to whom she is a proud cosplay/culture con mom. Her passions also include whisky tasting, shoe shopping, and travel.

Visit her at AngelPayne.com